RUTHLESS SINNER

A DARK COLLEGE BULLY ROMANCE

IVY BLAKE

PREFACE

Trigger Warning: This is a **DARK** bully romance and features bullying and dub/non con situations that might be triggering for some readers. Violence, drug use, alcoholism and disordered eating are also present.

If those are topics that are upsetting for you, then I'm afraid this might not be the book for you. Also, while this book has been edited, there's still the possibility that a typo might pop up somewhere. If you spot one, don't report it to Amazon, pop me an email at ivyblakeromance@outlook.com so I can fix the issue.

British English spellings and phrases are commonly used throughout this book.

1

GRACE

"Leave that one. I'll come back for it in a second." Dad pointed to the suitcase that I was having a hard time picking up. I let it rest against the car. I would not fight him on that one.

"I always forget how lovely this place is," Mom said as we walked towards my new accommodation building, her eyes roaming my bougie looking college campus.

Even though I'd spent a year at Oakwood Academy already, I still found it overwhelming how I got to see the beautiful campus every single day. The fact that I got to call it my home for most of the year was a massive bonus, too.

My eyes cast over the tall red brick buildings, glad that I now lived closer to them than I did the year before. I'd been adamant about getting an apartment closer to campus for my second year, because trekking to lectures and seminars when it was cold and dark lowered my motivation to go.

I'd assumed that I was going to keep living with my friend Violet, but when she found a place of her own that allowed her to stay all year round, I knew I had to get on with my application quickly so that I didn't miss out on the good apartments. I was happy that Violet had a place that she could call home, which meant that she didn't have to put up with her mom back home if she didn't want to, not to mention the fact that it was absolutely *gorgeous*. That didn't stop the fact that I knew I'd miss seeing her in the kitchen in the mornings and hearing her sing in the shower.

"In you go." Dad used the electric key card to hold open the door for Mom and me and let us walk in ahead of him. I noticed my parents exchange an unfamiliar look, but I was too excited to move in, so brushed it aside.

We walked up the stairs, passing other students with parents that were also helping them move into their new apartments. I knew it was going to be the busiest day for arrivals, but I wanted to settle in as soon as possible before the semester started. I also really wanted to meet my new roommate and get to know them so that we could start off the new academic year on the right foot.

Oakwood Academy randomly appointed roommates and no matter how many times I'd tried to get the accommodation service to give me a clue or idea about who I was going to share with, they wouldn't budge.

That's just how the system works, the woman on the other end of the phone had said.

We walked past a blonde family who smiled at us politely as we walked up the steps. I wanted to take the lift, but Mom was adamant about us all getting our steps in wherever possible. The heavy bags in my hands did *not* agree, but Mom wouldn't hear any of it.

"*He's* a handsome fellow, isn't he?" Mom hissed.

I was practically sweating as I hauled the bags up the stairs and was so focussed on not missing a step that it took me a moment to realise who she was talking about. I looked up to see a flash of tattoos and dark hair that made my heart flutter.

Elijah.

He was stalking down the hallway towards us, a stormy expression on his face, his eyes dark and intense. My breath caught in my throat as I took in his height and his muscly build. The darkness that he exuded was both intriguing and intimidating. I only knew him because Violet had started dating his roommate and friend, Nate. The one and only interaction we'd had together last year had been brief and cold, but the one thing that had stuck out most was how he'd been shirtless when he'd answered the door. Admittedly, I *was* a bit disappointed that he wasn't shirtless as he walked towards us.

Elijah drew nearer to us and my face broke into an involuntary smile. It was nice to see a familiar face, even if it was a scowling one.

I hope I wasn't staring.

"Hey," I said as I caught his eye.

Elijah looked down at me with a disdainful expression on his face and brushed past me without saying a word. *Ouch*.

"That was... awkward," said Dad.

I love it when he's so helpful and points out the obvious.

"Maybe he didn't hear you?" Mom offered. "He looked like he was in a bit of a rush." Mom and Dad exchanged a look that made my stomach pang. I shrugged in an attempt to detract from the discomfort I felt.

"Yeah, it's probably something like that," I said.

How fucking embarrassing.

As I lead Mom and Dad to my apartment, I couldn't shake the look that had been on Elijah's face. It had felt deeply personal. All I could hope was that I wouldn't have to experience it again. I hoped we wouldn't cross paths again or that Elijah would lighten the fuck up the next time I saw him. To be fair, Violet had told me that he'd given her the cold shoulder every time she was over visiting Nate, so at least I knew it wasn't a *me* problem.

"This place looks even nicer in person," said Dad once we'd walked into the apartment.

The living room and kitchen were wide and perfect for hosting parties. The furniture was new and in neutral colours that pulled the place together, making it look chic and cosy. My parents helped carry my things into my bedroom, which was *a lot* bigger than the one I'd had the previous year. I really had hit the jackpot.

I can finally put my Pinterest board to good use!

Once all of my things had been unloaded from the car, Mom and Dad said their goodbyes after making me promise to keep in contact.

"Don't forget to tell us all about your new roommate once you've met them," Mom said before she and Dad started their journey back home.

I was just as excited and curious as them to find out who I'd be spending the next year with. There was one box sitting on the kitchen counter when I came in and I had to fight against every nerve in my body that wanted me to dive in and find out *something* about my new roommate.

Instead, I busied myself with unpacking my belongings so that I could start making my new room my new home. At the bottom of one of my boxes, I pulled out a picture of me and Violet that we'd taken when we'd been at the fair over summer. The massive balls of candy floss that we held out in front of us partially shielded our smiles. My chest felt warm as I looked at the picture and remembered how long it had taken us to get one that we both liked and looked good in. I made a mental note to give Violet a call later.

I made my way to the kitchen and began unpacking my

pots and pans. I'd brought fewer things than I had last semester, after learning that I simply didn't have the time, while studying medicine, to cook all the fancy things that I'd planned to in my head.

I took out my favourite mug, a nice teal one that I'd picked out at a charity shop, and was grateful that it hadn't broken on the car ride to Oakwood.

"Oh, fuck no."

I nearly dropped my mug at the sound of the deep, gravelly voice behind me. When I finally got the courage to turn around, I saw Elijah standing in the kitchen, an annoyed expression on his face that matched the tone of his voice.

The sight of his chiselled face and muscly physique threw me off guard again, and I struggled to keep my wits about me as I tried not to stare. Besides, Elijah did not look happy to see me *at all*.

"What are you doing here?" I asked weakly, even though the big gym bag slung across his front told me everything that I needed to know.

"Apparently, I'm the unlucky motherfucker who has to share an apartment with you." Elijah grimaced. "I *specifically* said I wanted to live in a single sex apartment." He shook his head as he looked me up and down.

I tried my best not to buckle under his intense gaze. *We* were going to be *roommates*? There had to be a misunderstanding somewhere. I tucked my mug in the cupboard before I could break it.

"Maybe there's been a mistake," I said. I watched as Elijah scrolled through his phone, his dark brows knitting furiously as he tapped away at the screen.

What were the fucking chances that the two of us would be stuck together?

"Nope, it's fucking here in black and white," he growled. "Whatever."

Elijah stormed off down the hallway before I could say anything. My chest tightened when I heard him slam his bedroom door behind him.

I'd expected some awkward small talk over a cup of tea with my roommate to be the worst-case scenario. I'd certainly not expected *that*.

Interacting with Elijah twice in one day had really rubbed me the wrong way, especially because I felt like he was being unnecessarily unfair.

People didn't just *not* like me. Especially when I first met them. I was notoriously great at first impressions, but apparently Elijah was the outlier.

I took a deep breath, gathered up any semblance of courage I had left, and marched down the hallway to Elijah's room. Even if he was less than pleased about our living arrangement, there was nothing we could do about it. At least for the time being. I wanted to make the environment as pleasant as possible and that started with having a relationship that was, at the bare minimum, civil.

"Elijah," I called as I knocked lightly on his door.

I didn't know if he hadn't heard me or if he was ignoring me. Either way, I was met with silence and knocked again.

Elijah's heavy footsteps sounded out as he crossed his bedroom and flung the door open, a stormy expression on his face.

"What the fuck are you banging on my door for?" he growled. His dark eyes were barely slits and the tension in his shoulders was visible for all to see.

I took a step back, but not before I caught a whiff of his sweet, masculine scent. *Focus Grace, focus*.

"Do you want a cup of tea or coffee, by any chance?" My voice was barely a squeak, but I forced myself to smile and laugh politely.

Elijah clearly didn't appreciate my politeness.

"No." Elijah looked me up and down again before his lips curled into a sneer. Even as he made the cruel expression, my heart pounded in my chest.

"But do you know what would be great?" he said.

"What?"

"If you left me alone *or* found a new place to live," Elijah growled before he slammed the door in my face.

"Oh," the word collided with Elijah's door, and I stood still for a moment, taken aback by his unwarranted rudeness.

"I was just trying to be nice," I shouted through the wooden door.

"Well, nobody likes a try hard, so I suggest you stop," Elijah shouted back.

I scoffed and crossed my arms over my chest. I guess Elijah didn't get the memo that manners were *free*. Plus, I wasn't a *try hard*.

I understood being unhappy with the apartment situation, especially if he'd specifically requested to share with another guy. But I wasn't as bad as he was making me out to be.

Maybe he's just had a particularly bad day?

Even though Elijah's words stung and lodged themselves in my brain, I would not let them get to me. I was going to show him what a great roommate I could be. I was going to prove Elijah wrong.

2

GRACE

Elijah avoided me for the rest of the day as if I had the plague. After I'd packed away my things, I sat in the living room and watched TV, hoping he'd walk past and maybe say something or perhaps join me. Maybe he'd been stressed earlier, or was just in a bad mood. I held onto the hope that Elijah would apologise as I watched reruns of *Friends* on our fancy flatscreen TV. But as the hours ticked by and it got darker outside, I realised that any hope for an apology from Elijah was utterly futile.

I could smell something amazing coming from the kitchen, and my stomach rumbled in response. It was past my usual dinnertime, but I'd been waiting for Elijah to finish using the kitchen so that I could have my turn. When my stomach kept on growling incessantly, I decided I was well within my right to claim the space too. I was paying the same amount of rent as him, after all.

The smell got stronger as I walked into the kitchen and I could practically feel my self salivating. Seeing Elijah in a tight fighting shirt that showed off his back muscles and the intricate tattoos etched there didn't help, either.

"That smells great," I said as I walked into the kitchen.

Elijah grunted and continued putting food onto his plate without giving me so much as a sideways glance. Trying not to be offended by his unresponsiveness, I crouched down and grabbed my pot from my cupboard.

"What did you make?" I asked, in another attempt at trying to build some sort of rapport.

"Why do you talk so much?" Elijah snapped.

My gaze went to him and I saw that he was actually looking directly at me for the first time since I'd entered the kitchen. I shrunk back and stood up slowly.

"I don't. For goodness' sake, I was just asking a simple question," I shot back. I knew how defensive I sounded, but how was *I* the bad guy when I was just trying to imitate some small talk? Elijah sighed and grabbed his plate and cutlery.

"I don't like questions," he said pointedly before he left the kitchen.

A moment later, his bedroom door slammed behind him.

Ah, so Elijah found my company so unbearable that he couldn't even sit in the kitchen or living room to eat his dinner. Nice.

I sighed loudly, not caring if he heard as I began cutting vegetables for my stir-fry. I was grateful when Violet's name and face appeared on my phone screen.

Even though Elijah had already clarified that he didn't care about me, I still shut the kitchen door so that he couldn't overhear my conversation.

"Hey, how's the new place?" Violet asked when I picked up.

She'd been sounding a lot happier since she and Nate

started dating and even more so since she'd started her new admin job at Oakwood, which meant she wasn't constantly on her feet like she was at her last job.

"The *place* is nice," I said pointedly.

"How about your roommate? I know they could never be as great as *me,* but do they come close?" Violet giggled.

"You have nothing to worry about in that department," I sighed.

"What do you mean? Why are you being so coy, Grace? I need the drama!"

"Well, how's this for drama?" I turned the heat down on the stove. "*Elijah* is my new roommate."

Violet gasped. "As in Elijah Blackmoor? You must be joking."

"I wish I was," I groaned.

"Oh my God," Violet laughed. "How bad is it?" she asked after a moment.

"As bad as you can imagine... maybe worse." Violet had had more run-ins with Elijah than I had and none of them had been positive experiences either.

"Maybe he'll warm up once you guys have settled in." It was Violet's attempt at lightening the mood, but we both knew that Elijah didn't possess any ability to be warm in any way whatsoever. Today had made that fact *very* clear.

"That'll be the day that pigs fly and my hair is a normal colour," I laughed sarcastically as I twirled a strand of my pastel pink hair around my finger.

"I can't wait."

As I finished making my dinner, Violet and I chatted about our new timetables. She updated me on where things were at with her and Nate and when my stomach couldn't take the wait any longer; I knew it was time to stop the chatting and start the eating.

We made a plan to catch up during the next week before we said our goodbyes. My stir fry was delicious, even though eating alone was much lonelier than I'd expected. I usually had someone around me when I was eating, whether that was my parents at home or Violet, when we used to live together.

Knowing that Elijah was in the next room and actively *choosing* to avoid me unsettled me in more ways than one. But there was nothing I could do about it.

He'd already called me a try hard, an insult that had continued to play in my mind as if it was a song stuck on repeat. I couldn't stand the fact that he wouldn't even give me a *chance*. I'd thought our first run in last semester had been a fluke, but clearly, Elijah had written me off from the moment he'd set eyes on me.

Maybe his coldness wouldn't have gotten to me so badly if he wasn't so fucking attractive. It seemed like an awful waste to have those jaw dropping looks paired with such a foul personality. I hated to admit it, but it felt like even more of a waste to be living with someone as sexy as Elijah without being able to act on certain desires that my mind may or may not have been fantasising about without my permission.

Sexy or not, he was still an asshole. And if Elijah was going to engage in anything sexual with anyone, he'd made it crystal clear that it would definitely *not* be with me.

I woke up abruptly to the sound of the front door banging shut. My heartbeat sped up, and I grabbed my phone off my bedside table to check the time.

It was 3am.

My chest heaved, and I forced myself to slow my breaths as I listened out. Heavy footsteps flooded through the apartment, and I assumed they belonged to Elijah.

What if they didn't?

I shook my head and forced myself to lie back in my bed. We were at college. Of course, there'd be late nights. For all I knew, he'd probably been out partying. That wasn't weird.

Except Elijah seemed like the most antisocial person I'd ever met.

I flitted back and forth, conflicted on whether I should check up on the situation outside or mind my business and force myself to go back to sleep. The anxiety and curiosity won, so instead, I slipped my feet into my slippers and walked towards the door. I held my breath, nervous about what I might see.

My hand was poised, about to latch onto my door handle, when I heard the footsteps growing closer. They stopped outside my door and I drew my hand back. I held my breath and stayed completely still. After a couple of seconds, the footsteps continued down the corridor to Elijah's room before the door shut and muffled them.

Was he checking if I was in or if I was asleep?

Both possibilities sent a shiver down my spine and I couldn't quite work out why. I opened the door and stepped into the dark hallway. It was definitely Elijah. The scent of his masculine cologne lingered in the air, but it was also mixed with something else. I sniffed again. *Gasoline.* Funny, where would he be driving to at this hour? Especially if he'd been out partying. At the same time, Elijah didn't seem like the type to give a fuck about drink-driving laws, so it wasn't impossible.

A million questions went through my head, but I knew I wouldn't get any answers by just standing in the hallway.

Hell, I probably wouldn't get any answers by asking the man himself, but I at least had to try.

I heard Elijah stir in his bedroom and went to the bathroom so as not to draw suspicion to myself. As I brushed my teeth for the second time that night, I prayed he wouldn't come out of his room. When I was done, I tiptoed back to bed and struggled to sleep as thoughts about what Elijah could have possibly been up to at 3am in the morning consumed my mind.

When the actual morning rolled around, I got ready and made myself a coffee before I went to campus for my lecture. I was slightly sleep deprived yet still trying to figure out if there was a chance of easing the tension between me and Elijah, when the sound of him clearing his throat made me jump. My hand flew to my chest as I turned around and realised that Elijah had appeared at the kitchen door shirtless. I'd never be able to get used to his ripped body or his plethora of tattoos. I wanted to run my fingers over every single one and ask what each of them meant.

"Calm down, scaredy-cat," Elijah growled.

"I'm not a scaredy-cat, you're the weirdo who just snuck up on me," I retorted.

Elijah looked like he had barely slept, and yet he still looked ridiculously sexy. It wasn't fair. I'd had a shower and I probably still looked like a mess. I couldn't help but notice how low his shorts hung on his hips and I forced my eyes to return to my flask of coffee.

"And *you're* the weirdo who's fucking staring at me," he snapped.

"I'm not... *staring*," I said. *Great defence, Grace.*

Elijah snorted and brushed past me as he reached into

the cupboard for a mug. The blood in my veins turned into ice at his brief touch and the warmth that it had brought. The lingering smell of gasoline tickled my nostrils, and I fought back the urge to pry.

"Did you go out last night?" I asked in the most casual way that I could.

Elijah slammed the cupboard door shut and turned to look at me. He pulled his lips back over his teeth and I could tell that my question had hit a nerve.

"I don't see what that has to do with you," he spat.

"I'm just asking-"

"I don't know what you think this is, but we're not friends. We will not be sitting around telling each other secrets or having movie nights and tea together, so get that stupid shit out of your head, okay?" Elijah growled, his eyes flashing with danger.

"I know we're not friends," I said, even though his words shot daggers through my chest.

"And we're *never* going to be friends," Elijah sneered.

He looked me up and down, his gaze full of disdain. I shook beneath his stare and was grateful for the lid on top of my flask. I struggled to believe that he just simply wanted nothing to do with me. Elijah's words made me question everything about myself. I tried my best to keep my true feelings off my face as I held his gaze carefully with my own.

Was he always going to be this rude?

"I wouldn't want to be friends with such an asshole, anyway."

It was a cop out answer and I knew it was childish, but what else could I say to him?

"Good," I heard Elijah say as I walked out of the kitchen.

I focussed on making my way out the door before I could say something stupid back. There was no point. I didn't need to give him any more reasons not to like me. Clearly, he already had enough.

Me and Elijah had been roommates for a night and we still had an entire year left to go. As the seconds went by, I was growing less and less confident that things would get much better.

What a great way to start a new semester.

I instantly regretted not looking over the optional reading that had been uploaded online as I sat staring helplessly at the lecturer. I looked around at everyone else who seemed to know what was going on and cursed myself for taking shortcuts.

They weren't lying when they said that second year was a step up from first year. It felt more like a leap to me, but I wasn't about to admit that to my tutor. All it meant was that I'd need to do more studying and that I couldn't miss the extra reading. Not my idea of fun, but it would all be worth it in the end. I knew exactly what I needed to do. I just had to do the work and get my degree, and then I'd be one step closer to finally becoming a doctor. If only it didn't feel so far away.

As I left class, I texted Violet. I was glad when she said that she wanted to meet because I direly needed a pick me up. I walked into the cafe on campus and broke into a smile as soon as I spotted her curly brown hair.

"Grace!" she broke out of the line and walked up to me, throwing her arms around me in a big hug. I needed it. I squeezed her back tightly before pulling away.

"You look like you've had one hell of a day," Violet said. She eyed me up as we got in line.

"Don't even get me started," I said.

Violet's eyes lit up with mischief. "Oh, please do."

"So let me get this straight. You couldn't even get your charms to work on Elijah?" Violet teased, her lips open in an exaggerated 'o' shape.

I rolled my eyes at her and took a sip from my mug. "My power is clearly waning," I said. "He's impenetrable, and it's driving me nuts."

Violet chuckled. "It's barely been a week." I gave her a look, and she held her hands up in defence. "But I can only imagine how hard it is for you."

"I can't work or be calm in an environment like that," I burst out. "It's like I have to tiptoe or I'll piss him off. It's just so awkward and... unfriendly."

"You're always welcome to stay over at mine if you need a break," Violet said with a small smile.

"I appreciate it."

"I mean it, I want all the Grace time I can get!"

I nodded, even though I knew that Violet's place wasn't a quick fix. Even though it was lovely and more homely than my apartment, its distance from campus meant that it still wasn't the perfect escape. Spending the afternoon with Violet, though, was the perfect distraction I needed from my roommate situation. Paired with the coffee and fresh cake that I'd bought us from the display, it was basically perfect. Sharing stories and hearing her laugh at my jokes, even the terrible ones, reminded me that I wasn't as annoying or insufferable as Elijah wanted me to think.

The fact that I'd let a guy's opinion of me shake my

confidence in myself made me angry, and I would not let it happen again. Fuck Elijah and his opinions. I wasn't at Oakwood for him. What mattered most to me was hanging out with my friends and getting my medicine degree so that I could get the hell out of here and live the life I really wanted.

3

GRACE

A couple of days later, when I was in my room, I refreshed the page on my laptop screen. There had to be a mistake. The grade staring back at me showed that I'd barely scraped a pass.

Looks like that all nighter had been all for nothing.

Scrolling through the comments that my tutor had left me only threatened to send me into a deeper depression and because ignorance was bliss, I slammed my laptop shut and pushed it aside.

How had I fucked up so badly?

I *knew* second year was hard, but I was up for the challenge. Medicine was what I wanted to do, what I'd *always* wanted to do. It made little sense to be flunking after I'd had such a clean streak the year before.

I grabbed my phone off my dresser and called Mom. I counted seven rings, which were four more than usual, before she picked up.

"Hey, Grace, are you okay?" There was something off about Mom's voice, but I couldn't put my finger on it.

"I've been better. How are you?" I shot evil eyes at the

laptop sitting on my bed that held the truth of my poor grade. Mom paused for a moment and took a deep breath before she spoke.

"Actually, Grace, I have something I've been meaning to tell you," she said.

Goosebumps tickled my skin, and I sat up straight as if Mom could see me.

"Okay..." I said.

My mind raced as I thought about all the things that Mom might need to tell me. Were we moving house? Was Dad ill? Was Grandma ill? Was *she* ill?

"I know it's not the best time... well, it's never really the best time," Mom started rambling, and I started getting restless on my bed. I just wanted her to spit it out, to get whatever it was off her chest and out into the air so that I could figure out how to respond and deal with it.

"What I'm trying to say is that your father and I are getting a divorce."

My entire world split in half. The white walls that encased me started looking fuzzy as they closed in on me. *Divorce*. A word that was reserved for other people, other families, but not *mine*.

"Grace, are you there? Oh, honey, please say something," Mom said when I hadn't replied in two minutes.

My words caught in my throat. There *had* to be a misunderstanding. It *had* to be a joke. My cheeks were warm and wet and my brain was scrambled as I played Mom's words over again in my head.

"What do you mean?" I croaked out eventually.

Mom sighed. "I know it seems like it's coming out of nowhere, but trust me, it's not. Your dad and I thought we'd wait until you were older-"

"Did you think I wouldn't care or something?" I

snapped. I instantly regretted my harsh words and took a deep breath while I rubbed my temples. "Sorry, I didn't mean- look, I'm just shocked."

"Of course you are, Grace. But just know that we're still a family and we both love you and things aren't going to change," said Mom.

Lies. Of course, things were going to change.

"Why... why are you getting a divorce?"

I felt dirty asking, as if I was asking something taboo. But they were my parents, and even though their relationship was *technically* their business, I was a product of that relationship, so it was *technically* my business, too.

Mom was silent on the other side, and I waited to see if her answer would confirm my fears or not. Had one of them cheated? Cheating would certainly make things worse, but in all honesty, I didn't think that there'd be any reason that would be nice to hear.

"It's just not working anymore," Mom said. "We're not happy together, Grace." I noted the wobble in her voice and wished that I could hold her in my arms. Dad too. "People change and grow apart... I don't know what else to tell you."

My heart ached for Mom, for Dad and for me too. I couldn't imagine how they both felt, or how hard it must have been for them to come to their decision. But I couldn't stop myself from grieving the loss of my parents' relationship, a relationship that I'd believed to be perfect- to be the epitome of true love.

"I thought you loved each other," I sniffed.

I knew it sounded like an accusation, but I didn't mean for it to sound that way. I felt like I was losing brain cells as I tried to wrap my head around what she was saying. I'd seen the way my parents had been together my whole life, how they'd barely fought, how they'd been friends as well as lovers. We'd all been singing along to the radio in the car together on the way to Oakwood as if everything was just fine. Where had that all gone?

Each time I wiped the tears from my eyes, more fell down to replace them. I didn't want Mom to hear how upset I was- at both the divorce and how my course was going.

"We did... we do... Grace, it's complicated and I don't expect you to understand," Mom said, her voice barely louder than a whisper. "You probably won't understand this until you're older, but sometimes love isn't enough... and that's okay."

I let my tears fall freely because I didn't understand. Not when it came to my parents. My parents, whose love I'd strived for since the moment I was old enough to understand what they meant to each other.

"What's going to happen with the living situation? Christmases and birthdays?" It was the least important question shooting around my head, but it was the only one I could bring myself to ask.

"We're working on it. Your dad has found an apartment he likes, and he's letting me stay here. So home will always be here for you, Grace. And we're just taking things a day at a time... but we'll always be a family, even if we live in different places, okay?" Neither of us addressed the other question concerning who I'd live with.

"Okay," I breathed.

"I'm sorry to cut this call short, but I need to go, Grace. I know I just dropped a massive bomb and I'll be here to talk another time if you still want to," said Mom. "Are you okay besides all of that stuff?"

I cast my eyes back to my laptop. "Yeah, I'm fine. You go, we can chat later. I've got work to do, anyway."

We said our hurried goodbyes before I hung up my

phone. I stared at myself in the mirror for a few minutes. The colour had left my face and my eyes looked vacant.

I still couldn't believe what Mom had told me. It just didn't feel real at all. It felt like she'd been talking to me about another family, another set of parents that were splitting up. Not *mine*. My parents had been together since they were teenagers. I'd looked up to them and their relationship since I was a kid.

Divorce was such an ugly word, one that I never would have ever associated with them in a million years. I knew I felt angry, but I didn't even know who or what to be mad at.

My parents? Disney? Or was I angry at myself for not seeing the signs that must have been there?

I had an essay to hand in the following day that needed to get done, but every time I tried to type words on the page, Mom's voice cut through my conscience and reminded me that my family was breaking apart.

All notions of true love and happy families had been crushed in an instant, with just a few words. I rubbed my eyes and took a deep breath. Even though I'd gone on the call to tell Mom how much I was struggling and that I wanted to wallow in self pity, now I'd been spurred on by the news that she'd told me to try even harder.

One reason for that was because I didn't want to use my parents' impending divorce as an excuse. I was an adult, no one was going to accept that as a reason that might contribute to me struggling at uni. I also didn't want to worry my parents or make them feel worse than they probably already did. The last thing that made me want to try extra hard was fear. Fear of the future and what ifs.

What if I flunk university and don't become a doctor and am resigned to do a job I'm not good at and don't enjoy? What if I manage to find the love of my life but end up having to rely on them financially? What if we split up? What if...

Music began thumping through the wall, the decibels enough to shock me out of my downward spiral. Elijah. I waited for him to turn the music down, but of course he didn't. In fact, he had the audacity to turn it up so loud that I could practically hear every word that the singer was yelling down the microphone.

Fuck this.

I put my headphones on and turned my music up to the highest level, but it was still nowhere near loud enough to drown out the obnoxiously loud music coming from Elijah's room. It's like he *wanted* to piss me off.

I tore my headphones off and threw them on the bed, got up and flung my door open. I was outside Elijah's door in an instant and loudly knocked on the wooden door. I didn't care if he couldn't hear me over the noise or if he was deciding to ignore my knocks. I would not stop until he turned it down.

I'd had a shit day, and it was only going to get more shit because of the essay I needed to write. Elijah's bullshit was the last thing that I needed.

I wrapped my hand around the door handle and let myself into Elijah's room. His music got impossibly louder and the sound nearly made me cower in the corner. There was no way he was enjoying it and definitely no way that he was still going to have working eardrums by the time he was 25.

"Elijah!" I shouted over the music. He was sitting at his desk chair looking out the window, nodding his head in time to the music.

I shouted his name again, and this time he turned around, eyes flashing. My hands flew to my hips as Elijah stood up and made his way towards me.

"What the fuck are you doing in my room?" he snarled. "Get out."

I scowled back at him and pointed to the speakers in the corner of his room.

"Turn your fucking shit down. I'm trying to do my work," I snapped.

Elijah stared at me coldly. "You're trying to do work?"

"Yes, are you fucking deaf?" What little patience I had left for him was getting thinner and thinner by the second.

"Sucks to be you, then." Elijah shrugged. He pointed to the door. "Get the fuck out," he said bluntly.

I crossed my arms over my chest and continued staring at him, even though I could feel my heart speeding up in my chest.

Stand your ground, Grace.

"You're not the only person who lives here, Elijah, so why don't you stop being selfish for one fucking minute?" I nodded to the headphones sitting on his desk. "Use those, for fuck's sake."

Elijah rolled his eyes and closed the gap between us. He towered over me, and a gasp caught in my throat as I anticipated his next move.

"I told you to get out," he snarled, his dark eyes cold as stone.

"And I told you to turn your stupid music down," I snapped.

I could feel the heat radiating off his body, which was in stark contrast to the ice coming from his eyes. I waited for Elijah to shoot me an insult, but instead of hurting me with his words; he picked me up in one swift motion and slung me over his shoulder.

"Put me down," I cried as I balanced upside down. I tried not to think about the warmth of Elijah's body or his hands or how strong he was. I didn't want to be carried against my will, especially not by him.

"Stop moving so much," Elijah grunted.

I continued to squirm and try to break free, but Elijah's grip was firm as he marched across the hallway and into my room, where he threw me onto my bed as if I was nothing more than a sack of potatoes.

"What the hell?"

The sudden impact almost knocked the breath out of me and I looked up at Elijah from my crumpled pile on my bed with what was probably a very red face. I don't know what I'd expected when I'd gone to confront him, but it hadn't been *that*.

Elijah's eyes met mine and for a moment I thought I glimpsed hunger there. I was even more intimidated by his height as I sat on my bed, and the look on his face did nothing to quell my fears. Elijah's eyes roamed my body and lingered far too long for my liking. I noticed the muscle ticking in his jaw.

What was he thinking?

We were in my room... alone and he'd just thrown me on the bed like I was a newly wedded bride or something. I hated that I felt so flustered, but how could I not when he was looking at me like *that*?

When the prickling sensation that those dark eyes brought became unbearable, I was grateful when Elijah finally opened his mouth to speak.

"Stay out of my room," Elijah growled at me. His dark eyes flashed and his hands curled into fists as he stormed out of my room.

The question *or what?* teetered on the edge of my tongue, but instead I grabbed my pillow and threw it at the door. Elijah was already back in his room before it had a chance to strike.

"Well, keep the music down, asshole," I snapped.

I didn't care if the fucking bastard heard me or not. I *did* care that he'd felt so comfortable touching me when we'd barely exchanged words since we'd moved into the apartment. What I *didn't* care like was my reaction to his touch.

Pressing my hand against my chest, I willed my heart to slow down. Elijah wouldn't listen to me, and I wouldn't get any work done if I stayed.

Even though work was the last thing I wanted to do, I packed my laptop in my bag and headed to the library, where I could at least get some space from Elijah and hopefully my parents' divorce, too.

After a gruelling few hours of intermittently staring at my laptop screen and getting up for coffee and snacks from the cafe, I wrote something that resembled an essay. The quality of it was to be decided and looked over the following morning before it was due, but in the meantime, it was bedtime.

I checked the time on my phone and saw that it was just after midnight. I listened to my music as I walked to the apartment, making sure to take the quickest route home. As I neared my apartment building, I stopped in my tracks as I saw a tall figure in a leather jacket making their way down the steps.

Elijah.

Once he'd stepped outside, he took a quick scope of the surrounding environment. The fact that it was dark, and I was just out of his eye-line meant Elijah didn't notice I was there. I took an unexpected sigh of relief when he turned and walked off down the shadowy path that went behind the apartment building.

Where do you go every night, Elijah?

Part of me wanted to follow him, to see where he went off too, but the part of me that was in charge and had more sense was adamant about getting sleep after having had such a shit day.

I couldn't deny that a tiny part of me was afraid to find out what kept Elijah out so late. I was afraid that if I found out, I wouldn't be able to sleep soundly, knowing that he was only in the next room. Maybe ignorance *was* bliss.

4

ELIJAH

Thin ginger hair. A ratty beard that barely joined up. Crooked front teeth to match his personality. Filthy hands.

I watched as he rummaged around in his bag for a moment before he yanked out a crushed looking sandwich that must have been in there for days. The sight of his teeth sinking into the soggy looking bread made me want to vomit, but I held myself back.

He chewed like a monster, like a rabid beast feasting on flesh as opposed to bread, and God only knew what type of meat was in between the slices. His mouth was wide and food flew out of it and clung onto his beard, but instead of wiping it away, he simply tucked it back into his mouth for another round.

Filthy pig.

And it wasn't just his eating habits or the fact that I'd yet to see him wash his hands at all in the time that I'd been watching him that had earned him that name.

Once he'd finished devouring what I assumed was his dinner, he wiped his hands on his old as fuck cargo pants and stood up again. He stretched out his muscles and scratched his crotch before he turned to the toolbox on the bench behind him.

Even though I stood in the shadows, out of his direct eyeline, a part of me dared him to look at me, just once. It still astounded me that he couldn't feel my presence, or was too ignorant to notice. But I liked it that way. I liked that *he* was the prey this time.

For weeks, I'd tried to find out who exactly he was, and I was going off of very little information to start with. But that didn't stop me from trying. With some patience, late night walks and the internet, it wasn't long before I discovered more about the man who deserved pain and death more than anyone else in this world.

David Smyth. 32. Resident of Oakwood for 6 years. Mechanic for 4. Dropped out of high school in his senior year. A poor excuse for a human being.

I watched his stupid routine like I did every night. I counted the number of people that walked past each night. Three an hour until it hit midnight, then it was practically a ghost town. Which was perfect for me.

David tinkered beneath the hood of the Honda Civic he was working on and I felt the vibrations of his mobile phone as it rang. The excitement on his face told me that whoever was on the other side of the phone was someone he cared about a lot. Someone who'd miss him. Someone I couldn't wait to make worry about him.

His shift was due to finish soon. But the night had only just begun. Some might say that I'd grown obsessed with my new extracurricular activity. But the anticipation and adrenaline that ran through my veins was far too addictive for me to ignore. Far more interesting than my computer science degree. At least *this* posed some sort of challenge.

But what I reminded myself was that this wasn't about me or even for me. It was for her. All of this was for her. Even if she didn't know it yet, she would someday. And then maybe things between us would be different.

I unlocked my phone and looked through my messages. There'd still been no reply. I was beginning to think that she'd blocked my number, but those thoughts weren't helpful at all.

I caressed the knife in my pocket as I scrolled through the messages I'd sent most recently.

Please talk to me, Stella.
For fuck's sake, Stella, I'm sorry.
I'm going to fix this, I promise.
Stella?!!!

Hundreds of unanswered messages that told me exactly what she thought of me. To make matters worse, the only person who I could blame was myself. I was meant to be there. If I had been, then none of this would have happened and we both knew that.

My eyes flitted up to my target once more. The sheer sight of David made me sick. He put on his jacket before pulling down the shutter of the garage. I tucked my phone away and kept to the shadows as I trailed behind him.

As with every night, I needed to figure out if tonight was the right time to strike. If I got it wrong, then I would risk fucking everything up.

I dragged my feet up the stairs and let myself into the apartment. It had been a close one tonight, and all I wanted to do was pass out in my bed and not wake up until I absolutely had to. The late nights were killing me, but I couldn't stop yet. My sleep schedule would have to wait until I'd fully executed my plan.

I walked down the hallway and was about to turn into my room when I saw that the living room light was still on.

Fucking Grace.

I was about to turn it off when I noticed Grace sitting in her oversized pyjamas looking up at me.

"Hello, Elijah," she said with an unnecessary smile on her face.

The annoying bitch had stayed up for me.

"Turn off the light before you go to bed," I growled. I turned to go to my room. I hated small talk on a normal day, and combining that with Grace's overly peppy nature was my idea of hell.

"Where do you go every night?" Grace's words pierced through my skin and made me freeze on the spot.

No matter how many times I told her to back off, she wouldn't listen. I didn't like how she looked up at me expectantly with those big, hazel coloured eyes or how she was constantly happy as if she was always eating sugar or something. Grace's presence and persistent try hard behaviour made me feel sick. And I hated living with her.

"Did some of that hair dye seep into your brain or something?" I spat. I spun around on my heels and shot her a dirty look. "I told you, no questions."

"Well, excuse me for having questions when you're stomping around here at fucking 3am while I'm trying to sleep," Grace shot back.

She folded her hands over her chest and narrowed her eyes at me. I laughed bitterly. If Grace thought she could intimidate me, then she was dumber than I thought. She looked as intimidating as a Care Bear. If I wasn't so physically drained or tired of Grace's shit, I might have found the situation amusing.

"What I do is none of your business," I said. "Get a life and stop being so obsessed with mine." I heard her sharp intake of breath. I waited for Grace's comeback so that I could shoot her down once again.

"Are you selling drugs?"

Her question caught me off guard and I barked out a laugh. *Drugs*? If only it were that simple.

I looked Grace up and down slowly because I couldn't deny the ripples of pleasure that went through my body when she squirmed beneath my gaze. I allowed my gaze to linger on her chest, which she made even more effort to cover up once she realised.

"I didn't take you to be a junkie," I said. Grace's eyebrows shot up and her mouth fell open. A dirty thought crossed my mind as my gaze fell to her lips.

Nope, none of that.

I trapped a yawn in my throat and without another word; I turned on my heel and went to my room, slamming the door hard behind me. I found Grace so goddamn insufferable. How many times did I have to tell her I just wanted to be left alone?

And now she was on my back *again*. I paid for my place here and deserved to have my secrets. Besides, if Grace found out what I was really *doing*, she looked like the type to tell and not only would that fuck up my plans, I'd have no option but to destroy her for ruining everything.

I'd made various calls and trips to the accommodation office, but no matter how loud I raised my voice and told them that I urgently needed to change apartments, they wouldn't budge. They didn't deem my situation an emergency, and they told me they prioritised students that had *actual* problems. As if the pink-haired girl who lived in the room opposite mine *wasn't* a problem. I'd even gotten desperate enough to look at apartments in town, but I could barely afford to live at Oakwood already, considering I didn't have a mommy or daddy to pay for me to live like many other students, so that wasn't an option either. I was stuck with Grace in this stupid apartment until the end of the year.

It wasn't just her. I didn't like people. But especially not people that asked too many questions and kept trying to invade my privacy. That was the one thing most important to me in this world, apart from Stella. I hadn't wanted to live with a girl because I knew that some shit like this would happen. Plus, the distraction was unnecessary.

Even though she talked my ear off and continuously pissed me off, I'd be lying if I said I hadn't noticed how attractive Grace was. But I didn't care. I only cared about avoiding her and making sure that she kept out of my business. If I kept being rude and standoffish, she had to give up and leave me alone eventually. Most people did, but Grace didn't seem like most people.

All I wanted was the peace, quiet and space to do what I needed to do. I couldn't care less about my degree or making friends. Nate and Tristan were probably the closest I had to "friends", but that wasn't by choice. Nate and I were randomly put together as roommates last year and Tristan was around and knew where to get cheap alcohol and drugs, even though I stayed away from that stuff. But if I declined too many invitations to go out, the boys were always on my ass asking why. One thing I appreciated about them, though, was the fact that they didn't ask too much about my life before Oakwood. No one knew about that except Stella.

As far as I was concerned, Oakwood was only temporary, so there was no point getting too invested. It wasn't home, even if it was the closest thing to it. At least the only belts I saw here were the ones tucked away in my dresser drawer. My time at Oakwood was limited, and I had to focus if I wanted to get this shit right. I'd made too many mistakes already and I couldn't afford to make any more. Nobody was going to get in the way of my plans, not even Grace, no matter how hard she tried.

5

GRACE

"Good morning."

I said the words every day, even though they never got returned with anything more than a grunt or an eye roll. That morning was exactly the same. And all the mornings that followed it that month.

Every day Elijah would brush past me, barely acknowledging my existence. Every day we ate separately in our rooms and didn't talk to each other. He danced around me like I had the plague or something.

What was much more important than Elijah avoiding me was my degree. Writing assignments and learning new material at the same time was kicking my ass and no matter how long I spent in the library or looking over other people's notes, I just couldn't seem to get it.

Then to go back to my apartment, where I felt like a pariah, only made me feel even worse about myself. I couldn't bitch to my roommate about how I was feeling and felt bad dumping on my parents or Violet.

So I did the one thing I knew best. I ate out my feelings. In times of stress, snacking and baking became my specialities. It gave me something to do with my hands and mouth that didn't require too much thought or effort. And it felt fucking *great*.

The more Elijah ignored me and the more I struggled with my uni work, the more stressed out and unsettled I became. And the nights were no better. Every night I stayed awake until I heard him leave and then waited until he came back. I'd busy myself with baking something new every couple of days. First it was cinnamon rolls, then brownies, followed by cupcakes. Anything to keep my mind off the mountain of work I had to do and my aloof, absentee roommate.

And every night Elijah came back smelling strongly of gasoline, completely unfazed by both my presence and the sweet smells wafting out of the kitchen. I always left something out for him, a silent offering to call a truce, to start over, but every day the plate with his baked good stayed untouched, as did the note that indicated it was his.

I was halfway through a gooey chocolate brownie and a big mug of tea when my phone lit up. It was Dad.

"Hey, Dad."

"Hey, pumpkin, I hadn't heard from you in a while. How are you doing?"

His voice sounded cheerful, exactly like the Dad that had dropped me off at college at the start of the month. There wasn't a hint of divorce in his voice. Was he good at hiding his feelings, or did he simply not have any?

I looked down at the crumbs that had accumulated on my jumper and bed and was grateful that Dad hadn't insisted on doing a video call.

"I'm good, just still settling in," I said.

"How are you finding the course?"

"Challenging," I said after a moment. Dad chuckled.

"If my Gracie is finding something challenging, then it

must be worth the time. Make sure you're not pushing yourself too hard, though, okay?"

I nodded, even though I knew he couldn't see me. I wanted to ask him about Mom, but I didn't want to break the semblance of normality that we were cultivating on the phone.

"How's your roommate? I've been dying to hear all about them!"

I groaned at both the excitement in Dad's voice that I was certainly going to demolish and the thought of said roommate.

"Let's just say he's not really a people person," I said through gritted teeth. I had a lot more words that I could use to describe Elijah, but I still preferred not to cuss in front of my parents, no matter how understanding they might be.

"Ah, that's just most guys! He's probably in his shell and just figuring shit out." If Dad spent a few minutes with Elijah, he would realise that he was giving him *way* too much credit.

"Maybe," I sighed. I knew he wanted to ask more questions, to find out if he was boyfriend material and other stuff, but I was sure that he could tell I wasn't in the mood.

I put my half eaten brownie down on my beside table and chewed on my lip instead. Silence hung between us like cobwebs as we waited for the other person to make the move. Dad cleared his throat and took the lead.

"So, I'm sure you've spoken to your mom about... our separation." He sniffed. "I just want you to know that this changes nothing about us or how I feel about you, okay? I know it really sucks, but that's just life sometimes."

I wish I could see his face. I wish I could hear the words coming out of his mouth while he was standing in the same room as me. Life really sucked, and it sucked even more when it felt like the punches were coming constantly and out of nowhere.

"Who's decision was it?" I don't know why the words came out at all. There was no satisfactory answer, yet the little girl in me needed to know.

Dad sighed heavily. "In all honesty, I think your mom checked out of our relationship a few years ago. But I don't blame her, it's just... I thought it was a rough patch." Dad's voice was hoarse.

So Mom had been the one to initiate things. She'd been the one who'd fallen out of love. I scanned my mind for memories of signs of looks that I should have noticed, that I must have missed at some point. But it was no use. They were all laced with childish ignorance and blurred into one.

"That sounds really difficult," I whispered.

Dad made a noncommittal noise and cleared his throat. "I say all this to say that I wanted you to send me links to things you might want in your room at my place."

I could envision Dad scratching his head and grimacing to himself as the words came out. It was bound to be awkward, but there was no way around it. I hadn't even thought that far about Dad actually having a completely separate home to Mom. Two separate lives awaited me back home, and I barely had a grasp on the one that I was already living.

"I'll have a think," I said. I glanced down at my hands, which shook violently as the gravity of the future weighed down on me.

"There's no pressure and no rush. I just want things to be as nice for you when you come back h-" he paused. "When you come to visit."

"I appreciate it."

The conversation moved to other less stressful and life-changing things like the weather and TV before we said our awkward goodbyes.

After another sneaky brownie and some half-hearted work, I decided I needed a break for the night. I was at college, for goodness' sake, and even though I still wanted to be a doctor at the end of all of it, I still deserved some time off.

I texted Violet to see if she wanted to hang out. I was disappointed by the response that came back a few minutes later.

Sorry, it's date night. Raincheck for another evening?

I'd truly lost my friend to the relationship life. I was happy for her, but also slightly annoyed that I'd either have to call up someone else or go alone. I sent Violet a reply before I started getting ready.

No worries, babe. Have fun!

Once I'd put on some flattering jeans and a nice top, I looked through my contacts list to see if there was anyone that I could reach out to. As I kept on scrolling, I realised I felt too awkward popping up to people I hadn't spoken to since last semester. Sure, they probably wouldn't take it badly, but the threat of awkwardness stopped me from sending any messages.

I could have a decent night out on my own, right? It's basically a rite of passage, especially when you were single. People did it all the time in the movies, so I decided I would too. For all I knew, I could meet some new friends there.

∼

Once I'd put on a bit of makeup and grabbed my bag, I texted Violet my location and told her to ring me if she didn't hear from me after midnight. I grabbed my bag, slipped into my shoes and tiptoed out of the apartment, even though I wasn't sure if Elijah was even in or not.

The first bar that I came across was very loud, but they had cheap drinks going for their special student night, so I couldn't help myself. I settled myself in at the bar and was grateful for the cute bartender, who immediately took an interest in me.

"Your hair is really cool," he said with a kind smile as he made my two pornstar martinis.

"Thank you," I said, to both his compliments and the beautiful cocktails he put down in front of me.

We chatted for a bit before the bar became busier and he had to attend to more people. Abandoned by the only company I had, I took to people watching instead.

As the alcohol passed through me, I felt less and less awkward as the night went on. I flitted my gaze between frat boys sitting with a bunch of cheerleaders in the corner, giggling along to whatever the inside joke was as well as the adults that clearly frequented the bar every day after work.

It was interesting to come up with back stories for each individual person. That was, until they noticed I was watching them, of course. After my fourth cocktail, I felt like it was time to go somewhere else.

I remembered seeing signs towards a nice doughnut place nearby and decided to track it down. My bartender smiled and winked at me as I left and I'd be lying if I said it didn't make me feel good to get some positive attention.

I left the bar and started walking down the street. The world had started looking wobbly, but I was managing to keep my balance- just about. I looked down at my phone as I tried to work out what was going on with the map.

Where was this damn doughnut place? I took a left turn as instructed and was ready to cuss out my phone when it started redirecting me in the opposite direction and added 5 minutes onto my journey for good measure.

"What the hell is wrong with this thing?" I muttered to myself as I tapped at my screen, which had decided to freeze.

Fucking great. It was after midnight. I was out on my own, probably lost and getting cold. Not the bad ass single girl night that I'd expected, but the one I should have prepared for.

Just as my phone had decided to unfreeze, I looked up when I saw the flicker of something out of the corner of my eye. A tall figure was walking closely behind someone whose face I couldn't really see. I could recognise those muscly shoulders from anywhere, though. It was Elijah.

I squinted to try and get a better idea of what was going on. The guy in front of Elijah looked older than us, maybe early thirties- and it didn't seem like he knew he was being followed.

Why was Elijah following him?

The possible answers made me sick to my stomach, but they did nothing to make me turn around and go about the rest of my night.

I checked the time on my phone. Almost 1am. Was this what Elijah spent his nights doing? I wanted to call out his name, but I thought against it and instead followed behind at a distance.

My curiosity had peaked to an all-time high and all memory of the doughnut place had escaped my mind. When Elijah looked over his shoulder, I ducked into the shadows as quickly as I could and held my breath. When I was confident that he hadn't seen me and had walked on enough, I carried on following him. I wish I'd packed flat shoes because heels were *not* it when you were trying to be sneaky.

I was too far away to see what was in Elijah's hand but continued to follow him and the man towards what appeared to be a storage facility. I noticed a car sitting in the car park and wondered who it belonged to. It wasn't the light that made me stop in my tracks, fearful of being seen, but the motion of Elijah lifting his hand up above the man's head, something shiny and silver enclosed in his grip, before he brought it down on the man's skull with a sound that I'd never be able to forget.

My hands weren't quick enough to mask my scream as they flew up to my face. Elijah turned around in that moment, his dark eyes blazing with fire, his face one of a predator... a monster.

His angry gaze flitted from me to the man on the floor in front of him and back again. But I couldn't do anything but stare at the floor around the man's head where a pool of blood had started to form.

6

ELIJAH

Grace's blood-curdling scream was the last thing I wanted to hear while I stood over David's body. It was just my luck that my stupid, nosy roommate had followed me. I'd *made sure* that there weren't any witnesses. I'd checked so that this wouldn't happen. And yet she'd *still* found a way to fuck things up.

Grace's hand flew to her mouth and, with eyes wider than saucers, she shook her head and started walking backwards. It was like she thought she could disappear back into the night, rewind time and forget what she'd just seen.

I glanced down at David lying at my feet unconscious. Blood was running down the side of his head, but I wasn't worried. I'd done my research and knew that head wounds could be hella dramatic. He'd be fine. Grace was the one that needed to be dealt with.

"Don't fucking move," I hissed at her.

I looked around to see if there was anyone else with her. Grace looked far too dressed up to be walking around at such a time on her own. When I was confident that she was alone, my breathing returned to normal. Or at least as normal as it could be in such a situation.

Grace kept on shaking her head, and her pastel pink pigtails shook with her. I knew that look in her eyes, the look that people had when they discovered something dangerous or horrific. In Grace's case, this was both.

Think Elijah, think.

The most important thing was making sure that nobody touched David, and that I got him into the storage unit as quickly as possible. I'd set up everything beforehand and rehearsed it all in my head. It would take me a couple minutes, tops, to sort it at all out. But making sure that Grace didn't run off and snitch was just as important.

Fucking hell, why did women have to complicate everything?

"Is anyone else with you?" I hissed as I looped my hands through David's arms.

Grace shook her head. "No..." her voice wavered and I could tell that she didn't know whether to look at me or at David. "We should call an ambulance... the police..."

"Don't you fucking *dare*," I snapped. Grace jumped at the tone of my voice. I sighed. "Don't call anyone, don't do anything, just stay there, okay?" I said forcefully.

I needed her to understand how important the situation was. I needed her to know that she shouldn't have followed me, that she shouldn't have gotten involved, that she didn't understand the full story and never would.

"Elijah-"

"Grace, I swear to god if you don't listen to me," I growled.

"Okay!" she squeaked.

Her eyes darted to the metal pole I'd used to hit David over the head that now lay on the ground. It had fulfilled its purpose. I grunted and started dragging David towards the unit that I'd rented out, my eyes on Grace the entire time.

To my surprise, she stood completely still and simply watched me.

I pulled open the door and dragged David in, discarding him on the chair I'd set up in the middle.

I knew I was strapped for time, so set about quickly binding his wrists and ankles to the chair with cable ties as well as tying him up with thick rope to make sure that there was no chance of him getting out. To top everything off, I plastered a big strip of duct tape over his mouth. The motherfucker wouldn't be making any noise until I wanted him to.

I'd started renting the unit a month ago and had soundproofed the whole thing. I walked around the room to make sure that the panels were all in place and that all my utensils had been left untouched. When I was happy that David was firmly secured and everything was set up properly, I left the storage facility and locked the door behind me.

Now onto Grace. When I walked up to where she was, I saw she was on her phone, frantically texting. She looked up when she realised how close I was to her.

"I was just-" she squeaked out, but I grabbed her phone from her hand before she could finish her sentence.

"*OMG, Violet, you wouldn't guess what I just saw Elijah do,*" I read her text out loud, mocking her voice as I did so. Rage boiled deep inside of me, and I fixed Grace with my murderous glare. "This," I said, holding up her stupid phone to her stupid face. "This is not what I told you to do, is it?" I growled.

Grace shook her head and held out her hand for her phone. "Give it back," she said. She looked up at me with those desperate puppy dog eyes. This time they were filled with fear and, truth be told, I didn't hate it.

I chuckled and held the phone out to her. Before Grace's hands could wrap around the little silver gadget, I threw it onto the floor where it made a resounding *crack*.

"Fuck you, that shit was expensive!" Grace snapped as she bent down to grab it.

"Fuck *you* for not minding your business!" I growled.

"Did you just kill that guy?" Grace asked indignantly. I noticed how her bottom lip shook as she tried to maintain an air of confidence.

"Are you deaf? I literally told you it has nothing to do with you!"

"Elijah, just tell me the truth. What are you doing to that poor man?"

Grace's eyes were full of tears and remorse that was directed towards the wrong person. Her reaction pissed me off even more, and I knew I would explode if I wasn't careful. *Poor man*? Of course, she was dumb enough to think that *David* was the victim.

"Right, I'm going to the police and you can tell them the truth instead," Grace muttered. She turned on her heels, which she was clearly struggling to walk in, and ran in the opposite direction.

She must have been an idiot if she thought I wouldn't chase her. I was quick on my feet, but it barely took any effort to catch up with her, seeing as I was almost twice her size.

I could hear Grace's panicked breaths speeding up as she struggled to put distance between us. Before she could make it around the corner that would take her towards the main road, I grabbed her by one of her ponytails and dragged her towards me. I wrapped my arms tightly around her and walked back the way we had come, ignoring her cries and her squirming as well as her sweet vanilla scent.

"Get off of me!" she yelled. I could feel her heels kicking at my shins and squeezed her tighter in my arms.

Ignoring her kicking and screaming, I dragged her

toward my car. Once we stood outside of it, I unlocked it and gestured for her to get into the backseat.

"I'm not getting in your car," Grace snapped.

"It's cute that you think you have a choice," I said, pushing her into the car despite her resistance. It's like she forgot she was so much smaller and weaker than me. Grace folded her arms over her chest. Her lips pouted like a spoilt child, but the look in her eyes told me she was terrified. Of me.

"What's going on? Who is that man?" she asked.

"That's none of your business. You stay here and don't move," I snapped.

I slammed the door shut, muffling Grace's protestations, and locked the car before walking off to deal with David.

Now that I'd been interrupted, I had to work quickly. My plans had gone awry, and I needed to double check on David for my sanity.

I opened the door to see David's head lolling to the side, clearly still passed out. From where I stood, I could see that the wound on his head had started to clot. Satisfied that he would not move or break free, I turned off the light and locked the door again, checking twice more that it was definitely shut before I left.

Now back to that nosy bitch in the car.

I got back in the car, surprised to see that Grace had stopped banging against the doors and windows and was just staring straight ahead.

"You locked me in your car," she said flatly as I slid into the driver's seat.

"I did."

I turned on the engine and reversed out of the parking spot. I glanced at the mirror as I drove down the road that led to campus, catching Grace's eyes every few seconds. She still looked scared, but also very unimpressed.

"Who was that man? Why did you hit him over the head and why are you keeping him in that storage unit?" Grace asked.

I met her annoying questions with a fierce gaze in the wing mirror and silence. She wasn't getting a word out of me about David. She knew way too much already.

"If you don't go to the police, I will," she said after a few moments.

"No, you won't."

"You don't know that," she said haughtily.

If the situation wasn't so dire, I would have laughed at the look on her face. Grace truly thought she could intimidate and threaten me? She had to be on a completely different level of crazy.

"Oh, I'll make sure you don't," I said flatly.

We were both silent for the rest of the journey and when we pulled up outside our accommodation block, Grace was practically racing to get out of the car.

Good thing I don't like your company much either.

"Go inside and don't you dare go back to that place," I snapped.

"Trust me, I won't," Grace sneered at me before she slammed the door shut.

I waited in the car and watched her search for her keycard in her purse that would let her into the apartment. She cut her gaze towards me, brows furrowed in annoyance, before she let herself in. I waited a few moments before I drove back to the storage unit. I still had a long night ahead of me. And now I had another big problem to deal with.

How fucking fantastic.

7

GRACE

The sound of the metal pole when it hit the man's skull ricocheted through my ribcage. The empty look on Elijah's face as the man had fallen to the ground had burned itself into my memory and refused to leave. Those dark, empty eyes and lips that had twitched with something I struggled to put my finger on made it impossible for me to sleep.

My night had descended into something I never could have comprehended, and I'd been on edge from the second that I'd found seen with that pole in his hand. If he hadn't locked the car doors while he'd driven me back to our apartment, I might have jumped out just to get away from him. I'd tossed and turned in bed all night, wondering what I was supposed to do, how I was supposed to act now that I knew my roommate was more fucked up than I'd ever imagined.

And to make matters even worse, the motherfucker had cracked the screen on my new phone! How the hell was is supposed to explain *that* when my parents eventually asked? I didn't have the money to fix it right now and I sure as hell wouldn't ask them for it.

Morning rolled around, and I felt worse than I had in a

long time. My scalp still burned from when Elijah had dragged me by my pigtails. My skin still felt sore from when he'd manhandled me. I could hear him in the kitchen rattling around and I needed to go to the toilet, but I didn't want to bump into Elijah on the way. The longer I held it, the more my bladder complained. Life had to go on, even if I had discovered that I had the Devil as my roommate. I sighed and tiptoed to the bathroom as quickly as I could.

On my way back, I walked past the kitchen as quietly as I could, hoping that Elijah wouldn't notice me or would choose to ignore me like usual.

"Good morning."

Shit.

"Grace?"

There it was again, the deep, gravelly voice that I barely heard unless it was insulting me. I stopped in my tracks and went back towards the kitchen. Elijah leaned against the counter, a blank expression on his face, and in front of him were two mugs.

"What do you want?" I snapped.

I stood in the doorway, one foot in the kitchen, one outside it in case I had to run. I'd found out his little secret. I had something on him now. But now that I knew what he was truly capable of, I had to watch my back.

"I made you some coffee," Elijah said gruffly. He tilted his head towards the steaming mugs.

Even though the coffee smelled divine and was exactly what I needed that morning, there was no way in hell that I was going to accept anything from him. Not from someone who could hurt someone in cold blood.

"I'm fine, thank you," I said through gritted teeth.

"Please, I insist," Elijah pushed. This time, his voice was more forceful, even though his face stayed the same.

I walked towards him, my eyes on him the entire time.

Elijah watched me like a lion observing his prey, ready to pounce and feast when the time was right. I grabbed the handle of my mug and lifted it to my lips, noticing the flicker of satisfaction that crossed Elijah's face. Before any of the liquid could touch my mouth, I tipped the coffee down the sink.

"I said *no* thank you."

I gave Elijah a scathing look that dared him to bring up the events of the previous night, to bring up *anything* to do with all of that. The fact that he hadn't said anything made it feel like it was a dream or like it hadn't happened at all. But I'd seen it. I'd *heard* it. I'd heard the clang and the crack and I was afraid that I'd never be able to unhear it again.

"Suit yourself." Elijah snorted and brought his own mug to his lips.

Those dark eyes were on me once again, full of danger, full of challenge, forever alluring. I hated the certainty they held, the secrets they refused to share. But most of all, I hated how dirty they made me feel when I was trapped in their gaze.

I turned on my heel and flounced out of the kitchen. Clearly, I wouldn't get much out of Elijah. I'd barely gotten a reaction, and he didn't seem like he wanted to acknowledge his crimes. *Great.*

I needed to stand underneath the shower and scrub until all remnants of the previous night had disappeared. I grabbed my soap and towel and practically ran into the bathroom before Elijah could get to it first.

No matter how hard I scrubbed at my skin and lathered up the soap, I didn't feel clean. I caught my reflection in the mirror and cringed. Not only was I red raw from the burning water and from viciously attacking my skin, I couldn't help but noticed that my stomach was looking bigger than usual.

I pinched the fat there and couldn't believe that it was

mine. I knew that my bad snacking habits would have to catch up to me eventually, but I hadn't expected it to be so soon. I sucked in as hard as I could, and for a moment, I felt better about myself. But as soon as I released my breath, the truth was clear as day.

I jumped out of the shower and covered myself with my towel as quickly as I could. If there'd been any way to make me feel worse, seeing my reflection in the mirror had done exactly that.

I went to my room and looked for the baggiest clothes that I could find. Anything figure hugging or even moderately tight would just set me off again. I had to get it under control.

I pulled my sweatshirt over my head and jumped into a pair of tracksuit bottoms. My clothes swamped me and it felt good, well, at least better than seeing certain areas exposed.

It's okay, it's just a bit of weight. It's not the end of the world.

I anxiously checked out my face in the mirror. Maybe that was another chin that I could see...

No, I wouldn't do that. I wouldn't obsess over my body and make myself feel even worse. I just needed to get my stress under control and maybe bake and snack a little less. It was obvious which one had to go first.

I sat on my bed and took a swig from my water bottle, which had been sitting on my nightstand. I hadn't realised how parched I was and was grateful for the cool liquid as I glugged down the rest of the bottle.

When I stood up and began tidying my room, the world started to spin. *Weird.* I crouched down to pick up some dirty socks and nearly fell over as I tried to get back up.

What the hell?

I rubbed my eyes and blinked a few times as I tried to see through the blur.

What was going on?

My limbs felt heavy, and I was sluggish, almost like I'd had too many shots. But I hadn't had anything yet, not even breakfast. My heart raced and my breathing grew more shallow by the second. I swayed with the trees that were outside my window, moving back and forth like the breeze, like the ocean.

I looked towards the door. Maybe I could shout for help. Not like Elijah would help me, anyway. My eyes skimmed over my room and landed on my empty water bottle. The only thing I'd had since I'd woken up.

One minute my hands were filled with socks while my eyes were on my empty water bottle and the next minute, everything was black.

~

The smell of chlorine invaded my nostrils and made me gag. I felt the cool wet floor beneath me and had to force myself to come to. My eyes strained against the harsh light, but before they could open, the light disappeared and was replaced with a familiar face.

Elijah.

As he hovered over me, I was reminded of his sweet, masculine scent and the heat that radiated from his body. Blinking a few more times, I tried to sit up, but to no avail. Firm hands were pinning me down… Elijah's hands and no matter how hard I tried to fight against them, I couldn't win.

"You're just going to lose your energy if you keep doing that," Elijah said in a bored voice.

I opened my mouth to scream, a weak, croaky sound that was swiftly cut off by Elijah's massive hand. Its warmth and strength rendered me useless and even though I tried to bite him, Elijah stayed put.

"None of that." His dark eyes flashed.

The drum in my chest beat hard against my ribs as I tried to gather my thoughts. Elijah straddled my body and pinned me down easily while his hand kept me quiet. The sadistic sneer on his face only made my heart race more.

Why the hell were we at the pool?

The last thing I remembered was...

The water. Elijah must have drugged me while I was in the shower. That was the only thing that made sense. Then I passed out, and he took me to the pool.

"If you scream, I'm going to make you regret it," Elijah growled. He gave me a look that confirmed that promise as he took his hand away from my mouth.

"Let me go!" I shouted. It wasn't a scream, but Elijah clearly didn't appreciate the decibels, anyway.

"There'd be no fun in that," Elijah chuckled darkly.

It was the first time I'd heard anything that even vaguely resembled joy slip between those perfect lips of his. The sound was bone-chilling and seemed to echo around the swimming pool.

"What do you want from me?" I thrashed against him again, but Elijah stayed still and looked at me as if I was nothing more than a petulant child. "You drugged me, didn't you?"

A small smile appeared on Elijah's face. The sick fuck was enjoying my suffering far too much.

"I want to make sure that you don't snitch about what you saw."

There it was. The punishment for my nosiness.

"I won't," I said weakly.

In the moment I'd caught him, I'd wanted to tell someone, but after seeing the fire and fury in his eyes, I knew Elijah wouldn't let me go scot free after that.

He snorted. "You're just telling me what you think I want to hear."

Elijah slid off of me and I was about to get up myself when he grabbed me by my arm and dragged me across the floor.

"Ow, you're hurting me!" I cried out as my head bounced up and down on the uneven floor.

Elijah didn't care. He kept dragging me until we reached the edge of the pool. My hair was mere inches from the water. I took a deep breath and looked up at Elijah with pleading eyes. There was no way he was being serious. He'd scared me enough. I just wanted to get back to my day.

"No, please no," I begged when I saw that familiar glint in his eyes. "I swear, I won't say anything. I didn't see shit."

Elijah kneeled down beside me and stroked my hair gently. His face was blank for a moment and I held my breath in anticipation of his next move. Maybe he'd have a change of heart. Or better yet, maybe someone would see what he was about to do and make him stop. A girl could only hope.

"You might want to close your eyes," he growled. The words had barely hit my eardrums when Elijah yanked on my hair and submerged me under water.

No no no.

I gasped at the impact of the ice cold water. Elijah held my body down firmly with one hand so that I didn't fall into the pool and kept his other hand firmly in my hair. The chlorine filled my nose and made my eyes sting and every time I tried to push against him, tried to go up for air, Elijah held me firmly in the water.

Stars began swimming at the corner of my blurry vision and when I thought I couldn't take it anymore, he brought me up for air. I coughed and spluttered once I was back on land and shook violently as I stared at Elijah.

"I'm going to teach you to mind your business," Elijah growled. That sadistic smirk was back on his face.

I spat swimming pool water onto the ground in front of him and glowered with all my might. "Fine, I've got your message. Now why can't you let me go?" I coughed.

Elijah grimaced. Clearly, the sound of me choking on chlorinated water didn't please him, but I wasn't exactly the one to blame, was I?

"You're right, I could," Elijah mused for a moment. "But then that would be an awful waste."

Again, my limbs were too weak, probably because of the drugs he'd slipped into my bottle, to fight him. In a matter of seconds, he'd overpowered me again, and I found my head under water once more.

This time was worse, because I wasn't sure how long he'd keep me under or if he'd let me up at all. As I thrashed and screamed and swallowed gulps of water, I counted down the seconds that felt like hours.

Why hadn't I just left him alone? Why hadn't I just gone home?

He'd told me to leave him alone, he'd told me, and then I'd gotten involved in shit- I was implicated in a crime. A crime that had sent plenty of people to prison.

I was ready to take my final breath when my tormentor dragged me out of the water. Elijah discarded me on the floor like a smelly fish and stood up to stretch his muscles out as I struggled to get oxygen back into my body.

"That... was.... Unnecessary," I wheezed.

I coughed some more, not caring how gross it sounded. *He'd* done this to me. I shot Elijah the dirtiest look that I could muster, and he shot me one right back.

If I'd known the depths of Elijah's cruelty, then I might have asked to switch apartments earlier. *He* was the one in the wrong here, not me. I'd simply seen what he'd been doing. A simple mistake that had only made things worse. But this never would have happened in the first place if he hadn't been getting up to shady shit.

Elijah bent down and grabbed my chin with his finger and thumb. He brought his face, a picture of disdain, close to mine and bared his teeth at me. I shook from the cold. I shook with fear and uncertainty. I shook because of Elijah's touch... because he was so close. I tried to pull away from him, but his grip only became firmer.

"*I* decide what's necessary when it comes to safeguarding my secrets," Elijah spat, his eyes darkening as they searched my face. He released me and stormed away, leaving me in a crumpled heap on the floor.

"Why did you do it?" I shouted at Elijah's back, my voice hoarse. Elijah kept walking as if I hadn't said anything, slamming the door behind him like usual.

I wanted to know. I needed him to open up about this one thing. I couldn't allow myself to believe that he was truly a violent monster. Even if I had witnessed that side of him twice in the past 24 hours, I wouldn't be able to sleep knowing that was his true nature. Knowing that he was in the room across from me and could strike at any moment.

How far *would* Elijah go to make sure that his secret was safe?

8
GRACE

I stood with the other students who were waiting to go into the lecture theatre. Even though a whole day had passed, I still felt shaky after Elijah had drugged me and nearly drowned me. I'd slept awfully the night before and continued to avoid him at all costs.

I felt eyes burning into the side of my cheek and made the mistake of looking up. Elijah stood across the hall, his dark, hellish eyes fixed on me. I stared back, even though I felt even more on edge now that we were in the same vicinity. What was he doing in the medicine building anyway? Was he following me?

"Are you going to go in?"

I tore my gaze away from Elijah's and realised that the girl waiting in line behind me was impatient that I was holding up the queue. I was glad to have an excuse to put distance between me and Elijah again, and before I walked into the lecture hall; I took one last look to my right and found his dark eyes narrowed at me. The message was loud and clear.

I'm going to get you.

My attention flitted between my lecturer and the door.

I'd convinced myself that if I didn't guard the door with my eyes, Elijah would burst in at any moment and subject me to something just as bad, if not worse, than the cold swimming pool water.

∼

I was one of the last to leave once the lecture was over. A mistake I hadn't realised I'd made.

"Grace."

Elijah's voice met me as soon as I was alone in the hallway. I turned my back to him. I shivered from the ice in his voice and kept on walking.

"Grace, I'm fucking talking to you," Elijah growled.

I knew it was no use running away. He was bigger and stronger than me in every way and I'd have to face him eventually because newsflash: we still lived together.

"What?" I hissed as I turned around.

I wasn't prepared to bump face first into Elijah's big muscly chest and I was completely caught off guard by the heat and sweet, but dangerous smell that emanated from his body.

Elijah's lips curled into a cruel smirk. "I thought I'd check up on you," he said darkly.

His eyes trailed up and down my body, in that way that made me feel like he was undressing me in his head. I hated it, but there was nothing I could do, not against those dark eyes.

I pulled away. "How am I doing after you *spiked* me?" I spat. I brought my fingers to my chin and pretended to think really hard. "Well, I feel fucking horrible, thanks to you," I retorted.

Elijah licked his lips and cocked his head at me.

"Nothing to say? Cat got your tongue?" I snapped.

Before Elijah could respond, I turned on my heel to leave, but his big, firm hand flew to my wrist and forced me to stop.

"You're coming this way." Elijah's voice was hard, low, and serious.

I tried to pull away from his grasp, but it was no use. As he dragged me down the hallway and into an empty classroom, my eyes scanned to see if there was anyone who might interfere and rescue me.

"Elijah, you're hurting me!" I cried.

"Shut up," he grumbled in response.

Still gripping onto my wrist, Elijah shut the classroom door and pushed me up against it. He pinned my hands above my head with one hand and used the other to tip my chin up so that I was looking at him.

My breath caught in my throat, and my heart wouldn't stop racing in my chest. *Breathe Grace, breathe. He can't do anything to you on campus when there's so many people who could catch him. There's too much risk.*

"Couldn't this have waited until we got home?" I said hotly.

Elijah sneered. "That place will never be my home," he scoffed. "Besides, I enjoy catching you off guard. Your reaction is priceless."

I pulled away from him again, but his grip grew impossibly tighter. "Waste your energy trying to get away, I don't care," Elijah purred. "I have all day."

"Just say what you want already. I'm getting bored."

My voice was calm, but my thoughts were anything but. I didn't like the way that the feeling of Elijah's skin against mine sent electricity through my body. He was the same guy that I'd seen do awful things, who'd also done awful things to *me*, and I knew there were more things up his sleeve.

"Attitude, attitude," Elijah tutted. "I thought a few minutes in the pool would stop that, but apparently not."

I rolled my eyes at him. Elijah let go of my wrists and wrapped his hand around my throat, his eyes flaring with fire.

"You could get in trouble for that, you know? There was probably CCTV..." I struggled to breathe as his grip around my throat grew tighter.

"Maybe you're stupid enough to not think so far ahead, but I definitely did," Elijah growled. The insult stung, but I turned my focus to breathing instead of my feelings.

Elijah searched my eyes before his gaze fell to my lips. My eyes couldn't help but look at his lips, too. I found myself wondering how many people he'd kissed, and if he thought about kissing me as much as I thought about kissing him. My clit twinged as the thought of Elijah's lips on mine refused to leave my mind.

"Why are you doing this?" I wheezed.

It was *not* the time to thinking about kissing.

"I need to make sure you don't snitch." Elijah choked me harder.

I shook my head and gave him my most innocent look, even though he was hurting me.

"I won't snitch if you tell me why you did it. If you explain, I won't say shit."

It was a bold statement and a dangerous one. Elijah wasn't the type of guy that responded well to threats at all. His lips were at my ear, his warm breath sending me crazy.

"You're not going to snitch because you know I'll make your life hell if you even think about it," Elijah said.

I took in the situation and felt my lips spreading into a smirk. For a moment, the veil slipped, and I saw what was really going on. Sure, it was Elijah's hand wrapped around my throat, but it was *his* secret that was under threat, not mine.

I searched Elijah's eyes and through the hatred and aggression, fear floated there clear as day. If I told anyone about what I'd seen, who knew how long Elijah would end up behind bars?

"You have a lot more to lose than I do, Elijah," I breathed. And we both knew it was true. "Do your fucking worse. I don't care. Because I know the truth about you," I snarled.

Elijah's eyes darkened, and that chilling smirk returned to his face. "You're going to regret ever letting those words slip out of those pretty lips," he growled.

"Maybe you'll regret not telling me the full story," I said hotly.

A sharp rap at the door made me jump out of my skin. Elijah tightened his grip around my throat and he fixed me in his gaze. *Don't move*, his eyes said.

"Just a moment," he calmly called out to the person on the other side of the door.

Elijah moved me away from the door before he released his grip on my throat. I took in a big gulp of air as he walked back towards the door and opened it.

"Our class is starting now, so we need this room," said a female voice on the other side of the door.

"You can use it," Elijah said gruffly. He cast me nothing more than a sideways glance before he walked out of the room.

Asshole.

I felt awkward standing in the corner of a room that I had no reason to be in and when a group of students started milling in; I left before they could ask questions.

I brought my fingers to my wrist and my throat, feeling how tender the skin was there. Even though he'd caused me physical pain, somehow I still felt oddly satisfied. I actually had something over Elijah, some real leverage. But as I walked back to the apartment, the sensation of fear wouldn't escape me. I'd told him to do his worse, and going off of what I already knew about Elijah, I didn't think that there was anything that would prepare me for whatever his worse was.

∼

I blinked my eyes open slowly, confused when I realised it was dark outside. Shit. I sat up in bed and saw my discarded notebook and textbook sitting on the floor in a heap. What was supposed to be a two-minute breather had turned into a full on nap.

Shit. Shit. Shit.

My body must have needed it after all those sleepless nights. If only I could sleep when I was supposed to.

I'd woken up groggy, hungry and disoriented. And to make maters worse, Elijah's music was louder than ever. I yawned and threw on my jumper before I pulled open my door to confront Elijah.

I had not expected to see people spilling out of the kitchen and living room, drinks in their hands and dressed up as they spoke to each other. I closed my door as quickly as I'd opened it and slid onto the floor.

There was a party going on in the apartment.

What shocked me more wasn't the party itself, but the fact that Elijah must have organised it. Mr- I-Hate-People had enough friends to invite to a party? Of course, I was also pissed at the fact that he hadn't told me. Which was most definitely on purpose.

I weighed up my options. My stomach growled aggressively beneath my jumper. I'd eaten the other food that I'd snuck into my room. I needed to get to the kitchen or else I'd perish.

What if someone tried to talk to me? Or what if Elijah tried to drag me in and humiliate me? The ball of anxiety in the pit of my stomach grew bigger and bigger.

Think Grace, think.

A cheer went off in the living room. I didn't know why, but that didn't stop the pang that I felt in my chest. I hadn't been to a party since last semester and I'd be lying if I said I didn't miss them.

Moving in with Elijah and finding out about my parents' divorce had thrown me off my usual mojo and I hadn't accepted any invites to a single party because it felt like every night was meant to be used to catch up on my studies.

Fuck that.

I glanced at my closet and saw a hint of black silk peeking out from the corner. It was my apartment just as much as it was Elijah's. Maybe it wasn't my party, but I wasn't going to pass up the opportunity to get drunk and blow off some steam. Worst-case scenario, I would dip out and reacquaint myself with my bed.

I found a hip flask in my drawer that had some tequila left over from a night out I'd had over the summer with friends. I took a swig and winced at the taste, but took a longer one because I needed to play catch up with the other party guests.

Attacking my body with wet wipes, deodorant and perfume, I slipped into the dress and couldn't help noticing that even though it still looked good on me; it fit a bit more tightly than I remembered.

It's okay, it's not the end of the world.

I took another sip from my hip flask and tore my gaze away from the mirror.

I found a cute pair of shoes to slip on. It felt dumb

dressing up just to stay in my apartment, but it gave me something to concentrate on that wasn't depressing. I slapped on some mascara and lip gloss before I downed the remaining contents of my hip flask. I knew it wasn't the best idea on an empty stomach, but at least it would get me drunk quickly.

It was now or never. My head had started to feel fuzzy. I opened the door and walked straight into a couple that were making out.

"Sorry," I said too loudly. I wasn't sure if they hadn't heard me or didn't care about some random girl, but either way, they ignored me and carried on playing tonsil tennis.

I continued walking around, trying to see if I recognised anyone when I realised what was hanging off the walls and different articles of furniture.

My underwear!

Elijah had strung up my underwear, that I hadn't had the chance to take out of the washing machine, all over the apartment like birthday bunting. And to make matters worse, nobody seemed to be doing anything about it.

Could that asshole get anymore insufferable?

The embarrassment was too much to bear, especially because I knew that the party guests knew that the underwear couldn't belong to Elijah and I was sure that if anyone asked him, he'd be more than happy to tell them who it belonged to.

I needed another drink. Badly.

The music got louder as I walked towards the drinks table, where another bunch of unfamiliar faces swam into view. I poured myself a strong drink and quickly tossed it back before pouring myself another one.

I was grateful for the bowls of crisps sitting on the table, less grateful that they were in *my* bowls, but it was food. I nibbled on the snacks, glad to have something to line my stomach with.

I stood at the table, holding my drink in my hand as I scanned the room. The alcohol hadn't been enough to swallow all of my anxiety, but it had quelled it enough that I forced myself to walk up to a white-haired girl standing in the corner on her own.

She had an elfish look about her, a little pointed chin, pink cheeks and pretty eyes. She didn't look like she was into the party, what with the downcast expression on her face and the fact that she'd moved herself into a corner.

"Hey, are you okay?" I asked over the music.

The white-haired girl looked up and gave me a kind smile, but it didn't quite reach her eyes.

"Yeah, I'm alright. Are you okay?" She had a sweet voice, but I couldn't quite pinpoint where her accent was from.

"I live here and I didn't even know this party was going on," I chuckled, to lighten the mood.

The girl laughed and took a sip of her drink. "Oh really? It's a nice place. My roommate told me to come with her. I didn't know it was happening until like 30 minutes before." She nodded at a girl making out with a ginger haired guy near the door. "I'm Willow, by the way."

"I'm Grace."

We both smiled at each other and walked back over to the drinks table. As Willow and I got to talking about what courses we were doing and if we knew anyone at the party, her voice started lightening up a bit. I wanted to ask her what had made her so upset earlier, but knew better than to pry. I'd gotten into enough trouble already because of that.

"So, are you on the prowl tonight?" I teased. I raised my cup up to Willow before I took a sip.

Willow shook her head and her eyes darted to the corner of the room where the sofas had been moved to. I followed her gaze and noticed that Elijah was sitting in the corner with Nate and their other friend, Tristan, who I'd never spoken to before but only seen at parties.

"You got your sights set on one of them?" I asked. This time, my voice was a bit more guarded.

Obviously, Nate was going out with my best friend, but I had no reason to feel protective of Elijah. He was nothing more than my roommate and a nuisance. Nothing more.

"No, I just..." Willow ran her hand through her shocking white hair and sighed heavily. "Maybe I think Tristan's kind of cute, but I'm not going to do anything about it." She forced a laugh. Willow nudged me and gave me a pointed look. "What about you, Grace? Who are you after?"

I tore my gaze away from Elijah's corner and positioned myself so that my back was facing him and I couldn't betray myself by looking his way.

"I'm just here to have a good time," I said honestly.

"I'd love a second chance at that." Willow shrugged.

When the music changed, our eyes lit up with excitement as we recognised the song and before I knew it, we were on the makeshift dance floor, shaking our hips to the beat.

All thoughts of work, my parents, Elijah, his dark secret, and all the other bullshit that had been going on completely left my mind as I drank, danced, and sang with Willow.

9

ELIJAH

"We haven't heard from you in ages, man," Tristan punched me in the side and I winced.

"I've been busy," I said. I'd known that my absence at group hangouts was bound to come up again at some point, but that didn't mean I was any more prepared.

"How are you liking your new place?" Nate asked. He leaned back on the couch and took a long swig of his beer.

"I thought you were the worst flatmate imaginable," I said with a wolfish grin. "But now I live with Grace."

"No fucking way," Nate chuckled.

"Don't pretend that you didn't know."

"Okay, fair enough, Violet might have let it slip, but she didn't say much." Nate held up his hands in mock surrender, but his eyes flashed with mischief.

"Is it that bad?" Tristan asked before he snorted something off the back of his phone.

I grimaced as he shook his head. I still couldn't get why he was obsessed with that nasty stuff. From the moment I'd met him during fresher's week, it seemed like he was always on something. But that was his business and the more I stayed out of it, the more he'd hopefully stay out of mine.

A cheer went up near the speakers and I couldn't help but look over. When I noticed Grace dancing there with a girl that had long white hair, I felt my chest tighten.

Speak of the fucking she-devil.

I felt Nate nudge me in the ribs and I watched Tristan's eyes light up with glee.

"That's her, right?" asked Tristan.

"The very one," Nate replied.

I shook my head as I took in her outfit. The little bitch had gotten fully dressed up in a slinky black dress that clung too tightly to her curves and begged to be ripped off. I clawed at the sofa as my eyes trailed up her lean legs and lingered on her exposed cleavage before I found my way to her face.

The sight of Grace's face with her plush lips and wide eyes made me hard and hateful. I'd thrown the party to piss her off, not so that she could have a fucking fun time. I wasn't even having a fun time, so there was no way in hell that she was going to.

I couldn't take my eyes off of her as she shook her hips and danced with the other girl. She looked like she was having the time of her life. Meanwhile, I was struggling to chill out, knowing that I had a guy held captive in a storage unit that Grace knew about.

"So you're telling me you haven't hit that?" Tristan asked way too loudly.

I tore my gaze away from Grace and kicked him in the shin, but that did nothing to stop him. Clearly, whatever drugs he was taking had already had an effect on his brain and pain receptors.

"Nate, c'mon, you've got to agree with me. If you were living with Grace, wouldn't you-" Tristan was getting loud and obnoxious and I could tell that even Nate was getting sick of his shit.

"Dude, that's my girlfriend's best friend," he snapped. "But I think *you* should be all over her, Elijah," Nate said, shooting me a wink.

"You guys are fucking idiots," I grumbled. I took a sip of my drink, the same one I'd been holding all night.

"You're only saying that because you're not drunk enough," Tristan said.

He grabbed a bottle of tequila and was about to upend it in my cup, but luckily enough; I was quicker and could grab it out of his hand before he could start pouring.

"The fuck man? This is your party and you're currently being a massive bummer," he said.

"Yeah, what's up with you? Why are you not drinking?" Nate chimed in.

I clenched my fists so tightly that I was close to drawing blood. I'd thrown the party to piss off Grace and to get the guys off my back for being antisocial, and now I was under scrutiny, which was the last thing I needed.

"You must be blind because I am drinking," I said, pointedly holding up my cup. Nate raised an eyebrow and gave me a look that said *I'm not stupid*. I shrugged and took a long sip, only if it was to make a point.

I'd filled my cup up with mostly mixer so there was no fear of getting too drunk. The last time I'd been drunk, I'd let my guard down and made a selfish mistake that I knew I'd spend every day of my life atoning for. I wouldn't let that happen again.

"Maybe you need something to take the edge off." Nate nodded towards Tristan, whose face lit up instantly.

"What do you want, man? I've got downers, uppers-"

"I want to take a piss," I said, cutting him off.

I stood up from the sofa and made my way through the throng of people that were dancing in the living room. A few girls that I recognised from the parties that Nate and Tristan had thrown in the past tried to make intentional eye contact with me, but I ignored them.

My hand had barely wrapped around the bathroom door handle when I heard someone clear their throat behind me. I turned and looked down to see Grace standing behind me, a smug expression on her face, her cleavage inviting my tongue to explore it...

"I'm surprised that you have enough friends to throw a party," said Grace.

How was she speaking to me so confidently after what I'd done to her at the pool? After I'd threatened her multiple times and hung her lacy underwear all around the apartment? I eyed Grace's stature and deduced that she had to be drunk, or at the very least tipsy. The way she'd been practically hiding in corners and avoiding me since the pool incident told me that the only way she could talk to me could not be without liquid courage.

"I'm surprised that you don't look like a tramp for once," I replied.

Even though the insult wasn't true, both Grace and I knew that her choice to wear sweatpants every day wasn't a stylistic choice.

Grace's face screwed up, and she narrowed her eyes at me. Clearly, I'd gotten to her.

"I'd rather look like a tramp than-"

"Than what?" I challenged her. Grace and I were face to chest, and I found it amusing how much I dwarfed her.

"Whatever, you're not worth it," she scoffed as she turned to walk away. But I had other plans. I grabbed Grace's arm and pulled her towards me.

"Let me go, I want to dance," Grace whined.

I ignored her and dragged her into her room. The couples in the hallway were too drunk and too obsessed with each other to care about us. Once we'd gotten into Grace's room, I shut the door behind me.

"Ha ha, very funny. Now let me out," said Grace.

I crossed my arms over my chest and gave her an unrelenting look. Grace crossed her arms and mimicked my stance and expression. Even though she was trying to challenge me, I couldn't help but notice how fucking good she looked in her dress and heels.

Why couldn't she wear more stuff like that around the apartment? Her presence would be a hell of a lot more bearable if she did.

As if she could sense my thoughts, Grace took a step back towards her bed, trying to put as much distance between us as possible. I didn't blame her. The last time we'd been this close, I had wrapped my hand around her throat while she'd threatened to spill my secret. Grace deserved to be afraid.

"That's right, sit on the bed like a good little girl," I purred.

"Elijah, stop, it's not funny," Grace breathed as I took a few steps towards her. She fell onto the bed in her haste to get away from me, and I couldn't help but marvel at the sight of her lying down. The way that her dress rode up her thick thighs was hard to ignore.

Fuck.

Grace gasped, her hand flying to her dress as quick as a flash- but not quick enough. I'd seen the flash of her lacy underwear, and it had been enough to set me into a trance.

With her eyes wide and lips parted, Grace looked like a meal that I had to devour in its entirety. If she knew the depths of the grotesque fantasies that flitted through my mind every time she walked past me in her shorts or towel, then she would be nothing short of afraid. Even more afraid than she already was.

"Elijah," Grace breathed, and I barely heard her over the sound of my racing heart.

Sickness. That was the only thing it could be described as, the thing charging through my veins. It was sickness that possessed me in that moment and led me to pounce on Grace before she could even think about moving away from me.

"Ow," Grace cried as I pinned my arms above her head.

I pressed myself flush against her and scanned her face for any signs of struggle. Grace's expression went from fear to lust to anger in seconds. And I loved every single moment.

My eyes dropped to her mouth once again, and I felt my cock twitching in my pants at the thought of all the possibilities.

"Get on the floor," I snapped.

Grace narrowed her eyes at me and pursed her lips. "I thought you wanted me on the bed like *a good little girl*?" she said in a mocking voice.

I flashed Grace a cruel smirk and dragged her off the bed, her arms flailing as she tried to fight against me. There was no use. I easily pushed Grace to her knees.

"Happy?" Grace glowered at me.

Even though the look on her face suggested that she'd be happy to witness my murder, my cock had other ideas. Having her face so close to my crotch made it hard to think straight, made it hard to think about anything at all that didn't concern Grace.

Grace's body, Grace's mouth, her eyes, her perfect cheekbones. All of it. I had to have it. I had to own it. I felt like I'd stepped out of my body as I pulled down my zipper and took my erect cock out of my pants.

"Elijah, no..." Grace whimpered as her eyes landed on my erection. Her eyes widened as she took in my length and

I knew from the flush that took over her face that she was imagining it sliding inside of her.

Grace tried to stand up, and I pushed her right back down to the floor where she belonged. I pressed the tip of my cock right up against her perfect pink lips, which she had clamped shut.

Grace shook her head and gave me a pleading look. Her eyes darted around her room, probably to see if there was anything she could use to assist her escape.

"Don't you dare think about anything except putting this all in your mouth," I breathed.

Grace whimpered, her lips still firmly shut, and in the spur of the moment, I wrapped her pink hair around my hand and gave it a good pull. Grace's mouth flew open in pain at the sudden movement, which gave me the perfect opportunity to thrust my dick into her mouth.

Pleasure shot through my body at the sensation of Grace's warm mouth. The sight of her struggling against my grip on her hair and my length in her mouth gave me a sick satisfaction that I couldn't even comprehend.

"Stop squirming and suck," I ordered her.

I held Grace's scared eyes with my own. The flicker of innocence I saw there was something I wanted to break, something I needed to destroy.

"Suck my fucking cock or I'll make you regret it."

The animalistic side of me was out and in full force, and I was in no mood to play. Like the good submissive girl I knew she was, Grace relaxed her mouth and started sucking on my cock gently.

"Good girl," I moaned as I wound her hair tighter around my hand. "Now use your hand to pleasure me as well."

Grace started jerking me off as she sucked me. Meanwhile, my hips started bucking involuntarily.

"If only you put your mouth to good use like this all the time," I purred as I grabbed one of Grace's breasts through her dress.

She narrowed her eyes at my comment, even though a hint of pleasure flitted across her face.

"You like being touched here, don't you?" I breathed as I slipped my hand into her dress. Grace moaned when my hand met her warm skin and pebbled nipple.

Something about her moans and the fact that she was enjoying it too much made me tear my hand out of her dress. It wasn't about Grace; it was about dominance and the record needed to be set straight. There couldn't be any confusion about that.

I grabbed onto the sides of Grace's face and fucked her mouth until I could feel my orgasm building. As tears streamed down her face and the moans continued to escape her throat, my balls begged to be emptied.

"*Fuck!*"

I braced myself for the orgasm that threatened to take over my whole body. As my cum left my balls, I thrust myself deeper, harder and faster into Grace's mouth. The sight of her choking on my cock sent my ego into overdrive. I liked a girl that couldn't back down from a challenge, and Grace seemed to be the queen of that.

"You better swallow every drop," I growled, shuddering as the last bit of my load came shooting out.

I need to push her to her limits, to see how far she's willing to go. I needed to break her down so much that she wouldn't even dare to tell anyone about what she saw.

I'd saved up a lot of cum, specifically for a moment like this, and Grace had been the perfect target. I pulled myself out of her mouth and refastened my pants, a smirk on my face as I noticed the cum dribbling down Grace's chin.

"Every single drop, don't you *dare* make a mess now," I cooed.

Grace shot me evils and to my surprise she tilted her head back and swallowed what was left of my load.

Fucking hell, as if she could get any hotter.

"Are you happy now? Do you feel like more of a man?" Grace said coldly.

I blinked at her as I tried to comprehend what she'd said. Her words had wiped away the pleasure and satisfaction I'd felt sheer moments before. I hated her for taking that away from me.

"What? Don't know what to say?"

Grace looked up at me through tear-stained eyes, eyes that I'd forced her to keep wide open while I'd shoved myself in her mouth.

Grace was still on her knees and looked like she was in complete shock after what had happened. I was just as shocked as she was. I'd dreamt about her submission for consecutive nights, but I would never have been able to anticipate just how delicious it would be.

So why did the feeling of guilt threaten to ruin everything?

"You talk too much," I muttered.

Grace's lip trembled, and I watched as a bead of cum escaped from the corner. My pants tightened once again.

No, that's enough for tonight. Don't be greedy.

Before I could stop myself, I brought my thumb to Grace's lip and pushed my cum back into her mouth where it belonged. I could barely focus on how warm her tongue was on my thumb as she continued staring at me with those sexy eyes of hers.

"And that's to make sure you stay quiet," I said, my eyes locked on hers the entire time.

Grace's brows knitted together and she bit down hard on

my thumb before I could pull it out of her mouth. The pain shot through me and I scowled as I returned to my full height.

"Looks like the bitch needs a gag next time," I growled. Two small beads of red decorated my thumb, courtesy of Grace's canines.

"I'll be happy to buy one for you then," Grace snapped as she finally got off her knees and stood up.

Even though she had a fierce edge to her voice, I couldn't help but notice the slight wobble in her tone.

I couldn't stand to be in Grace's presence any longer. Ignoring the throbbing sensation in my thumb and whatever Grace had to say next, I stormed out the door, only focussed on getting as far away from Grace as possible.

I hated how Grace made me think, and I hated the way she made me feel even more.

Fucking her face and forcing her to submit had felt so amazing in the moment, so why had I felt so disgusted with myself afterwards?

Because it means you're no better than him, my conscience taunted.

If David was a monster for what he'd done, then what did that make me?

10

GRACE

I'd stared a hole into the floor where Elijah had forced me to my knees the night before. I hadn't left my room since he'd been there. Since he'd made me give him a blowjob. Since he'd humiliated me.

Even though hours had passed, I could still feel Elijah's thick length in my mouth, no matter how many times I'd tried to rinse it out with the old water that sat on my desk. I knew my neighbours below had *not* appreciated me spitting out my bedroom window.

I sat up in my bed, still dressed in the same dress from the party, feeling achy and exposed. What had meant to be a simple party, a laugh, had turned into a realisation of who Elijah really was. Of *what* he was, and what he was willing to do to make sure I was afraid of him.

I knew he was dangerous, and every chance he got, he would show me that. It was time for me to believe it.

I was about to leave my room and go to the bathroom when I heard the floorboards creak outside my room. I held my breath and waited for Elijah to pass. Every inch of my body froze at the thought of his presence.

What the hell had happened last night?

I hated myself for not screaming louder and for not fighting him more. But what I hated myself for most of all was the fact that I hadn't hated what he'd done to me. At least not *completely*.

I knew it was crazy, but there was something... alluring about being made to follow orders, especially such degrading ones. But it was all confused because I hated Elijah's guts and knew he hated mine, and yet he'd clearly enjoyed it a lot. Even if he'd tried to keep his face as neutral as possible. The fact that I'd been able to make him lose control and drop the stone wall for even a second had not gone unnoticed.

What did it all mean?

The smart part of my brain knew that it was a warning, and that if I didn't heed it, things would only get worse for me.

But the other part of my brain wondered if it would happen again. We were roommates after all, and Elijah had shown time and time again that he didn't care about privacy or morals. He could barge in at any time, force me to my knees and demand that I sucked him off again.

As if I'd thought that our living situation couldn't get any worse or any more awkward.

∽

I didn't see Elijah for five days, but I knew he was in the apartment because I heard him walking around and closing the door in the morning when he was back from doing whatever he did to that man. Like the party, Elijah had become a ghost and even though I couldn't see him, he still haunted my every waking moment.

I didn't sleep for five days. The bags under my eyes were getting worse by the day, so bad to the point that

Violet commented on them when we met up at the library.

"What's going on with you? I don't mean to be rude, but... you do *not* look good," Violet winced.

Stifling a yawn, I flicked through my textbook and ignored her concerns.

"Grace, I'm being serious," Violet hissed.

"I just have a lot of work, that's all," I said, knowing that I was lying through my teeth.

I wasn't struggling to sleep because of work. Even though it was piling up again and get increasingly more difficult, that wasn't the only thing giving me anxiety. I couldn't sleep because of Elijah.

The image of him towering over me, pulling on my hair and fucking my face was burned into the back of my eyelids and I couldn't get rid of it, no matter how hard I tried.

"How are you supposed to take care of other people if you can't take care of yourself?"

I knew Violet was only teasing me, but I couldn't shake the momentary pain that shot through my chest at her words. Because ultimately she was right.

Was I really sacrificing my grades and career over Elijah and what he might or might not do to me?

I sighed heavily. "I think I might have insomnia." It was a half truth, but it was better than admitting to the degrading things I'd been made to do.

Violet put her pen down on her notebook and widened her eyes in pretend shock. "No way, you should have said." I rolled my eyes at her. "But seriously, why don't you just pop a Xanax? You'll be out in no time." Violet shrugged nonchalantly.

I looked around at the other students on our library floor to make sure that no one was listening in on our conversation. I hadn't thought about using drugs to get my sleeping back on track. I'd just accepted that I was resigned to sleepless nights until the end of the year or until Elijah or I caved and moved out.

"I don't even know where I'd be able to get some," I hissed.

Another half lie. I was pretty sure that someone in my contact list from my first year partying days could get some, but it felt too weird to reach out all of a sudden.

"Don't worry, I can give you someone reliable."

I breathed out a momentary sigh of relief before the anxiety washed over me again, my textbook completely ignored.

"Isn't it like too risky?" I asked.

My mind was running at a million miles a minute as I thought about all the ways that things could go horribly wrong. What if this "reliable" person snitched and got me kicked out of Oakwood?

Violet chuckled and shook her head. "It's literally only Xanax, relax. Here, just text him. He should reply before the evening."

My phone vibrated as Violet sent me the number that would guarantee me a good night's sleep. I thanked her and saved it into my contacts list. I knew I'd still obsess over whether I should make the call for at least another hour, but I was grateful to have the option.

∼

"What are you doing here?"

I turned around and walked straight into Elijah's warm, hard chest, where his sweet cologne tormented me. I jumped back and cleared my throat as I got myself together. Memories of the party flashed through my mind. Elijah's hand in my hair, his cock in my mouth as he dominated me and forced me to submit...

"I pay to go here. I can stand wherever I like," I snapped.

My heart thrummed frantically in my chest now that it knew my tormentor was near. I was meeting a random guy to buy drugs, but the amount of fear and anxiety I felt about him was no match for the amount I felt when Elijah was in my presence.

I checked my phone to see if the dealer had any updates about his arrival. I was getting cold, hungry, and impatient. The lack of sleep had truly caught up with me and I just needed to get back into bed before I did anything stupid. Elijah quirked an eyebrow and tucked his hands into the pockets of his leather jacket.

I prayed to God that he wasn't the person I'd been messaging for drugs. If Elijah turned out to be the dealer, I'd be beyond mortified.

"A girl like you shouldn't hang around here," Elijah spat.

What did he mean by a girl like me?

"What do you want, Elijah?" I snapped impatiently.

Elijah's eyes flashed with danger and a sprinkling of lust. As his eyes roamed around my body, no doubt remembering how great it had looked in my tight party dress, I pulled my jacket tighter around myself.

"I want to know how long you think you can avoid me for," he breathed.

I took a step away from him, but Elijah closed the distance in an instant, pushing me up against the wall of the old gym building. His tall frame trapped me, and the joy it brought him only made me angrier.

"I'm not avoiding you," I said coldly. I didn't have the energy to deal with him. *Where was the fucking dealer?*

Elijah chuckled darkly. "You're a terrible liar, Grace. And I don't like fucking liars."

Before I could realise what was happening, Elijah's hand slowly began making its way up my thigh and towards my centre.

"Good thing I don't care if you like me or not," I hissed. I tried to squirm away from his touch, but Elijah's big hands were firm on my body, holding me in place. I maintained eye contact with him, even though I wanted to look away from his burning gaze.

"You look like shit. Have you not been sleeping?"

"That's none of your business," I snapped.

"I bet the memory of me face fucking you is the reason you can't sleep," Elijah purred, his fingers teasing my clit through my clothes.

"Get off of me," I cried.

Elijah pushed harder and began swirling circles into my jeans. I wanted him to stop touching me, but I didn't want the heat that he'd conjured up there to disappear.

"I know I'm right, and so do you." Elijah's eyes darkened as he slipped his other hand up my jumper and trailed his big hand up my bare waist.

His touch scorched my skin and oxygen no longer flowed to my brain as easily as it had before. Elijah's hand latched onto my breast, catching me off guard as he began massaging it roughly with his palm.

Elijah's eyes were on me the entire time as he massaged my clit and breasts while I struggled not to melt against his touch. He didn't need to know how good he could make me feel, especially when I knew he'd only use it against me.

"You're scared that I'm going to do it again."

I was more than scared. I was *terrified*.

"I-" the words were trapped in my throat. Elijah cocked his head to the side and a cruel smirk appeared on his face.

"But you *want* me to do it again."

I opened my mouth to respond, but stopped when Elijah slipped his fingers into me.

Oh no. It felt so fucking good that I couldn't stop the moans that escaped my mouth.

"That's a good girl," Elijah purred as he pumped his fingers in and out of me.

I couldn't believe that we were doing this outside, in public, where anyone could just walk past and see us. It was like my rational mind was on holiday and all I could think about was whether Elijah would grant me a release or not.

"You're so fucking tight and wet," Elijah breathed, his breath hot on my skin. His lips were inches away from mine and I couldn't resist.

I tilted my head forward and was about to close the gap when Elijah withdrew his hands from my body, wrapped a hand around my neck, and pushed me away from him. The sudden motion took me by surprise as I banged my head against the wall.

Elijah dropped his hand and stepped away from me as if I smelled bad or something. Ashamed, flustered, and confused, I looked up at the glower on Elijah's face. *What the hell had just happened?* It was like the lights had gone off in his face and the familiar, haunting darkness was back.

"What's your problem?" I asked.

I wanted to go back to the moment before. I'd been so close to orgasm- Elijah must have known that. Why had he backed away from the kiss? My chest felt like it was in ribbons, but I kept my face as blank as possible. I'd made the mistake of being vulnerable in front of Elijah far too many times already.

Elijah narrowed his eyes and looked me up and down before he turned on his heel and walked away without another word, taking any answers he may have had for me with him.

Shame flooded my body. Shame at what we'd just done, at what he'd done to me, as well as the shame of being rejected. Why had I thought for even a minute that Elijah would want to kiss me?

From the sexual encounters that we'd had, it was clear that Elijah was only interested in humiliation and domination and nothing else. I'd been a fool to think that he'd want to kiss me. Especially after everything he'd already done to me.

So why had I wanted it so badly?

I knew that a deep, dark part of me craved Elijah's attention and his touch, because it was better than his silent, stony coldness.

But was it really?

The dealer arrived a few minutes later while I was still trying to get my breath back and wrap my head around what had just happened with Elijah. Luckily, he didn't care about anything except his cash, and once he'd given me my pills; he disappeared into the night like Elijah. He wasn't a talker, and for once, I actually appreciated that.

I hoped the pills would stop me from staying up all night thinking about Elijah's words, his smell, and how his hands knew exactly the right places to touch on my body.

I was getting more and more desperate. I needed to forget, for my own sake, before it was too late.

11

GRACE

Angry that I'd put myself in a position for Elijah to reject me, when I got home, I pulled my laptop out and opened a blank Word document. As I waited for the Xanax to kick in, I let my fingers fly across the keys, documenting everything I'd seen Elijah do that night. I needed to get it all down before I edited it properly to make sure it made sense. Then I'd share it with someone. Maybe it was stupid and reckless, but how much worse could things really get from here? I wasn't thinking about the consequences, only thinking about getting all the shit off my conscience.

Whether I'd go to the police first or start small by showing Violet, I knew I was implicit in Elijah's crime by keeping quiet. That man had a *family*, and even though I wasn't sure if Elijah had hurt him or actually killed him, it didn't matter. There had to be people worried and looking for him. I started a paragraph describing the cruelty that Elijah had inflicted on me to keep his secret, but passed out before I could finish my confession.

I woke up the next morning feeling slightly groggy but relieved that I'd actually had a full night's sleep. I checked the time on my phone and realised that I'd slept for ten hours straight. I got myself ready and went to the kitchen.

I went to throw a tissue in the bin and nearly screamed when I saw it hadn't been emptied *yet again*. It was the same story, every single fucking time, and it was getting on my last nerve. The only reason I kept caving in and emptying it was because I couldn't stand the smell, and I hated trying to balance things on top of the trash that was already there. Apparently Elijah didn't care or loved pissing me off more than he liked a clean smelling kitchen. I didn't know what he'd thrown in there, but the bin wasn't just an eyesore, it was a fucking health hazard.

"Elijah!" I shouted from the kitchen. Of course, I was met with silence, even though I knew the bastard was in.

Sighing, I dragged myself out of the kitchen and knocked on Elijah's door loudly. Moments later, the door opened to reveal a glowering, half naked Elijah. It was the first time I'd seen him since he'd rejected me the day before.

"Are you on your fucking period again?" he snapped.

"No, but clearly you're being a misogynistic pig, again," I shot back.

Elijah went to shut the door, but I stopped it with my foot before he could. Gritting my teeth together, I met his vicious stare with my own.

"What the fuck do you want?" Elijah growled, his breath hot against my skin. His mouth was mere inches away from mine and the way his gaze kept flitting between my lips and my eyes told me he was thinking about the last time we'd been that close to each other.

Focus, you're here to tell Peter Pan to fucking grow up and empty the bin not to journey to Neverland.

"You need to take the bin out," I said, snapping back to reality.

Elijah scoffed. "I don't need to do anything. You can do it."

"I did it last time!"

"And since you were so great at it, do it again," Elijah sneered.

I let out an exasperated noise. I was on the brink of pulling my hair out. I took a step back and tried to calm myself down.

"You put more shit in there than I do, anyway. The least you can do is take it out. Especially because it fucking stinks!"

I guess calming down didn't work.

Elijah took an exaggerated sniff of the air before that cruel smirk teased at the corner of his lips. "I can't smell anything, seems like a you problem."

"Elijah-"

My sentence was cut off before I could finish by Elijah slamming the door in my face. Mom had always said that issues should always be sorted out in person and as soon as possible, especially when you were sharing a space with someone. Elijah was clearly the sort that thought otherwise.

Annoyed, slightly embarrassed and at risk of running late to class, I tied up the bin bag and put it outside of Elijah's bedroom before I grabbed my things and went to campus.

It took every ounce of my being to not just take it to the bins outside, especially when I saw that something was leaking from it. But the pettiness won, and I needed to show Elijah that I was serious. I didn't care if he could knock people out and hold them hostage, or even kill them. Roommate etiquette still existed.

∽

Thursday was my least favourite day of the week because I always had so much on. With back-to-back classes and lectures, I was on the brink of spontaneous combustion following all the information that I'd been exposed to.

Luckily, when I had a break between classes, so did Violet, and we met at a cafe to complain and catch up. She was having issues with her mom, wanting her to babysit her brothers, but she couldn't take time off work. I finally plucked up the courage to tell her about my parents' divorce, not that I was hiding it from her or anything. What with everything else going on, it didn't seem big enough to bring up.

"Oh my gosh, how are you handling it?"

I shrugged. "Fine, I think. I'm just trying to concentrate on what's going on here." *And watch my back for Elijah.* "I think if I was at home, things would be a lot worse."

Violet gave me a sympathetic look. She reached her hand across the table and placed it over mine.

"I'm here if you ever need to vent, okay?"

"I'm assuming Nate will be too?" I couldn't help myself.

"What? No, of course not," Violet laughed uncomfortably. "I'm not spending that much time with him, am I?"

"Spending that much time with whom?"

I snapped my head up to see Nate standing behind Violet. He must have crept up on us when we weren't paying attention. Towering over Violet even more than usual because she was sitting down, he gave her a quick kiss before turning to me.

"You alright, Grace?" Nate asked.

"I'm good. I actually need to get going."

I excused myself, not because I didn't like Nate, or because I was unhappy for Violet, but simply because I wasn't a fan of third wheeling.

Violet and Nate didn't seem to mind my hasty exit and

continued chatting away merrily. They were clearly besotted with each other and I was happy for them, especially because they'd had one hell of a time to get to where they were. Even though they'd overcome their problems to be together, the cynic in me always thought about the potential or possibly inevitable end of their relationship. Hell, if my parents had split up after being together for over 20 years, then what chance did Violet, Nate or I have at love? I knew it was just fear talking. So why was a small part of me worried it could be true?

∽

I was relieved to be done with my hectic day and ready to go home. I had to drag my legs up the stairs to my apartment. Ready to just pass out on my bed, I was not prepared when I unlocked the front door.

The smell of weed hit me instantly, and I was surprised that the smoke alarm hadn't gone off yet from how much of it swirled around the apartment.

"Elijah, what the fuck?"

Elijah was sitting on the sofa, which was a rare occasion considering the fact that he preferred to spend his time in his room where he wouldn't have to talk to me. His back was facing me as he played some fighting game on the PlayStation.

"Calm down Grace, there's no need to shout," Elijah replied without looking away from the screen.

Was he fucking serious? Not only was he doing drugs, but he was smoking inside, which was *literally* against Oakwood Academy's rules!

"You can't smoke in here!" I exclaimed. My eye landed on the green glass bong sitting on the floor by his feet. "Especially not that."

Elijah paused the game and looked to see what I was referring to and I finally saw his face fully. His eyelids were heavy, and he looked less tense than usual. If I hadn't been so pissed at his actions and worried that we might get in trouble with security, then I might have allowed myself to calm down.

"I can do whatever the fuck I want," Elijah said in a lazy voice. He brought the bong to his lips, a lighter to the bowl and took a long drag of the smoke.

"I am *not* dealing with this," I snapped.

I cringed at the bubbling sound that the water in the bong made and marched off into the kitchen. I noticed that as I walked past his door that the bin had been taken out. About fucking time. Maybe Elijah responded well to certain types of confrontation.

I boiled the kettle and made a cup of tea to have with the brownies that I'd made a couple of nights before. As my tea brewed, I opened the fridge to take the brownies out. But when I opened the fridge, the shelf that they'd been on was empty.

Prick.

"Elijah, where the hell are my brownies?"

I marched back into the living room and saw my pink Tupperware filled with nothing but crumbs on the floor. Elijah looked at my face and brought his hand to his mouth to mock my shocked expression.

"Who knows where they could have possibly gone?"

I clenched my fists together and stopped myself from jumping on him and pummelling his stupid happy high face until it was blood red. How dare he help himself to *my* food?

"You're so fucking annoying!"

"And you're a great baker, Grace," Elijah smirked at me

and took another rip of the bong. He blew a thick cloud of smoke into the air. "You should make some more."

"You should go to hell," I snapped.

"And I think next time you bake, you should wear a little maid costume and let me watch." Elijah's eyes held mine the entire time, and I blushed fiercely at the words that came out of his mouth.

Even though his eyelids were heavy, that didn't stop the darkness and predatory hunger in his eyes. Visuals flashed through my mind at Elijah's words... visuals that were *not* safe for work in the slightest.

Elijah coming up behind me while I whisked the batter, his body pressed against mine, lips on my neck, his hands running up my thighs, under my skirt...

"In your fucking dreams," I snapped before *my* daydreaming could get any worse.

Before Elijah could make me blush any more, I turned on my heels and went to my room. I opened my door and was immediately hit with the most disgusting stench I had ever encountered. It only took one look at my bed to know why. Contrary to the relief that I'd had moments before, Elijah had *not* taken the bin outside. Instead, he'd upturned the trash bag's entire contents onto my bed.

I felt weak as I looked at the new sheets that I'd bought recently and only put on my bed earlier that week. They were utterly ruined and who knew if the shitty Oakwood washing machines could get all the stains out? There were bits of egg, mouldy fruit, tomatoes and God only knew what else. I wanted to cry, and I wanted to vomit, but my body had other ideas.

I screamed. And when I heard Elijah laughing in the other room, I only grew angrier.

I hated him. I hated the fact that I lived with him. I hated how he made living with him feel like a punishment. I hated how cruel he could be. I hated how weak I felt around him. *I* was meant to be the one with the upper hand. I knew his darkest secret, so why was I the one going through hell? I fucking hated it all.

If Elijah wanted to play, then we could play. And since he was so adamant about me baking more treats for him, I would. And I'd make sure that there was a special surprise just for him, one that I thought he absolutely deserved.

12

ELIJAH

That fucking bitch.

Because Grace had slipped something into the brownies she'd left in the kitchen, I was out for two days. I'd been amused when I heard her singing and baking in the kitchen the day after she'd had her little meltdown about me eating her brownies. Little did I know she had never intended for the second batch of brownies to be for herself. Fucking bitch.

Two whole days meant I hadn't been able to check on David or feed him. He was going to be a fucking nightmare when I finally went to see him. Time was running out, and I was behind on my plan - and that was Grace's fault. I needed to make my mind up and act soon before it was too late.

I'd spent way too much time on the toilet and cursed Grace's name every time I felt a cramp. I even cursed her when there wasn't enough toilet paper. It was horrible. And what was worse was that she had clearly been enjoying my misery, even though she tried to force herself to have a blank face when we ran into each other in the kitchen or the hallway. I knew exactly what was going on in her mind. She thought she'd won. Which meant that she'd probably let her guard down.

I heard the door close as Grace left the apartment later that afternoon. I waited a few minutes in case she forgot something and came back before I let myself into her room.

I was instantly hit with a wave of sweet vanilla that seemed to emanate from every corner of her room, which was in particularly pristine condition. I was impressed that she'd managed to clean up everything after all the trash I'd dumped on her bed. Her screams when she'd discovered the present I'd left her hadn't messed with my high in the slightest. In fact, Grace's discomfort and annoyance brought me a sense of joy that I couldn't even begin to explain.

I'd let myself into Grace's room many times since we'd first moved in together. It was practically my rite of passage. At first, it was out of curiosity, but then the trips became more frequent as I tried to search for things that I could use to blackmail her.

I rummaged around in her drawers and broke into a smile when I found a little plastic bag in her underwear draw. Two pills stared back at me. *What a terrible hiding place.*

Grace knew that if they got into the wrong hands that her time at Oakwood would be over. I was sure that the college wouldn't be too happy to hear that one of their future doctors was engaging in illicit activities. It would be a shame for her to get suspended...

My eyes landed on the laptop sitting on her desk. *Bingo.* She was stupid for leaving it behind and in such an obvious place, so it only made sense for me to go through it. I put the bag of pills on the desk beside her laptop as I lifted the screen. Luckily, I'd known my way around computers since I was a kid, so it wasn't hard to bypass all the locks she'd put on it.

I was ready to spend the rest of the evening browsing through Grace's online life when my eyes zoned in on a document that she'd been writing in before she'd put her computer to sleep. It was entitled *My Confession.*

My eyes skimmed over the words on the screen, and I couldn't believe my eyes. Everything in pure detail, or as much as she knew anyway, detailing the moment that Grace had seen me knock David out and the events that had happened since then. Hundreds of letters and words outlining my guilt, my heinous behaviour.

I felt the blood rushing through my body, fuelled by pure anger and hatred. The dumb bitch was trying to snitch. What I was most angry about was the fact that Grace thought I wouldn't find out about her secret plan. When people tried to cross me, or even so much as thought about it, I made sure that they paid.

I *knew* that something like this was going to happen. And I knew I had been too lenient with her. Even after all the shit I'd put her through, she still thought that confessing would be a smart thing to do?

Blinded by rage, I stood up and was about to throw Grace's laptop at the window when an idea crossed my mind. Breaking Grace's computer wouldn't make her keep her mouth shut. She could probably afford to get a new one where she could type up more confessionals.

I was going to get her where it hurt.

Reporting her for having drugs wasn't enough, at least not yet. If I did that and she got suspended, the chances were that she'd go to the police and snitch on me once she no longer had anything to lose. No, I had to do something that scared Grace enough that she wouldn't dare test me again.

I pulled up the internet on her laptop and quickly found the portal where we handed in all our assignments. I looked at the deadlines and saw that she had handed one in at 1am this morning.

Poor Grace must have been up all night trying to finish that essay.

There were 30 minutes left until the deadline, which meant that the portal would shut if I didn't act quickly.

I chuckled to myself as I opened the assignment that Grace had sent. After a few minutes of research, I found another med student's essay on the exact same topic and submitted that to the assignment portal.

Once I got the notification that the new file had been submitted in the place of Grace's old one, I cleared my history, closed Grace's laptop and sat back in her desk chair. Pleasure and vengeance ran through my body and I felt more alive than I had in days.

I could only imagine the look of horror and confusion on Grace's face when she got an email regarding her plagiarism. What made things even better was by the time she found out, it would be way too late.

The bag of Xanax pills stared up at me. If Grace didn't heed *this* warning, then I'd have no choice but to take things even further.

∾

"You left me for *two days*!"

"Calm down, I'm here now," I snapped as there the strip of duct tape I'd removed from his mouth onto the floor.

I'd swung by the store before going to the storage unit and held a shopping bag in my hand with water, a sandwich and a bunch of other random shit.

I was glad to see that David was exactly where I left him. He smelt even more wretched than he had before and I was so close to puking up my guts. I didn't hide my grimace, and neither did David. He didn't look happy to see me in the slightest.

"Let me out, you asshole!" he yelled.

"Woah, you could at least ask how I'm doing," I smirked. David's scowl grew even deeper. What an *ugly motherfucker*.

I sat down on the chair opposite David's and started going through the items in the bag one by one. Holding each one up so that David could see before I put it back in the bag.

"You starved me for two days. You didn't even give me water, you son of a bitch!" David's voice cracked as he raised his voice at me.

David kicked at the floor and rocked back and forth on his chair, his face red raw. His lips were cracked, and he had thick, dark circles around his eyes. He glowered at me, but I couldn't feel an inch of sympathy for that monster.

"I don't think that's the worst thing considering what you've done," I said pointedly. I poured the water from the bottle into a glass that I picked up from the floor.

David spat at my feet. Clearly, he was asking for it.

"You want some water? Here you go. Drink it from this glass."

David stared up at me as I walked towards him with a glass of water in my hand. He side eyed me as I held it out in front of his mouth.

"What if it's got poison in it?" he asked.

"Poisoning you would be a fucking mercy and I'm not granting you any of that," I growled. David winced, and I pushed the water closer towards him.

"Do you have a-a straw?" David stuttered.

"You have five more seconds to drink from this cup like a fucking dog or you're going to go without it for three days," I barked.

"Please-"

"5-4," I started counting, ignoring the sound of David's protests.

"3-2..."

I stopped when David thrust his tongue into the cup to get the water. Smiling, I watched him struggle for a few more seconds before I took the taser out of my pocket and pressed it to his neck. David jumped back and yelled out in pain, the glass of water pushed aside, now on the floor in pieces.

"Motherfucking piece of shit," I snapped.

I kicked David's chair over onto the floor and climbed onto him while he was still fastened to the chair and began tasing him again.

David jerked and squealed and every time he got louder, I tased him and kicked him until he shut up again.

There was nothing but red and sheer bloodlust. Red exploded all over David's face and body, as well as the floor. Even when he stopped crying out, I couldn't stop myself.

Kick. Tase. Kick. Tase.

I was a monstrous machine, keen to enact my revenge, but this was only the start. The motherfucker deserved a lot more than I'd given him. He needed to suffer more than he'd made her suffer.

I pushed my hair out of my eyes and stood up to my full height. David remained shaking on the floor, his eyes black and blue. I wiped my blood on my t-shirt and then tore it off and threw it into the corner.

As I grabbed another shirt from my bag, I heard David's weak voice as he struggled to speak. I'd done some damage to his chest and lungs and I hoped it was permanent.

"Please, let me go, I'm sorry.... Please forgive me, it was a mistake... I'll do anything, please-"

I slipped the clean shirt over my head and shot devilish eyes in David's direction.

"You can keep begging like a pathetic fool, but it's not going to get you anywhere."

I turned around and walked away, picking up my bag and jacket in my haste.

"She- sh-she b-b-begged," David spat out, a sleazy tone in his voice. He chuckled to himself like a sick psycho. Every muscle in my body tensed up as David's words hit my ears. Someone was begging to be killed.

"You want to repeat that?" I barked as I turned around.

"N-n-no," David said in a shaky voice.

I took in the sight of the thin strands of hair plastered to his bloody forehead, his broken nose, and bruised eyes. He looked desperate; he looked apologetic and possibly even remorseful. He looked like a man that was sorry, truly sorry, and wanted to be forgiven for his actions. For his *mistakes*.

Setting my bag and jacket back down on the floor, I grabbed the crowbar that sat in the corner and walked towards David, my pace speeding up as his screams got louder.

13

GRACE

Elijah went back to avoiding me like I had the plague. I'd expected him to retaliate after the laxative brownie incident, but he hadn't struck yet. I walked around the apartment and around campus, looking over my shoulder as I wondered if I was finally free from his wrath or if I hadn't seen the worst of it yet. Despite my anxiety, I was pretty damn proud of myself for pulling it off and surprised that Elijah had fallen right into my trap.

After class, I walked back to the apartment to have some lunch. I'd been having lunch on campus with Violet for the last couple of days and I knew my student loan wouldn't be able to sustain my habits for much longer if I kept going the way I was. I heard Elijah humming a tune that I didn't recognise as I walked to the kitchen. It was the first time we'd been in the same place in over a week.

"You feeling any better?" I snarked.

I leaned against the kitchen door frame and stared at Elijah's muscly tattooed back. I started wondering how much the ones on his spine had hurt to get done.

"Last time I checked, you were living here, so..." Elijah

looked me up and down with a sneer on his face. "That's a resounding no."

His words stung, but not as much as the look on his face or the way that he turned his back to me again, as if I was nothing more than a speck of dirt.

"I always forget how lucky I am to have such a lovely roommate like you," I said before I locked myself away in my room.

I threw my bag on my bed and went over to sit at my desk. I connected my earphones and opened up my laptop. At least my room was the one place I felt somewhat safe from Elijah.

I looked through the news and then rewatched a lecture from earlier in the week as I took more detailed notes. I was still feeling burnt out from the last assignment I had to do. I knew all nighters were a rite of passage as a college student, but I hated them with a fiery passion.

A couple of hours later, I heard an email entering my inbox. I checked to see which spam account or scammer had graced my emails, but when I clicked on my email icon, my mouth dropped when I saw what waited for me.

Urgent + Cause for Concern: Plagiarism in most recent essay.

I blinked several times, but the words didn't shift or disappear. Plagiarism? The email had to be sent in error because there was no way in hell that I was being accused of *plagiarism* when I'd spent hours grafting on my last essay.

My hands trembled as I opened up the email and scanned my eyes over its contents. I could taste the bile coming up my throat and had to force myself to hold it back.

I was being accused of stealing my work from another student. But I knew that wasn't true. Admittedly, I had been sleep deprived and running off too much coffee, but I'd checked every single reference and made sure that I'd put the right things in quotation marks.

I was desperate to pass, but not desperate enough that I'd ever *cheat*. But the words were there and so was my name. I hurried over to the assignment portal, confident that I knew I'd checked my essay at least twenty times after I'd submitted it. The essay was still titled the same, but when I opened the document up in full, my breathing stopped completely.

The words that stared back at me weren't mine. The title of the essay was the one I'd chosen, and the content was similar, but I knew for a fact that I had not seen that essay on my screen before that moment, let alone submitted it.

I felt sick to my stomach, but knew that there had to be an answer somewhere. There had to be problems with the assignment portal, right? I couldn't be the first person who had had a mix up like that.

Wracking my brains for answers, I checked the time the essay had been submitted. That's when everything clicked into place. I'd gone out for a walk when the newest copy- the *stolen* copy- had been uploaded.

And when I'd left... Elijah had still been in the house.

That motherfucking asshole had taken things *too* far. It was one thing to threaten me, but to threaten my education and my future? All I saw was red. My skin also crawled at the idea that Elijah had gone through my laptop. It utterly horrified me that he'd invaded my privacy. What kind of psycho would do something like that?

I wanted to go through all my documents to see if he'd tampered with anything else, but the fire inside me had other ideas. I marched straight to Elijah's room and let myself in. He was sitting on his bed reading a book and as soon as he looked up and saw me, his face turned to stone.

"Get the fuck out of my room," he said in a low warning voice.

"You went through my laptop and submitted a stolen essay, pretending it was me!"

It wasn't a question and even though I knew that whatever answer Elijah gave me wouldn't change anything; I stood at the foot of his bed, my hands on my hips and a fierce glower on my face.

Elijah calmly set the book down on his bed, then simply smiled before laughing. I curled my hands into fists as I looked at his joyous expression.

"There's nothing fucking funny about this. You could have gotten me suspended!"

"Well, there's nothing funny about that little confession you were writing," Elijah shot back. His face was once again a picture of icy fury.

"I don't know what you're talking about." But the waver in my voice gave me away. Plus, what was the use in lying when he'd already violated my privacy?

"Then *I* don't know what *you're* talking about."

Elijah stood up and walked towards me. I took a step back towards the safety of the door, wanting to be as far away as possible from Elijah's bare skin and tattooed muscles. With every step I took, Elijah closed the gap immediately. This carried on until he'd edged me out into the hallway.

"Why were you in my room in the first place?" I was trying my best to keep my voice even, but the lack of distance between us made it difficult.

"Why did you follow me that night?" Elijah snarled.

"I didn't-"

"If you play stupid games, you get stupid prizes."

Goosebumps erupted on my skin as Elijah looked me up and down.

No, I wouldn't let him intimidate me. I wasn't the one in the wrong. Maybe I should have anticipated that Elijah was more psychotic than I thought and kept my laptop safe and out of reach.

Maybe I should have heeded all his warnings and cast out any idea of confessing the truth. But the guilt had eaten me up so much to the point that I just had to get it out. I hadn't gotten far enough to decide if I had the balls to actually send the confession to anyone, but Elijah had already found it and the damage had been done.

"What reason could you have to hurt that man?" I yelled. "Is your little secret worth jeopardising my education and my *career*, Elijah? Because I know for a fact that if the tables were turned, you'd be thinking the same thing."

"Don't pretend you know me, because you don't," Elijah growled at the same time as he pushed me up against the wall so hard that the back of my head smacked against it.

"Fine. But what I know is that you're an arrogant tiny dick asshole who clearly has nothing better to do than ruin my life," I snarled.

The fire in Elijah's eyes flared up again, and his face contorted into a furious expression. Before I could stop him, he grabbed my hand and pressed it against his crotch.

I recoiled when I felt the large hardness growing there. I tried to pull my hand away, but Elijah gripped it hard, his eyes burning holes into mine. He'd proven his point that he wasn't small by any means.

But why was he hard at a time like this?

"Tiny dick, my ass," Elijah spat. "You, on the other hand, are an annoying bitch, hellbent on sticking your nose in where it's not wanted and making everyone like you," Elijah snapped in return. "Not to mention you have a drug problem."

Shit. Of course, he'd found the pills when he'd been through my room.

Elijah didn't have to make the threat to let me know

exactly what he was thinking. His words were like arrows slowly puncturing my chest, and I held back my tears. He knew how much he was hurting me. He didn't need more validation.

"I don't have a drug problem! And whatever this is that you think you're doing... This isn't a game, this is my life!" I cried.

"You're telling *me*? You're the one who thinks this is a fucking game!" Elijah roared and slammed his fist into the wall beside my head.

I shook from the rage in his voice and the impact that his fist had made. It had only been mere inches from my head. *Was he actually going to hurt me?*

Angry and scared, I froze in place as I tried to come to terms with the state of affairs before me. It didn't matter how sharp my tongue was, Elijah was bigger and stronger than me, and probably angrier, too. If I wasn't careful, things could get out of hand really quickly.

"Let me go," I said finally, not making eye contact.

Elijah's hands were on either side of my head and whichever way I turned, they trapped me. I didn't want his bare skin pressed against me, or his face mere inches from mine. I needed to be free from Elijah's cologne and body heat, and even more so from his scathing words and cruel eyes.

"I didn't think you'd be stupid enough to cross me," he said, his breath warm against my cheek.

"You're the stupid one if you think that no one's going to find out what you did to that guy," I retorted. "Or what you're doing to him."

Rage and annoyance flickered across Elijah's face and his fist connected with the wall once more, making me jump again. His reaction let me put two and two together. The man was still alive and I could only imagine what horrible things Elijah did to him when he snuck out of the apartment each night.

"Fuck this," Elijah spat.

To my relief, he took a step back, freeing me. Showing me his tattooed back, Elijah stormed into his room without saying another word. My heartbeat was louder than the slamming door and even though I was glad to not be trapped beneath Elijah's body, I suddenly felt cold at the absence of his touch.

We hadn't gotten any closer to resolving our problem and, as far as Oakwood was concerned, I'd been stupid enough to plagiarise my essay.

The fact that I'd thought for just a second that Elijah had even a shred of humanity in him made me feel ashamed. Of course, he felt nothing for me. I was nothing to him but a nuisance.

I went to my room and sat at my desk. Through my angry tears, I set about trying to see how I could fix the mess that Elijah had made. I couldn't tell my tutor the actual truth. He wouldn't believe me, especially when there wasn't any proof.

No one had seen me go out for a walk, so as far as my tutor was concerned, my alibi was completely false. All I could do was beg for another chance and hope that because it was the first misdemeanour on my record the department would go easy on me.

14

ELIJAH

"Good morning. How did you sleep?" I asked David as I closed the storage door behind me.

From the chair that he was still strapped to, David looked at me through narrowed eyes, unable to say anything because his mouth was sealed shut with duct tape.

"You're a quiet one today, aren't you?" I taunted.

I walked up and down in front of him, my hand in my pocket as I caressed my newest toy with my fingers.

David stared back at me with hateful eyes, hidden by swollen folds of skin. I gathered my utensils that were arranged in the room's corner and lifted the bucket full of water. I ignored David's muffled cries as I dumped it over him. It wasn't enough to get rid of his grotesque smell, but it would have to do for now.

I tossed the bucket aside and reached for my baseball bat. David's eyes were wide with terror as I brought the bat down onto the sides of his abdomen repeatedly, ignoring the cracks that echoed around the room.

This is all for Stella. If only she knew how sorry I was and that I'd let no one else hurt her again. This is all for Stella...

Over and over again. I was in a sweaty frenzy and my

clothes stuck to my skin as I let David feel my wrath, let him feel only a mere morsel of the horror I had in store for him. My mind drifted back to the memories of my past that I'd locked away, out of reach.

I lay curled up on the ground of the tiny room that would never really be mine, begging for mercy while the belt came down on my back repeatedly. It didn't matter how much I screamed out; he didn't want to stop. He was bigger than me, had more power than me. At least when he beat me, he got his anger out on. I made sure he never hurt her, no matter how much I hated the sound and feeling of the belt buckle on my skin. At least it was me and not her. I'd learned to stop crying pretty young as soon as I learned my tears did nothing to stop the beatings or remove the sick smile on his face. Tears and screams did nothing but signal weakness. I couldn't be weak, not when she needed me to be strong.

I tossed the bat aside and crouched down beside David. I tore the duct tape off his mouth and let the blood drip out onto the concrete floor. I pulled out a new strip of duct tape from the roll I kept in my pocket and taped David's mouth shut again. Silent tears ran from his eyes, but the forced remorse in them prevented me from giving a shit.

I turned David over so that he was facing upwards before dragging him, chair and all, to the wall that had the plugs on it. After I'd gotten David into place, I got my tools together.

"I'm feeling in a pretty artistic mood today," I said to David as I connected the tattoo gun to the wall.

I poured the ink into it and then hovered it over David's head. His eyes widened in horror and I chuckled at the fear on his face.

"I thought you could be my canvas," I said.

I turned the tattoo gun on and the buzzing sound filled the room. I slowly moved it across David's face, lazily moving it up and down, hovering it over his eyes and his lips- slowing down when he flinched because it brought me a sick swell of pleasure. Pleasure I'd only ever felt around Grace.

No, this was different. But was it really?

At the last second, before the tip of the tattoo gun touched David's eyelid, I moved it down and got to work tattooing his hairy, flabby chest. David failed to make a sufficient noise behind the tape. I kept the tattoo gun pressed to his chest as he bucked his hips and arched his back. Whether he'd realised what I was writing or was simply trying to escape, I didn't care.

I turned the tattoo gun off and let it drop to the ground, taking a step back to marvel at my work when it was finally finished. The letters were jagged and uneven from David stupidly trying to put up a fight, but he deserved it. I watched David's chest rapidly rise and fall.

"I think this suits you perfectly," I said. "And you get to stay on the floor tonight."

David flinched and groaned when I kicked the chair and tried to break free from his restraints. It was a waste of time, and it was time that he realised that.

The bleeding letters of the word *RAPIST* on David's chest were the last thing I saw, and David's muffled screams were the last thing I heard before I locked the door behind me.

15

GRACE

A few days later, the apartment was so fucking cold it was unreal. I'd been tossing and turning in my bed for hours, snuggled up in multiple jumpers and gloves to get some heat. But nothing was working, and I swore I could feel icicles forming on the end of my nose.

I'd gotten up and checked my radiator twice, and after the third time of convincing myself that it was heating up, I went searching for answers. At this rate, there was no way that I was getting to sleep. I made my way into the kitchen, blanket and all, and froze even more when I saw Elijah standing at the boiler, his back turned to me.

"Hey," I squeaked.

Elijah glanced over at me and smirked at my attire. I tightened my blanket around me and tried to look as calm as possible.

"The boiler is out and maintenance doesn't open until tomorrow morning," he said after a moment. Elijah closed the panel for the boiler and turned his full attention to me.

My eyes danced over his sleeping shorts, which made his legs look fucking incredible. I cleared my throat and returned my gaze to his face once the realisation that my room was going to be the North Pole for the rest of the night dawned on me.

"That's ridiculous. Surely this is as an emergency?" I said indignantly.

Elijah ran his hands through his hair and I couldn't tell if the tiredness in his eyes was from a lack of sleep or some other reason. I bit down on my tongue to stop myself from asking about the guy that he was holding hostage. The way he'd reacted to me bringing it up when I'd confronted him the other day had told me that the topic was completely off limits.

"Fuck if I know why they do the things they do," Elijah grumbled. He eyed my blanket again. "How cold are you?" he asked after a moment.

Elijah's dark eyes filled with something I couldn't quite put my finger on. "Oh, I'm not cold at all. I just like wearing all my clothes at the same time," I said sarcastically.

Why the fuck would he *care how cold I was, anyway?*

Elijah rolled his eyes and walked past me, his slippers slapping on the floor until he reached his room. So much for the sympathy card. My chest heaved with disappointment, although I shouldn't have expected anything different.

I boiled the kettle and made myself a cup of tea. Warming myself up from the inside, no matter how temporary, was better than nothing. My teeth chattered and my hands shook as I set about making my tea before I went back to my bedroom. A knock on the door a few minutes later startled me out of my drifting thoughts. Before I could answer, Elijah opened the door, his head and torso peeping through the gap.

"Fucking hell, it's freezing in here," he said, his eyes darting around my room. I still didn't like him entering unannounced, and not just because I felt uneasy in his presence. I knew it was irrational, but I didn't want him to think that I was a slob. I'd just had a busy day.

"While I appreciate you stating the obvious, I need you to get out and close that door behind you because you're letting the heat out," I snapped.

Elijah snorted. "What heat?"

"I'm being serious!" I took an indignant sip from my mug to show Elijah exactly that. Underestimating how hot it would be, I ended up scorching my tongue, which only made me more annoyed. It was late, I was tired and cold and having to deal with Elijah was the cherry on top of the fucking cake.

Elijah scoffed and shook his head. "Look, I have a small electric heater-"

"Bring it in here, then!" I exclaimed.

"Oh no, I'm not giving it to you." Elijah shot me a look and my spirits sank. He ran his hands through his hair and sighed heavily. "Look, if you want to come and use it for a few minutes... I guess you can." He gestured to his room.

Was Elijah really inviting me into his room of his own volition? His expression told me he wasn't sure why he was making the offer either, but it continued to float in the air between us.

"It's okay, I'll probably warm up soon," I said lamely, even though what I really wanted to do was sprint into Elijah's room and curl up in front of this so-called radiator he had.

"I won't make the offer again, so stop being an idiot and just accept it. My room is there, you can have some heat. And then the maintenance guy will come tomorrow, okay?" Elijah's voice was stern and his eyes were dark.

"Okay..." I drawled. My mind raced ahead as I thought about all the small parts. *Where would I sleep? What would we talk about? Was it a good idea to accept such an offer from my enemy, even if I was freezing my ass off? What if something happened between us?*

"Hurry, I'm fucking tired and I don't have all night," Elijah snapped.

"Alright, calm down," I shot back. But despite his hurrying, I jumped off the bed and grabbed my blanket. My desire for warmth was a lot greater than my desire to be on Elijah's good side.

I followed him into his bedroom, immediately enveloped in his familiar scent. It was dark, except for the small slither of light from the moon that peeked through the curtains.

Elijah had a double bed just like me, but his looked smaller. In the darkness, I could see the outline of a massive stack of books that sat in the corner. I wanted to run my fingers over all the titles and pick his brains about his favourite ones, but the fists held at Elijah's side told me that his room was not a space for chit chat.

"I guess I'll take the floor," I said.

My eyes fell to the rug beside Elijah's bed. It didn't look particularly comfortable, but it was the only way I could think of staying safe and out of his hair while I accepted the favour from him.

"Don't be stupid, take the bed," he said impatiently. He grabbed a pillow from the bed and chucked it onto the floor, where he began making his 'bed.'

"Thanks for your hospitality," I snarked through gritted teeth.

I awkwardly climbed onto Elijah's bed and slipped underneath the blanket. I felt like I didn't belong, like I was invading somewhere of the upmost private. Ironic how he didn't seem to have the same problem when it came to *my* stuff. The way that Elijah shot daggers at me while I tried to get myself comfortable did not help make me feel any better.

"Do you usually sleep with the light on?" I asked after a few silent minutes.

I heard a growl deep in Elijah's throat as he stood up and went to switch the light off without saying a word.

"Thank you."

I knew that the polite thing to do was to look away as Elijah took his shirt off, but the slither of light coming through the curtains danced over his tanned, tattooed body and made me forget all about my manners. Elijah tossed his shirt onto his chair and stretched out his chest while I glued my eyes to his rippling muscles.

Maybe it was a good thing that we weren't sharing a bed.

"Why are you taking off your shirt if it's fucking freezing?" I blurted out before I could stop myself.

"Why are you policing my bedroom attire?" Elijah shot back as he got down on the floor and lay down in his makeshift bed.

I turned over on my side, so I could scowl at him even though the chances of him seeing it were very slim. It was the thought that counted.

"Must you always answer a question with a question?" I said.

"Must you always ask annoying questions?" Elijah sighed.

I lay on my back and faced the ceiling, trying my best to focus on the fact that I was warming up instead of my frosty host who lay on the floor.

"I get really hot," Elijah said after a few minutes of silence.

"What?" I asked, having lost myself in my thoughts.

"That's why I don't wear a shirt." Elijah cleared his throat and turned over onto his side. I cast my gaze at him and saw the outline of his muscled back facing me.

Sighing deeply, I turned over onto the opposite side, so I was facing away from him. Even though I tried to put as much distance as possible between me and Elijah, I was hyperaware of his smell and his warm body near mine.

It wasn't like I'd expected us to chat away into the night when he'd offered up the radiator in his room, but the silence was torturous. In that silence, my brain whirred as I tried to figure out what was going on in Elijah's mind. While he stayed silent, I tossed and turned as I struggled to relax and get comfortable.

"For God's sake, just pick a position and stay in it for more than two minutes," Elijah growled.

His sudden interjection startled me. I'd convinced myself that he'd fallen asleep. Clearly, I'd been keeping him awake. Or maybe it had been his thoughts or his upcoming night time activities that had been keeping him up.

"It's not my fault that I'm not a lifeless robot," I said coldly. I hoped that my subconscious would absorb Elijah's annoyance and keep me tossing and turning all night to piss him off.

"Be careful what you say when you're in my room, unless you want me to teach that filthy mouth of yours a lesson again."

My breath hitched in my throat and I contemplated between burrowing myself deeper into Elijah's sheets and returning to the safety of my ice cold room.

"Good," Elijah said when I didn't reply.

Instead of scaring me off or disgusting me, Elijah's threat intrigued me. The silence that fell over us only became more excruciating as I tortured myself with ideas of Elijah teaching me more lessons against my will.

What the hell was wrong with me?

This was *Elijah* that I was thinking about. The asshole who'd almost gotten me kicked out of college. The asshole who'd tried to ruin my life. The asshole that had forced me to my knees and face fucked me until I cried, but *somehow* made me ache for his touch.

The fact that my body could betray my morals was scary, and a little fucked up. I pulled my blanket tightly around me, imagining myself in a straightjacket. I'd been worried that Elijah would pounce on me the second he saw a moment of weakness. But in that moment, my weakness was the one thing that I knew would betray me and make me jump on him.

Keep it together, Grace. Just stay in the bed and it will be fine.

I spent the rest of the night listing all the possible reasons why climbing on top of Elijah and riding him until the sun came up would be a bad a bad idea. I repeated the list of the things I hated about him over and over again in my head until I eventually drifted off to sleep.

The low click of the door during the early hours of the morning made me flutter my eyes open slightly to see who was there. When I looked down at the floor beside the bed, I saw it was empty. I checked the time on my watch. 2am. Elijah had gone to the storage unit.

Even though he'd been going for a while, it was still hard to wrap my head around what he actually did when he went there. He never told me, and I knew that asking was a personal death sentence, but that didn't stop the nightmares. Nightmares of Elijah doing way worse to that man than he'd ever done to me.

As I lay back down in the bed of the guy that had hated me since the day we'd met, I sank into the sweet smell of him. I shut my eyes tight and forced myself to think of happy thoughts, but Elijah's cruel smirk kept popping into my head no matter how hard I kept trying to push it away.

16

GRACE

I woke up the next morning feeling groggy but warm. I felt pressure and heat against my back and almost jumped at the sound of light snoring in my ear.

Elijah.

Oh my God, oh my God, oh my God. I had to be dreaming. There was no way that I was sleeping in the same bed as my roommate. The same roommate that had made it his life's mission to make me regret ever sticking my nose in his business. *That* roommate. He must have gotten into bed after he'd come back early in the morning.

Without making any drastic movements, I lifted the blanket and saw that Elijah's arm was slung over my waist. As I looked closely at his intricate tattoo sleeve, I thought about the fact that there was no way that we'd fallen asleep spooning. The last thing I remembered was that he'd been on the floor just before I closed my eyes. The next thing I knew was that we'd woken up in bed together.

Granted, it was his room, and I was sure that the floor hadn't been comfortable, but waking up beside him with his face pressed into my hair and his dick pressed into my back.

Oh my.

I shifted slightly and heard a small moan escape Elijah's throat as I 'accidentally' pressed into his erection. I momentarily freaked out as I wondered if Elijah could read my mind, which was why his body had reacted accordingly. That was until I remembered that a lot of guys had erections in the morning. It was completely normal. Awkward but normal. Awkward and oh my gosh, how could I possibly forget that Elijah was *packing* down there?

A fluttering sensation started in my heart and then made its way to my stomach. Feeling Elijah's body pressed into mine and the way that his heat encased me was weirdly comforting and borderline arousing. Which made little sense after all the shit that he'd done to me, but what was that saying? Was my flesh really that weak?

I certainly felt weak as I lay in Elijah's arms and he started grinding his erection against me. I didn't know what to do, but my pulsating pussy sure as hell did. One part of me wanted to shake him awake and tell him to get off of me, thank him for letting me use his radiator and disappear off to my room for the foreseeable future. The other part of me, the part that was feeling especially horny and pent up, wanted to grind back, no questions asked.

"Elijah?" I called his name softly to see if he was awake.

Another low moan escaped Elijah's lips and was then followed by a light snore. He was still asleep. Elijah's breath tickled the back of my neck and I turned around slowly so that I could look at him properly. When I was finally face to face with Elijah, his arm still slung over me precariously, I saw how calm and non-threatening his face looked when he was sleeping.

Elijah's long, thick eyelashes cast shadows onto his high cheekbones, and it took every strength in my being not to bring my fingers up to them. Yes, he was sexy, but seeing him in that position made me realise that Elijah was agonisingly beautiful.

As if he could sense me staring at him, Elijah's eyes flew open. All sense of calmness seeped out of his face and was replaced with confusion and fury once his eyes met mine.

"What are you doing in my bed?"

Shit, busted.

"You told me to sleep in here. I-I thought you're sleeping on the floor!"

"You try sleeping on it and you'll see how uncomfortable it is." Elijah's face was red and suddenly on guard again.

"Are you forgetting that you were the one who offered to sleep on the floor?" I shot back my defences up again, once more.

"Why would I do that?" Elijah snapped. My eyes darted to the radiator sitting on the floor and Elijah's gaze followed mine.

"Right."

He sighed heavily and reached over to turn it off. We were lucky that our bills were included in our rent or else our electricity bill would probably be through the roof.

"Seems like you're the one who got into bed with me," I breathed.

I meant for it to be a light-hearted joke, for Elijah to roll his eyes or tease me in response, but of course, there was none of that. Elijah was barely listening to me. Instead, he stared down at his phone screen, at something there that had clearly caught his interest.

"Everything okay?"

Elijah's eyes flickered up to me. "I've got to check up on some shit," he said bluntly. Even though I met his response with silence, I knew it was time for me to leave.

Elijah didn't have to tell me to leave because his body did it for me. There was no way that I could have felt any more distanced from him. I picked up my blanket and walked towards the door. I'd made a mistake of entering Elijah's world once. I wouldn't do it again. Unless I wanted to feel shit about myself after.

∽

I was grateful when Elijah left the house, even though every time he did that, he took my brain with him, too. For all I knew, he could be going to class, but he could also be torturing the man in that storage unit.

The fact that I knew where that man was and that Elijah was holding him against his will made me feel sick. What if he had family or kids that were out looking for him? I'd checked the local news every single day, anxious that I'd see the man's face with MISSING letters above it soon. But nothing. With the casual way that Elijah left the apartment and refused to talk about him, it almost felt like I'd hallucinated the whole thing.

The only thing that reminded me it was true and very real was the sound of Elijah showering every single night when he got back. Even though he tried his best to get rid of it, the smell of blood was pungent and hard to get rid of, no matter how much soap and bleach were used.

Even though I hadn't been the one to hit the man, that didn't stop the guilt from eating up my insides and the fact that I was complicit in the whole thing. But Elijah's warnings had been brutal and clear: fuck with him and he'd fuck with all chances I had at being a doctor. Was I selfish in wanting to protect my future while Elijah denied someone else of theirs?

It wasn't exactly something I could pop into Google or ask the Oakwood Academy counsellor. I sighed heavily as I got out my ingredients from my cupboard and set about making a chocolate fudge cake.

I put on a recording of my most recent lecture as I tried to keep the material fresh in my mind. An hour later, I'd cleaned everything up and the fudge cake smelled delicious as it cooled down on the kitchen counter.

"You're baking again," I heard Elijah's voice waft down the hallway and into the kitchen as he closed the front door behind him.

It sounded more like an accusation than a question, so I ignored him and began icing the cake. I still wasn't happy with how he'd acted when I'd woken up beside him that morning. The feeling that his face and the tone of his voice had left inside of me was more than the fear he conjured up in me on a daily basis. Well, almost.

"What is it?"

I jumped at the realisation that Elijah had joined me in the kitchen. To my surprise, I squeezed the piping bag too hard, accidentally sending chocolate icing flying out everywhere.

"Chocolate," I said awkwardly as I tried to clean up as calmly as possible. Elijah chuckled, but kept watching me from afar.

"You want a slice?" I asked once the silence grew agonising.

Elijah's eyes flashed, and I saw a muscle tick in his jaw.

"First sleeping in my bed, now baking for me?"

"I didn't bake *for* you, asshole," I snapped defensively. "I didn't think you'd want me to anyway after last time."

I watched Elijah's face as the memory of the laxative brownies and their aftermath reentered his conscience.

"Well, we're not going to be doing any of that shit, okay?" Elijah growled.

I put down the piping bag and turned to Elijah and

allowed the rage and confusion that was boiling up inside of me to overflow.

"I don't get what your fucking problem is. You're the one who started things with me first. *Every* time," I said indignantly. Elijah's face remained passive, but his dark eyes glared at me and dared me to go on. "And you didn't want to talk about it, which is fine."

I bit down on my bottom lip. It was definitely not fine, and there was so much more I wanted to say to Elijah, so many questions I wanted to ask him, but knew that I'd lose him if I even tried.

"But waking up in the bed that *you* told me to sleep in and offering you cake *because I'm polite* is where you seem to have a problem?"

Elijah's face screwed up. He was clearly uncomfortable at the words that were flying out of my mouth.

"I've kept your fucking secret, haven't I? Can't you be nice to me or even pretend to be for just one minute? I promise it won't kill you," I said in a sickly sweet voice.

"I'm not doing this with you," he snapped. Elijah turned around and began walking out of the kitchen.

"That's right, walk off like a pathetic loser because you know I'm right," I shouted at his disappearing back.

When Elijah didn't say anything, I got back to icing my cake. His little tantrum wasn't enough to ruin the fact that the chocolate fudge cake was the best consistency and texture that I'd ever made. I raised the piping bag to fill in the last bit on top, when Elijah came storming back into the kitchen.

"What do you want now?" I asked boredly. I refused to look at him as I continued icing the cake.

I could practically feel the heat and aggression radiating off of Elijah's body. But I wouldn't give him the satisfaction of my attention.

Before I knew what was happening, Elijah came up beside me, grabbed the cake tin with one hand, and threw the whole thing at the wall.

"What the fuck is wrong with you?" I yelled.

The kitchen was a mess now and the hours I'd put into baking had gone completely to waste. I went to the corner where the destroyed cake lay and glared at Elijah. Elijah's nostrils flared, and his face spread into a cruel sneer.

"What, are you going to cry like a pathetic loser now that your cake is ruined?" he said, mocking my voice and hand gestures as he parroted my words from moments before. Angry tears pricked at my eyes, but I forced them back before they could fall.

"You know what? You can torment me all you like, Elijah. But just admit that it's because you're too stupid to come up with anything better."

Venom dripped from my voice and I waited for Elijah to lash out. I watched as his lips pulled over his teeth and his eyebrows knitted together furiously before he stormed out of the apartment, leaving me to deal with the cake fiasco on my own. I shouldn't have expected anything different.

Elijah's momentary lapse in kindness and judgement had come to a certified end, and I wouldn't hold my breath hoping things would change between us.

17

GRACE

I'd realised that since I'd started living with Elijah, I hadn't really given any other guys a shot. I knew that there was a small part of me that had half hoped my fantasy of getting with a hot roommate would come true, but it was far from it. It was stupid for me to hold on to that idea, especially when there was a high likelihood that Elijah was getting his rocks off somewhere else, *with someone else*.

Since Elijah had been so adamant about the fact that there was nothing going on between us, I decided it was only right to find someone to confirm that.

The next day, I spent nearly an hour curating my Tinder profile with Violet's advice. She picked out the pictures that best showed my looks and personality at the same time. She also cut down my 'about me' section by more than half, which I initially wasn't happy about, but Violet said that it was better to be mysterious than look too eager.

Noted.

I spent the rest of the day swiping; between classes, during lectures, heck, even on the toilet. The dopamine receptors in my brain were on fire and loving it, even more so when I kept getting matches. *This is a piece of cake!*

There was one guy who I somehow matched with, even though I didn't remember swiping on him, who popped up asking for my Snapchat in a matter of minutes. That's when I discovered how useful the blocked button was.

∼

I sat in the cafe pretending to work on my laptop when I matched with a hot brunette who played football. His name was Mason, and he looked like the stereotypical heartthrob that would have dominated television in the 90s and early 2000s. Mom would be all over him in an instant if I were to bring him home.

Woah, slow down Grace.

I took a deep breath and was about to type out the first message when Mason saved me the pain and sent a message first.

Hey, I can't believe you go to Oakwood too! I would have remembered seeing such a beautiful girl on campus ;)

I found his message cheesy but sweet, and the way that my lips spread into an involuntary smile made me cringe and realise that it had been way too long since I'd properly entertained a guy. I pondered over my message before I replied.

Aw thank you! You're not so bad yourself ;)

Mason's reply came back in a matter of seconds.

You free to hang out tonight?

Straight to the point, I liked it. I was done with playing games I hadn't even consented to. All I wanted was an easy lay with a nice guy. Was that so much to ask for? *Is it what I really want or are am I just telling myself that to feel better?* I pushed aside my conscience and responded to Mason.

Yeah. How about we have a drink at my place??

I stared at the screen for an entire minute before his

message came in. I breathed out a sigh of relief as I'd been half expecting him to deny my request or ignore it.

Fucking hell, Grace, grow a pair.

Mason finally replied.

Sounds good to me ;)

I cast my mind to the evening that lay ahead. I ironed out all the possible scenarios that could go down and went over the emergency plan with Violet in case Mason was weird or anything.

Even though I wasn't looking for a hookup with the explicit intention of pissing Elijah off (who even said it would, anyway?) if he heard or saw Mason at the apartment, I couldn't deny the fact that I'd be amused at the expression on his face.

~

I'd just about finished getting ready and making my room 'hookup' friendly when the doorbell rang. I spritzed on a bit of perfume and went to let Mason in.

As soon as I opened the door, Mason's face broke into a wide smile. I took in his face and his body, an exact replica of his profile. Tall, muscly and brunette with a footballer's physique and a little dimple in his chin. I shouldn't have been *that* surprised that he was who he said he was, but too many reruns of *Catfish The TV Show* had taught me to be cautious.

"I brought some beer, just in case," said Mason, holding up the 4 pack in his hand.

"Great!" I said. I ushered him into the apartment, sure that Elijah was out.

"You look even better in person," he chuckled.

"Thank you," I giggled.

I did a curtsy which luckily made Mason laugh, but as I

righted myself, I felt a wave of embarrassment wash over me. I looked around the living room, which suddenly felt unfamiliar and overwhelming because I had a new guest in it.

"Do you want to watch something?" I asked lamely.

Mason's eyes darted towards the TV and a slightly disappointed look crossed his face, but he quickly replaced it with a smile.

"Sure."

I turned on the TV and sat on the sofa as I began flicking through channels for something appropriate to watch. Mason sat beside me, slightly closer than I would have liked, but I reminded myself to breathe. He wasn't a serial killer, and if anything happened, I knew how quickly rumours could spread around campus.

Mason cracked open his beer, and I grabbed my bottle of wine from the kitchen. I quickly poured myself a glass, and took some long sips, hoping that the liquid courage would make me feel less on edge.

"So, have you been on many dates?" asked Mason.

I drained the rest of my glass and topped it up again with more wine.

"I haven't been on many dates, no," I said, chuckling at his use of the word 'date'. We both knew what he really meant, but I was in the mood to tease him. "You're my first one, actually. From Tinder that is." I raised my glass at him.

"You've got to be lying," Mason said, poorly disguising the surprise in his voice as he raised his can to clink it against my glass.

I played with a loose strand of my hair, realising that I needed to dye my hair again at some point, when the true meaning behind his words sunk in.

"Are you implying that I'm a *slut*?" I said, plastering a

look of fake horror onto my face. Mason shook his head and held his hands up, clearly missing the joke.

"No, of course not. I didn't mean- I just- oh my gosh, I'm so bad at this." Mason was getting more and more flustered as he tried to explain himself. I found it hilarious and placed my hand on his arm to show that it was okay.

After a rocky start that proved that we had vastly different senses of humour and interests, I realised Mason was definitely a pretty face first and personality second.

Elijah might be an asshole, but at least he's interesting

Fuck Elijah, I couldn't think about him tonight. I had to focus on getting laid and getting Mason out of here before an awkward encounter with Elijah happened.

My eyes kept flitting to the clock and the door in anticipation of Elijah's arrival. I didn't keep track of his schedule, bar his nightly 'errands', so I felt super on edge, not knowing if or when he'd show up.

"Is your roommate in?" Mason asked.

"No, it's just us right now."

"Is it cool that I'm here?" Mason had a wary look on his face. *Poor guy*.

"Yeah, of course it is!" I blurted.

He was definitely picking up on my anxiety, which I thought I'd been masking pretty well with my wine. Mason's face relaxed, and we both finished our drinks and I let him talk my ear off about how much he was looking forward to the newest Marvel film after the commercial that had come on the television.

I hadn't seen a single Marvel film and didn't want to be rude, so tried to listen politely, even though I just wanted to get the whole knocking each other's boots thing over and done with.

"Sorry, I'm chatting so much, I don't mean to bore you,"

Mason said sheepishly after what must have been my tenth 'yeah'.

"Nah, not at all," I said.

The wine was definitely kicking in and even though I was feeling a bit sexually frustrated, the more that Mason had talked, the more I'd started to second guess myself.

C'mon Grace, you need to do this. Fuck Mason so you can get Elijah out of your fucking head. Even better if he finds out, then he'll know that you seriously want nothing to do with him.

"You want to see my room?"

Shit, how cringey had that sounded?

Mason's face lit up eagerly. "Yeah, sure," he said. We stood up, and I led him down the hallway.

I'm actually going to do this.

When we reached my door, I stopped, suddenly horrified at the fact that I might have not put my laundry away.

"Wait here a second," I told Mason.

"No worries."

I opened my door, just a crack, so that Mason couldn't see, and slid inside. Spying a stray pair of underwear on the floor, I gave it a sniff before realising that it was clean. I carefully folded it and tucked it away into my drawer.

Catching my reflection in the mirror, I was amazed that I still looked pretty put together, despite how tipsy I felt. I smoothed my hair back into a ponytail and readjusted my skirt, which kept threatening to ride up my thighs.

Stay calm, you can do this. Just relax and it's all going to be okay.

I made sure that the condoms were in a discreet yet accessible place before I spritzed on a bit more perfume. I was so nervous, you would have thought it was my first time. As I checked my reflection one last time, my attention was snatched by the sound of the front door opening. Shit.

I practically ran to my bedroom door and flung it open to see Elijah and Mason standing in the hallway together.

"Who the fuck are you?" Elijah had a furious expression on his face. He stood a few inches taller than Mason, who I could tell was feeling both intimidated and confused.

"He's with me," I said at the same time that Mason said,

"My name is Mason, who are-"

"Get the hell out of my apartment," Elijah snapped aggressively, cutting us both off with his deep, loud voice.

Mason looked between me and Elijah, clearly trying to figure out what was going on between us.

"Don't talk to my guest like that," I scowled at Elijah. I turned to Mason and gave him an apologetic look. "Come on, let's go-"

"Are you deaf?"

Elijah was practically seething as he grabbed Mason by the collar of his shirt and shoved him against the wall.

"Stop it, get your hands off of him!" I cried.

I was completely horrified. I thought that if Elijah came back, the worst thing he'd do was get in a strop and go to his room. I hadn't thought for a second that he'd *put his hands* on Mason, especially since he was only standing in the hallway, which was pretty inoffensive.

"I don't like trash in my house," Elijah gritted out. "Leave." Elijah pushed a stunned Mason roughly towards the door.

"I-I-G-Grace, who is this guy?" he stammered as he slowly made his way to the door. The hurt expression on his face made my stomach turn. How could I even begin to explain to him?

"He's my roommate," I said. "I don't know why he's being such an asshole." I turned to Elijah. "Don't you have other places to be?"

Elijah's lips pulled back over his teeth and, even though

he closed the gap between us and towered over me, he turned his head to face Mason.

"She's not going to fuck you, so you better get the hell out of here before I get my hands on you again," he snarled.

My mouth dropped open, and I was completely at a loss for words. Confusion, humiliation and anger mixed together in a tumultuous cocktail in the pit of my stomach.

Mason's eyebrows shot up and nearly disappeared into his hair. Without saying another word, or even grabbing his remaining beers, he opened the door and practically ran out, allowing it to close behind him.

"Why the hell did you do that?" I snapped at Elijah once we were alone again.

His hands were in fists by his side and his shoulders heaved up and down as he stared daggers at me. Scratch that, I wasn't even sure he could see me. He looked so fucking angry I could practically see the smoke coming out of his ears and nose.

"Hello? Do you want to fucking explain yourself?" I clicked my fingers impatiently at Elijah.

Of course, he couldn't just leave me alone for one evening. He could go days, hell *weeks* of not showing me any real interest, and the minute that a guy turned in my direction, all hell broke loose.

"Don't you dare click at me!" Elijah roared as he pushed me up against the wall and pinned me with his hands. The sudden motion sent a rush of adrenaline through me and I struggled to move against his aggressive hold.

"Move!" I said.

"Why was he here?" Elijah glowered, ignoring my request.

I looked him dead in the eye, into those dark pools that held wicked secrets and a tortured past that I couldn't even begin to understand.

"Answer me, Grace!" Elijah shook with rage while I shook with fear at the sound of his voice.

"I don't have to tell you shit!" I spat.

Who did he think he was? Why did I have to give him all the answers while he barely gave me anything?

"I don't like the idea of anyone touching you... it makes me *sick*," Elijah snarled, his eyes dancing across my face. They settled on my exposed cleavage before they made their way back up to my face, where they lingered on my lips for just a moment.

No. There was no way that he was getting territorial. Not when he'd made it very clear that he didn't want me like *that*.

"It's not up to you, Elijah." I let out a frustrated breath. "Why do you even care, anyway?" I said after a moment.

Elijah shut his eyes and released an exasperated breath. When his eyes snapped open again, I saw that there was pain there, which was quickly replaced with anger.

"Answer me, Elijah!"

I held my breath as I waited for his answer, aware that I'd crossed a line by mocking him to his face. Elijah raised his fist in one sharp movement and punched the wall beside my head, making me flinch. I yelped, even though he hadn't touched me. *But he could have*. It hadn't been the first time he'd lashed out like that. I had to admit to myself that no matter how much I fought back; I was still afraid of Elijah. Especially because every time I felt closer to understanding him, he sharply pulled away, and I felt like we were back to square one.

"Never bring him, or anyone else, back here again," he said through gritted teeth.

Elijah continued staring at me, his body pressed flush against mine as our breathing and heartbeats synched up.

Elijah peeled his body away from mine and stormed

down the hallway and into his room, leaving me to be a quivering and lonely mess against the wall. Another door slammed into my face.

When I turned to look beside me, I noticed that Elijah's fist had left a dent in the plaster. I knew we'd have to answer to the damage when the end of the college year came, but that was the last thing on my mind.

Elijah found the idea of anyone else touching me... sickening. What he'd inadvertently said was that he wanted to be the only one touching me. Like I was his toy, his possession. I knew it was wrong. I didn't want to be someone's property, especially not someone like him, but deep down, I knew I was lying to myself.

Even though I didn't want to admit it, Elijah had laid a claim to me that day he'd forced me to my knees and fucked my face. And as far as he was aware, that meant that my mouth, my *body,* was reserved for him and him alone.

But why couldn't he just come out and say it?

18

GRACE

"Fucking hell, I'm going to scream!" I exclaimed as my computer froze for the third time in ten minutes.

"And I'm going to fucking scream if you don't shut the hell up." I looked up to see Elijah standing at the kitchen door, a grumpy expression on his face.

He'd been in an even worse mood than usual since his showdown with Mason the other night. Since he refused to explain himself, I refused to give him the attention and kept to myself. It hadn't been easy avoiding him, especially because I felt drawn to him every time he stepped into the room.

"Well, if you had an exam in two days and your laptop was playing up, I bet you'd be having a fit," I shot back. I pressed a few keys sporadically on my keyboard and my laptop decided to cooperate again.

"What's your test on?" Elijah grumbled as he set about making himself a cup of coffee.

"I don't think you have enough brain cells for that," I said. I rearranged my flashcards to avoid looking at him.

"It doesn't look like *you* have enough."

I rolled my eyes and started muttering underneath my

breath as I refreshed my knowledge for my test. I got three answers wrong in a row and nearly tore up the deck. I looked up at the sound of Elijah sniggering at me.

"What?" My scowl deepened at the sight of his pleasure in the presence of my misery.

Elijah shrugged and slowly brought his coffee mug to his lips. It was agonising, and he knew it. When he had decided that he'd tortured me enough, he joined me at the kitchen table.

"Touch anything and you're dead," I warned him. Elijah's eyes flitted over my carefully arranged notes and textbooks, and I could see the hint of mischief dancing in his dark eyes.

"How about we make this studying thing a lot more fun?"

"How?" I narrowed my eyes at him. Knowing Elijah, whatever he had up his sleeve, would probably be to my detriment. Despite that fact, I still wanted to know.

Elijah sat back in his chair and took another drawn out sip of his coffee. As he set his mug down on the table, his eyes met mine and that same dangerous smirk returned to his chiselled face. He gestured to the flashcards in my hand.

"Let me help you."

I ignored Elijah's outstretched hand and held onto my flashcards, suddenly feeling very overprotective of my work. I knew I was smart enough to be at Oakwood and to get onto my course, but the thought of proving that intelligence to Elijah terrified me.

"I'm not a masochist," I shot back. "What's in it for you, anyway?"

"The quicker you get through these flashcards, the quicker you can stop complaining about having to study. Then I can get some peace and quiet," Elijah said, with emphasis on the 't.'

"I'm not convinced. It's my right as your roommate to annoy the hell out of you until the day you move out-" I began, but Elijah cut me off before I could finish.

"For every flashcard you get wrong, I'll give you an orgasm," Elijah purred.

I nearly choked on air, unable to believe the words that had come out of his mouth. Elijah's tattooed muscly arm was still outstretched in front of me. *An orgasm for every wrong answer?*

My mind danced over the idea. It was a bad one, so why was I so hesitant to say no?

"Unless you're not confident in your abilities?" Elijah teased, with one eyebrow quirked.

The hunger and the challenge in his eyes were too much to bear. My chest felt hot and tight and I knew I couldn't waste any more time arguing about how I should study for my test.

"I'm confident," I snapped. Elijah scoffed, and I cleared my throat as I braced myself for the question that was most pressing. "Let's say that I *theoretically* get an answer wrong. How and when would these orgasms be administered?"

Elijah chuckled for a moment before his face went still as a stone. He leaned across the table, bringing his warmth and masculine scent with him, and pressed his thumb to my bottom lip. I shivered beneath his touch, even though his hand was warm as he scanned my face.

"I'll give you those orgasms whenever I want, *however* I want, and probably one after another to see how much you can handle," Elijah growled before he pulled away from me and resumed his position in his chair.

Holy fuck.

Could Elijah tell how pent up I was just by looking at me? I mean, I had called over Mason with the specific intention of getting a few orgasms out of him. Looking at Elijah sitting across from me with a cruel smirk on his face, offering to give me orgasms of his own volition? It was too much to compute.

"Maybe this isn't such a good idea-"

Elijah grabbed my flashcards from my hand and started going through them one by one, asking me the questions that I'd hastily scribbled onto them. I had a good run of four correct answers before I got one wrong.

"You're smarter than that, c'mon," Elijah said as I struggled to remember the answer. "Or did you self sabotage on purpose?" he asked, his eyebrows raised suggestively.

"Of course not," I snapped, but my defensive tone didn't stop my cheeks from burning.

We carried on, the pressure on now that Elijah's forfeit was on the table. It felt like everything I'd been taught had coincidentally displaced itself from my memory.

Every time I got something wrong, Elijah chuckled sadistically and added to the tally that he kept on the sheet of paper in front of him. I heard his phone buzzing in his pocket.

"I need to take this," he said quickly, standing up from the kitchen table.

Elijah threw the flashcards on the table and they fell into a rainbow spiral in front of me. I felt my heart drop in my chest, upset that our time together had ended, only just realising how much I had actually been enjoying it.

What about my orgasms? I wanted to say. But instead, I watched Elijah disappear out of the kitchen, his phone pressed to his ear.

"Fucking hell, not again," he groaned into the phone. I had no clue who he was referring to, but my curiosity peaked. Did it have something to do with the man in the storage unit?

"Why can't *you* pick him up this time?"

That was the last thing I heard before Elijah disappeared into his bedroom. I knew he didn't want me to know who he was talking to or what he was talking about, but that didn't stop me from wanting to know what was going on.

Alone once again with a bunch of work left to do and no orgasms, I looked down at the table in front of me. My study materials looked even less appealing than they had moments before.

19

GRACE

After a long day of lectures and seminars that left me with barely any energy, I couldn't wait to get back to the apartment, shower, and pass out in front of some Netflix. I peeled off my clothes, wrapped my towel around my body, and made my way to the bathroom. I heard Elijah shuffling about in his room, but that was nothing out of the ordinary.

I turned the heat up really high and got out all the fancy soaps that my parents had gifted me for Christmas. Lathering the soap suds all over my body, I started humming to myself as I let the water run over me. My humming was cut off when I heard the door opening.

When I looked up, the sight of Elijah stood at the door, staring at me, scared me stiff. I rushed to cover my body with my hands, but the intense look in his eyes told me I couldn't hide from him.

"Get out," I said, annoyed at how weak my voice sounded. "Hello? I'm showering here!" I said more forcefully when Elijah made no attempt at moving.

As if he'd snapped out of a trance, Elijah's eyes darkened and I watched his Adam's apple bob up and down in his throat when he swallowed. The water from the shower wasn't loud enough to conceal the growls coming from Elijah's throat.

What was he thinking?

Hot and exposed, I stared at Elijah, willing him to leave the bathroom even though a part of me didn't want him to go anywhere. There was something oddly sensual about the way that he watched me- like he couldn't decide if he wanted to hurt me, devour me, or both.

"Get out, Elijah," I said again. "Please."

I needed him to leave before something happened. Something like the night of the party. Possibly even something worse.

"Turn off the shower and come here," Elijah ordered me, his face passive.

"What?"

"Are you fucking deaf? Get out of the shower and come here now. Before I make you."

The hardness in his voice made me shiver with fear, and I found myself following his instruction. It felt like my body had a mind of its own as I turned off the shower and stepped onto the bath mat. I grabbed my towel and wrapped it around myself, even though Elijah had already seen enough of my naked body.

Elijah's eyes were on me on the whole time and my heart was in my throat when I turned around to face him, my hands tight on my towel. The light danced over Elijah's tattooed muscles as he walked towards me, bringing his warmth with him. I watched the muscle tick in his jaw and scanned his face for a sign of anything. I was scared to breathe, scared to do anything that might anger him, especially when he had that crazy look in his eye.

Elijah's hand shot out and tore off my towel before I could stop him. He threw it on the floor and I crossed my hands over my private parts.

"You can't hide from me," Elijah growled as he grabbed my arms and roughly pulled them away from my body, exposing my swelling breasts.

My nipples hardened when they were hit by the cool air, and perhaps for another reason. Elijah's eyes flew to my nipples and in a split second, he'd crouched down and brought his mouth to my breasts. His rough hands were all over my body, hungrily searching as I stood naked before him. He sucked and licked and teased my nipples and I hated how good it felt.

"Elijah," I breathed. I needed to stop him before things went too far.

Ignoring me, Elijah wrapped his arms around my thighs and hoisted me over his shoulder like a caveman. He walked me into my room, where he flung me onto the bed.

Being thrown around like a rag doll would never get old.

"What are you d-" I started, but Elijah cut me off with his sharp tone.

"Shut up and spread your legs," he snapped.

My words caught in my throat and I tried to cover my naked body up before Elijah got to me. But of course, he was stronger, and I was no match against him.

Elijah peeled my hands off of me, grabbed onto my ankles and pulled me further down the bed. Ignoring my gasps and attempts to escape him, he pushed my legs apart and stared down at my exposed slit.

"Fuck," Elijah muttered underneath his breath, his eyes full of animalistic lust.

My chest felt tight with fear and desire, but I stopped trying to escape Elijah's hold when I noticed the look on his face. I waited for him to make the next move.

"I didn't like seeing you with that dickhead the other day," Elijah growled.

He got on his knees and began kissing up and down my

thighs while he ran his big, warm hands over my body. His touch sent heat coursing through me and I hadn't realised how much I'd been craving it.

"His name is Mason," I said, trying my best to keep my voice even as Elijah's lips brushed against my skin and teased towards my centre.

"You should thank me."

"What?" I asked incredulously.

"For saving you from him."

I sat up and gave Elijah a confused and angry look.

"I don't think *he* was the one I needed saving from," I said pointedly, as the memory of Elijah punching the wall sprung into mind.

Elijah's eyes darkened and his grip on my thighs became tighter. He held my gaze as he traced his tongue around my clit, but not on it. My breath caught in my throat and I knew I was going to surrender to him in a matter of moments.

"I saved you from a mediocre orgasm," Elijah breathed, his breath warm against my clit. I felt like I'd die if he didn't press his lips against mine.

"Is that so?" I said breathlessly, my voice barely more than a whisper.

Elijah looked at me like he wanted to ravage me, like he wanted to consume my body until there was nothing left. The sight of his head between my legs was already enough of a turn on. I didn't know how I'd be able to cope if he used his tongue on me.

"I'm going to force you to cum on my tongue, hard, for making me wait to taste your sweet pussy for so long," Elijah purred. "And for forgetting all those questions wrong yesterday."

So he was going to stick to his promise. Holy fuck.

"And the fact that you're dripping wet for me tells me you've been waiting for this for a long time."

Elijah dove headfirst into my pussy before I could stop him. I struggled to hold back my moans as Elijah lapped up all my juices with his warm, wet tongue.

"Elijah," I breathed as I tried to pull away from his mouth. It was too much, it was too good. I needed to make him stop before I got carried away.

"Be a good girl and stay still," Elijah ordered me.

He came up for air for just a moment, his dark eyes ravenous and his face full of animalistic desire for me. For my pussy. Elijah continued licking and sucking with all his might, surprising me when he slipped two fingers inside of me and started pumping gently.

"Oh my God," I whispered. I tried to fight them, but my eyes shut against my will as I surrendered to my feelings of ecstasy.

I was so conflicted between my hatred for Elijah and how badly I wanted him, *needed* him to keep pleasuring my body the way that he was. And I think a part of him knew that and felt the same way, too.

Elijah picked up the pace, started sucking on my clit harder and pumping his fingers in and out of me more quickly. My eyes flew open, and I looked down at Elijah's head, the sight of him and his enjoyment making me buck my hips as I neared my orgasm.

"What a greedy little slut," Elijah chuckled darkly. "What if I stop now and don't let you cum?"

"No, please don't do that!" I cried. The fact that my voice sounded so desperate and submissive only turned me on more, in ways that I never could have imagined.

Elijah smirked and fucked me with his fingers even harder, this time slipping in another finger so that my pussy had to stretch around them.

"Beg like a good little slut and I might let you cum," Elijah purred.

I hated that he had so much control over me, but I needed to finish. I was so close and I felt like I'd die if I didn't get to reach orgasm.

"Please, let me cum," I said.

"Make yourself sound *pathetic*," Elijah barked.

"Please, let me cum. I'm begging you!" I cried.

Elijah locked his eyes on me and smirked because he knew that I was only seconds away from the edge. But he also knew that he had the power to ruin my orgasm if he wanted to. I pleaded with my eyes, my legs shaking uncontrollably as my orgasm dangled in front of me. I needed Elijah to say it, to give me the order that would finally set me free.

"Be a good girl and cum for me, Grace."

I released everything inside of me and gave into Elijah's command. I shook violently as the orgasm careened through my body and set fire to every fibre of my being. Elijah's eyes were on me the entire time, watching me intensely as I came, which only strengthened my orgasm.

"T-t-thank you," I stammered once I'd gotten my breath back and the aftershocks of the orgasm had subsided.

Elijah raised his fingers to his lips, the ones that he'd filled me up with mere moments before, and slowly sucked them until they were clean. I stared at him with wide eyes, too stunned to speak. I glanced down at his crotch and saw his rock hard erection poking through his jeans.

"I told you I don't do mediocre," said Elijah before he turned and walked out of my room before I could offer to return the favour.

What the hell had happened there?

I lay back on my bed, naked, confused, and flustered. I watched the door, waiting for Elijah to burst back in and fuck me until I forgot everything.

Even though he wasn't in the room anymore, I could still

feel his lips all over me, and I knew I needed more. My skin burned with the memory of Elijah, from his touch, that had lit up all my nerve endings and made me forget my name.

The monster I knew as my roommate seemed to have too many faces to count. I was losing track of them all and losing my mind as I tried to figure out where I stood with each one.

Elijah was the king of mixed messages, but he'd been loud and clear. He'd been *waiting* to eat my pussy, to conquer it. That explained why he'd lashed out when he'd seen me with Mason. Something about his jealousy and the fact that he had gotten so possessive of me and of my body set my insides on fire.

Elijah had always walked down the dark path, and now I was willingly following him. He'd introduced me to the dark and delicious, unlocked a craving for it that I'd never known existed within me. I was scared of what would happen if I got to explore that side of me again.

Especially because the only person I wanted to explore it with was *him*.

I knew things would be much worse and a lot harder if I didn't get to explore that side again. Something had awakened inside of me and it wasn't going to sleep any time soon.

20

GRACE

The next morning, I walked into the kitchen to get my coffee. After fighting with my stupid laptop for most of the night, I decided I deserved at least one nice thing. As I waited for the kettle to boil, I noticed the light bouncing off something shiny. My attention went to the kitchen table where a white box sat, still sealed in plastic, next to a textbook that I'd left out.

Ignoring the whistle of the kettle, I approached the laptop as if it was a wild animal and looked over the specifications. It was exactly like the one that I'd been looking at getting when I eventually had the money.

What the hell?

When I looked closer, I realised that there was a small Post-it note that read *Grace* and nothing else in cursive writing.

Elijah had bought me a laptop.

I buckled under the weight of all the different emotions that erupted inside of me. I was confused; I was angry, my heart felt warm, I felt weirdly hopeful because a gift meant...

Slow down, Grace, way too many emotions over a damn laptop.

I heard Elijah's bedroom door open and heard his slippers on the floor. I put as much distance between myself and the laptop and pretended to focus on making my coffee like usual.

"Hey," he said when he came in.

I noticed he was shirtless and almost drowned my coffee in milk. Elijah's attention was on the fridge, and I was glad that he hadn't noticed my mishap.

"Hey," I said, forcing myself to stay calm.

Elijah's gaze flitted to me before he returned his attention to the fridge. The events of the previous night stood between us, as did the brand new laptop on the kitchen counter. One minute he'd been eating my pussy and the next, he was replacing my laptop? What the *hell* was going on?

"Is this for damaging the wall?" I asked as soon as Elijah shut the fridge door. He blinked a few times before he flitted his gaze between me and the laptop on the table.

"Oh, that?" he said boredly. "No, that's so that you can finally shut the hell up and stop complaining about your old one."

"Oh, well thanks," I said lamely. "I can't guarantee I'll be shutting up, though," I said to his back as he walked out of the kitchen.

"It was worth a try." I swore I could hear a smile through Elijah's disdainful tone even though he was trying his best to seem unbothered.

I couldn't believe that he'd gone out of his way and gotten me a *laptop*. I didn't even want to think about the price or where he might have gotten the money from because then I knew I wouldn't be able to accept it. I weighed up my options and eventually decided that morality wasn't going to win. I'd gotten a new laptop that seemed to come with no strings attached. Sure, it had come from the same guy that had been bullying and blackmailing me and also happened to give me amazing orgasms, but it meant that I didn't have any more excuses to avoid doing the assignment and exam revision that awaited me.

I sat down at the kitchen table and started unboxing my new gift with all the excitement of a child on Christmas day. It was time to get to work.

∼

I walked out of the exam hall triumphantly even though I'd completely guessed the last two pages. I was just glad that it was fucking over. I messaged Violet, and we made a plan to meet at her house for the party that was happening in Oakwood Forest later that evening.

When I got back to the flat, I had some food, did some cleaning and called Dad. He was fully settled into his new apartment, but still went over to see Mom for dinner, which I found odd but understandable. Mom had seemed really withdrawn when I'd spoken to her on the phone a couple days before, so I was sure that the dinners they were having were probably quite an awkward affair.

Probably still not as awkward as my situation with Elijah. At least my parents knew where they stood with each other.

The mere thought of Elijah made my cheeks burn. The image of his head between my legs as he grabbed onto my thighs with his tattooed hands had refused to leave my memory. They way he'd managed to look so animalistic yet so tender at the same time..

Don't get ahead of yourself, you can never have him. Besides, he doesn't even want you like that- it's just his way of controlling you.

Even if I wanted to convince myself that Elijah had wanted to go down on me, and that the laptop he'd gifted me was some sort of sign, I had to accept the reality that he probably got off on my submission and the fact that he could treat me anyhow, but always have access to my body.

It was a degrading thought, and I knew I had to stop him from touching me and fight back harder, but it was hard to keep saying no when Elijah looked like *that* and could use his fingers and tongue in such amazing ways. I shook my head, hoping to clear it of all its confusing thoughts as I went to open the door for Violet.

∼

I had settled on a short denim skirt and a crop top at Violet's request that we dress similarly, so she didn't feel awkward wearing a skirt. I had tried to protest that I felt awkward too and that we should just change into something else. The wind whipping against my legs as we walked to the party made me regret listening to Violet.

Oakwood Forest was a short walk away from campus and it was where loads of students, of all years, went to party and get up to shenanigans. When we got to the forest, the smell of weed mixed with alcohol and the sound of thumping music were the first things we noticed before the groups of students. The shots of tequila we'd had on the way over made the whole thing look slightly less intimidating, but not completely. Either way, it was time to let loose and *party*.

"Should we sit by the bonfire?" Violet asked as she looked up from her phone. From how she'd been checking it every few minutes, I knew Nate was at the party or would arrive soon.

"Yeah, let's go!" I said. I grabbed her hand, and we made our way through the party until we'd arrived at the bonfire. Violet pointed out a space on one of the logs and we squeezed on it together.

"How are things going with you and Elijah?" Violet's voice cut through my daydream as I stared at the fire.

"What do you mean?" I squeaked, turning to look at my friend.

Violet chuckled. "Are you guys still at war? That must be so exhausting if you are." As I lifted my cup to my lips, the memory of Elijah's head between my legs resurfaced.

"I guess you could say that," I said with a shrug.

"You can always change apartments, Grace."

"I swear they're full or something," I said, remembering a conversation I'd heard Elijah having with someone over the phone while I'd been in my room.

Violet gave me a confused expression. "Of course they're not full. There are many reasons why people need to move out, so they always leave some spare. There's still time for you to ask if things are getting really bad. I know it sucks, but the option is there."

I focussed on draining the rest of my drink so that Violet couldn't see the expression on my face. Even after everything that Elijah had put me through, there still hadn't been a moment where I'd seriously considered moving away from him. I just couldn't bring myself to do it. I felt compelled to stay. Even if he ignored me for five days in a row, I knew a day would come when he'd break and speak to me. And for some reason that I couldn't put my finger on or didn't want to admit to myself, I craved those days, no matter how few of them there were.

"Yeah, I'll check it out," I said with a forced chuckle. Luckily, it was enough to quiet Violet.

When the music changed, we stood up and danced together along with a group of physics guys that stood nearby. We were busy dancing and grinding when Violet's phone lit up with a text message, casting a ghostly white glow on her face as she checked it.

"Sorry to bounce, but Nate said he just got here, and he wants me to meet him over there." Violet gestured to some trees on the left-hand side of the forest as she spoke.

The poor girl had an embarrassed expression on her face. Usually, I'd press her for more details because my nosiness was a curse, but for once, I didn't want to think about how she was getting some consistently while I only got the occasional crumbs that Elijah decided to bless me with. On *his terms*.

"You go get your man," I said. I gave Violet a lazy hug and kiss on the forehead and watched her as she disappeared into the woods.

I turned my gaze back to the jumping flames and let my mind wander. After a few minutes, some more people came to the bonfire and sat down around me in their various groups and pairs.

I chatted to a pair of girls beside me, first years, who'd been invited to the party by some football guys they refused to tell me the name of. Even though they were bubbly and nice enough, I was half relieved when they stood up to meet these so-called footballers. Pouring myself another drink from the hip flask in my purse, I nearly choked on the liquid when a guy sat down promptly beside me.

"Hey gorgeous, how are you?" he asked with a big smile on his face that looked more threatening than kind.

"Oh, I'm okay, just waiting for my friend. You?" I said

warily. I was only asking to be polite. I had no interest in having an actual conversation with him.

"A pretty girl like you shouldn't be on her own. You should be dancing!" he exclaimed, grabbing me by the arm.

"No, I'm okay, I'm a bit tired actually," I lied, trying to pull away from him.

The guy shook his head and laughed forcefully. I wasn't sure who exactly he was trying to convince that he was having a good time, but I was getting annoyed at Violet for leaving me.

"C'mon, just one dance. Then we can sit down and talk if you like. How does that sound?"

It didn't sound like the *worst* thing. I looked towards the trees, but there was no sign of Violet or Nate. Knowing them, they were probably having sexy times in there. Who was I to rain on their parade?

"Fine, I'm going to get a drink first, though," I said.

Even though I was already starting to feel quite drunk, I knew I needed more if I was going to get through a dance and a conversation with the weird guy that kept hounding me.

"I'll grab you one!" he said eagerly. "Here."

He dug into his backpack, which was on the ground beside his feet, and passed me a beer. From experience, mixing beverages had rarely turned out well for me, but it was sealed and I'd run out of booze, so I decided I was willing to risk it. We cracked our beers open together, and I took a long drag of mine while the guy watched me.

"I'm Mike, by the way," he said, raising his can towards me.

"Grace." I tapped my can against his and then drank some more. It tasted worse than I'd expected and the fact that it was a little warm too definitely didn't help.

"Now for that dance you owe me." Mike waggled his

eyebrows and even though I was rolling my eyes, I let him pull me up to standing.

Mike was a terrible dancer, but a very enthusiastic one and I didn't even bother hiding my laughter as he had what could easily be mistaken for a seizure in time to the music.

Time started to blur as the music got louder and the alcohol started to hit. Before I knew it, I was dancing longer than I'd planned to and Mike was handing me more drinks and encouraging me to down them with him. My pride wouldn't let me back down and say no, even though I knew I'd regret it in the morning. I winced after my last drink and shook my head at Mike.

"No more," I said, noticing that my speech was now fully slurred. "I need to find Violet."

Mike nodded at me. Or was it in time to the music? My eyesight had started to get blurry, and the world seemed to spin. I stopped dancing and looked at the floor as I tried to get my bearings. A bunch of people were dancing and chatting loudly around me. A lot of faces I didn't recognise, but some that I did.

The one thing that sucked about having parties in Oakwood Forest was that there were no toilets, so I couldn't even go and splash water on my face or get some peace and quiet. Or at least a semblance of it. I pulled out my phone, but my fingers felt numb and the words and numbers on my screen all seemed to blur together. I needed to find Violet.

Ughhh I shouldn't have drank so much.

"Can you help me find my friend?" I asked weakly. "Or some water, but mostly my friend."

"Sure, after this song," Mike said, a massive grin on his face as the music changed once more. I was going to have a word with the DJ or whoever was controlling the music, to get them to stop just so that I could hear myself think.

Why the hell had I agreed to dance with Mike in the first place?

My phone slipped out of my hand and I bent down to pick it up.

"You alright?" Mike's voice sounded like it was coming from another room.

"Yeah."

Mike's smile was the last thing I saw before everything went super blurry before turning completely black.

21

ELIJAH

My phone buzzed angrily in my pocket and I ignored it while I continued to clean up David's excrement. Of course, he was human, if only just, which meant that he had to go to the bathroom *somewhere*. Some days, I let him sit in his own filth, just to torture him a bit more, but I'd quickly learned that it was more hassle for me than for him. In fact, I was convinced that the sick fucker enjoyed making a mess for me to clean up.

When he needed to go to the bathroom, I made him go in the bucket that I'd placed in the corner of the room so that he could feel like the animal he was. I held him on a leash and was equipped with a taser for when he got too confident and stupid and tried to break free.

I'd shoved a needle into David's arm and sedated him so that he wouldn't cause any more trouble. I was sick of hearing his voice, sick of him and annoyed that no matter how much I punished him, the situation hadn't changed. There was nothing that I could do to change the past or make it go away. But I felt like I'd be failing Stella even more if I didn't at least try.

My phone wouldn't shut up the entire time, so after I'd

washed my hands and made sure that David's restraints were as tight as possible, I picked it up.

"What?" I barked into the receiver.

"Dude, you need to come to Oakwood Forest. Grace is *not* in a good way," said Nate in an urgent tone. I stood up straight and cast my gaze towards David. He was completely out cold.

"I'm on my way," I said before I hung up the phone.

My chest felt tight as I thought of all the things that had could have happened to Grace. It had to be bad enough for Nate to call me, even though he knew how much I disliked her. I didn't like being interrupted when I was doing something important, but I knew that the tightness in my chest would only ease once I'd figured out what was wrong with Grace.

Who knew what she could do or *say* with a bunch of alcohol in her system?

I checked the time on my watch. It was just after 2am. Locking the door behind me, I tucked my phone away and ran the whole way to Oakwood Forest.

∽

The music flooded my ears as soon as I arrived. The stench of sweat and alcohol mixed together in a way that made me sick. I scanned the crowds of students dancing and making out until I spotted Violet standing near the forest's entrance, a worried expression on her face. I marched towards her, and when she noticed me, she looked somewhat relieved.

"Thank God you're here," she breathed.

I ignored Violet and pushed past her, moving through the crowd of people dancing and towards Nate and two other girls that were standing around Grace's unconscious body.

"What the hell is wrong with her?" I growled, looking to Nate for answers.

"Everyone's overreacting. I think she's just really drunk," Nate said gruffly.

I glanced down at Grace and took in her very short skirt and skimpy top. A surge of jealousy took over my body as I wondered if anyone had looked at her too long or touched her while she'd been dressed that way.

Why do you even care? They're just clothes and she's just your annoying roommate.

"Is she going to be okay?" asked a girl standing over Grace who had a bunch of glitter on her face.

"Shouldn't we call an ambulance? I think we should!" exclaimed her friend.

I scoffed and scooped Grace up into my arms, ignoring the sweet scent that radiated off her body.

"I'm taking her home," I said.

"Can I come with you? To make sure she's okay?" Violet squeaked, suddenly appearing at Nate's side. Or maybe I just hadn't noticed her.

"No, she'll be perfectly fine," I growled. I suddenly remembered why I found Violet annoying. She was just as overbearing as Grace.

Nate shot Violet a look before he wrapped his arm around her shoulders and nodded at me.

"You better get her warmed up," he said.

"I'll text her in the morning," Violet said as I began walking towards campus.

I carried Grace the whole way back to our apartment, across the college campus and past students who were on their way to or from the library to study and other students who were getting back from their nights out.

The whole time, she barely stirred, and I held her close to my body to ensure that she didn't get too cold. I glanced down at her every so often to make sure that she was alive. After I unlocked the front door and let us into the apartment, Grace came to. The sound of the door banging behind us must have done it.

"Toilet, please," she groaned.

I stood behind Grace and held her pink hair back as she kneeled on the bathroom floor and emptied her stomach into the toilet bowl.

"You don't have to be here. This is gross," she said weakly before she threw up again.

"Just focus on being sick," I told her.

Grace moaned again and wretched into the bowl, but nothing came out this time. It seemed that she'd gotten to the bottom of her stomach. She sat up and leaned her head back against the wall, closing her eyes. Even though her makeup was smudged and she smelled of sick and alcohol, she was still the most beautiful woman I'd ever seen in my life.

Tearing my gaze away from her, I grabbed the glass of water and a slice of bread that I'd taken from the kitchen and passed them to her.

"Have these, you'll feel much better," I said.

Grace opened her eyes and when she spotted the water and bread, she shook her head and pouted at me.

"I can't eat or drink anything or I'll be sick again," she groaned.

"No, you'll be sick if you don't have anything and you'll wreck the lining of your stomach," I said more firmly.

I pushed the water and bread into her hands and guided them to her lips. Grace was too weak to fight me, and it wasn't long before she opened her mouth to let me feed and hydrate her.

"Someone doesn't know their limits," I snarked once she

decided she couldn't take anymore. Grace shot me an unimpressed look and held her head in her hands.

"It was all Mike's fault, not mine." Her voice was muffled, but I froze at the sound of her words.

"Who's Mike?"

"I don't know, some guy at the party who kept giving me drinks and making me dance with him," she said. A growl escaped my throat, and I launched into protective mode.

"What's his last name? Did you see him slip anything into your drinks?" My words came out thick and fast, my mind whirring as I put all the pieces together.

The sick fuck had probably been trying to get in her pants.

"Did you have sex with him? Did he force himself on you, Grace?"

Grace shook her head and winced at the tone of my voice. I knew I was getting loud, but I couldn't help it. If someone had touched her, taken advantage of her, I had to do something about it.

"No, I don't think we had sex-"

"You don't *think*?" I seethed.

I cast my gaze down to Grace's skirt, which had ridden up her thighs. I swallowed hard at the sight of her lace panties.

"What do you remember from the party?" I gritted out, slowly getting more and more impatient. Grace covered her ears and shut her eyes like a child.

"Stop asking me questions and let me go to bed," she said in a petulant voice.

I was about to press her for more questions but could see how tired she was and decided against it.

Grace struggled to her feet and even though I could feel a storm brewing up inside of me, I swooped her up into my arms like I had before and carried her to her room.

"I can walk by myself," she said in a sleepy voice.

"Be quiet, you," I said gently.

I took her to her room and laid her down on her bed. I rummaged through her drawers for something that she could wear to sleep in. I found an oversized top that would be good enough.

"I need you to take off your clothes, Grace," I said awkwardly. "Grace?" I called her name again when I didn't get a reply.

When I reached the bed again, I realised she was fast asleep. *Great.* I looked down at Grace's party clothes and the t-shirt in my hand and swallowed hard. I couldn't just leave her like that.

Taking a deep breath, I carefully undressed her, slowly, so that she didn't wake up. Grace's head lolled to the side as I peeled her top off of her to reveal her bare breasts.

Fuck.

I thought about the last time I'd seen Grace's body, naked and fresh out of the shower. I wanted to put my lips on her breasts again and my tongue on her pussy like I had a few days before.

Focus.

Pushing my fantasies aside, I focussed on getting her denim skirt off, which was a bit more challenging because of how round and plump Grace's ass was.

A great problem to have.

Once I'd taken off her clothes and left her lying on her bed in her thong, the perverted thoughts started up again and I tried to push them away. I felt an aching sensation deep in my balls as I stared at Grace's mostly naked body. She was so fragile, so clueless. *I could do anything to her.*

I cradled Grace gently as I slipped the shirt off her head and slipped her arms into the sleeves. Once she'd gotten under the covers, I took a step back and looked at her. *Really* looked at her.

Even though Grace was passed out, she was still a picture of beauty. She looked so delicate, so breakable. Even though she'd been the only girl I'd ever met that had tried to match and one up me, in that moment, I remembered she was just a person. And I felt this overwhelming desire to protect her. I don't know where that desire came from, but it seemed to get stronger every single day.

Hell, Grace had been the only person I'd ever bought a gift for. Sure, it had been because her constant complaints about her old laptop pissed me off, but I knew I'd be lying to myself if I didn't admit that her reaction hadn't melted the shards of ice lodged in my chest just *a little bit*.

My eyes wandered over Grace's long eyelashes, which curled slightly at the ends, before trailing down the slope of her nose and landing on her full pink lips. The same lips that I'd forced my cock between.

The thought of someone else taking advantage of Grace made my blood boil. Hell, the mere idea of her *being* with anyone else made me mad as fuck, and I couldn't explain it. Even if I hadn't told her, I hadn't needed to. Those lips were mine to do with as I pleased. As was her body. That was the only explanation for the feeling in my chest. I couldn't ignore my need to possess Grace entirely. My pants tightened and even though I wanted to feel her tongue on me again, I forced myself to pull the blanket around her and make sure that she was warm enough.

"I didn't know you could be... nice," Grace hiccuped and giggled lightly before she turned over on her side, where she began snoring again in a matter of seconds.

Nice.

I scoffed. No one ever used that word to describe me. Clearly, she was still drunk and wouldn't remember what had happened between us when she woke up the next morning. Things would be back to normal again.

Grace, of all people, knew I wasn't nice. How could I be nice when I was holding David hostage and torturing him every chance I got? How could I be nice after all the shit I'd done to her? What I'd done to my sister?

Now is not the time for a pity party.

Even though I had business to attend to, I waited to make sure that Grace was properly asleep and that I'd put her water somewhere she'd be able to find it easily in the morning before I closed her door quietly behind me.

∼

My body was tense the entire way to Oakwood Forest. The party had died down a little bit and there were far fewer people around than there had been earlier. It surprised me to see Nate and Violet still there, huddled on a bench together.

"Hey man, is Grace okay? "Nate called out to me.

"She's fine." I was about to walk past him when I got an idea. "Do you know a guy called Mike?"

Nate and Violet exchanged looks. "Why?" Nate asked me warily.

I didn't have time for any of this. "Do you know where to find him, yes or no?" I snapped.

"I think he's near the bonfire," Violet squeaked. The only time she'd ever been helpful in her life.

"See, that was easy, wasn't it?" I snarled, before I turned on my heel and went towards the bonfire in search of the asshole called Mike.

When I got to the dying bonfire, there were two guys and a girl dancing around it, obviously drunk out of their minds.

"Hey, someone else to join the party!" One guy cheered, and his friends cheered with him, opening the circle so that I could join. The guy who'd spoken to me had a face that just pissed me off, but it was that stupid smile of his that did the heavy lifting.

"Which one of you is Mike?" I barked.

I watched as the face of the guy who'd spoken to me fell. A sick feeling of satisfaction swirled in my stomach.

"Me," he said, his voice noticeably a lot quieter than it had been seconds before. He cleared his throat and tried to put on a tough voice. "Who's asking?"

I closed the gap between us, and Mike's friends started chatting anxiously behind him. I towered over the dickhead that had given Grace drinks all night, probably with the intent of taking advantage of her.

Mike's nose cracked as my fist connected with it, and even though he fell to the floor, I didn't stop with one hit. I got on top of him and let my fists get to work, all the while ignoring the shouts and screams around me.

22

GRACE

My eyes flickered open, and I flinched at the light streaming through my window. I flinched even more at the sight of Elijah sitting on the end of my bed.

"Drink this," he said.

Elijah pushed a glass of water into my hand and his eyes were on me the entire time. The last time he'd had any contact with something I was going to drink, he'd spiked me and I'd woken up next to the swimming pool. My parched throat decided it was worth the risk and so I quickly gulped down the water before I could change my mind.

"Thanks," I croaked. I set the empty glass down on my bedside table and turned back to Elijah.

"How did I get back here?" I asked him when he refused to explain.

"I brought you back."

"But you weren't at the party."

I cast my mind back to the previous night, and I was confident that I hadn't seen him. I'd seen the occasional tattoo sleeve, but none of them had belonged to Elijah. I'd been *sure* of that. Besides, parties didn't seem to be Elijah's thing unless he was throwing them with the specific intention of pissing me off.

Which meant that there must have been a specific reason he'd gone to the party.

"Nate called me and I came to pick you up," he said bluntly, his dark eyes burning into mine.

"Thanks," I said sheepishly. "You didn't have to do that-"

"Get some rest," Elijah said, cutting me off. He flexed his knuckles, and I caught sight of dried blood dusting them.

Noticing my attention on his hands, Elijah shoved them into his pockets as he stood up and left my room without another word.

When had he gotten those marks on his knuckles?

My mind went to the man that was still trapped in the storage unit. I shuddered at the thought and decided that my brain was too frazzled to think about all that dark stuff while I nursed a terrible hangover.

I looked down at my body and realised that I was in my old pyjama top that had just come out of the wash. I hadn't remembered getting changed, which meant that... Elijah had to have changed me.

He must have seen me naked again. But this time it had been different because I'd been passed out and didn't remember a second of it. My cheeks burned with embarrassment as I thought about the state I must have been in the previous night.

I am not drinking again for a long time.

I grabbed my phone to distract myself and clicked on the most recent message from Violet.

Did you hear about what Elijah did to Mike?!

I frowned at the message, wracking my brains to try and place a face to the name Mike. The annoying smiley face popped into my head again and I shuddered. But why would he and Elijah have any reason to be together?

No, what happened??

Violet's message came back instantly.

He beat him up and then just walked off like it wasn't a big deal.

I gasped and reread the message to make sure that I'd read it correctly. But it was there in black and white and I didn't need Violet to fill in the pieces for me. At some point the previous night, Elijah had not only saved me from the party, but he'd also beaten up Mike, and I assume it was because of me. *Great.*

I honestly don't get what's up with that guy.

And it was true. That was the second time that week that Elijah had physically assaulted someone because they had tried it on with me. Had Mike even been trying it on with me?

I had a blurry recollection of him giving me lots of drinks, but nothing more than that. And I physically felt okay, so he can't have forced himself on me. Someone at the party probably would have realised. It was all so confusing and my head was already hurting without having to think about Elijah's violent outbursts.

I planned to scroll through YouTube for only a few minutes, but of course I fell down into a spiral of videos. Eventually, I pulled myself out of bed, took some painkillers, and hopped into the shower.

My memory of the previous night was a complete blur. I remembered getting to the party, but I remembered little after that point. Even though I'd had some food and water, I still felt a bit out of sorts, so I stayed in my room for the rest of the day.

∽

A knock on the door made me jump. I closed my laptop and walked over to the door. I pulled it open to reveal Elijah standing at the door, shirtless, with nothing but his boxers on. Looking up, I noticed that his hair looked jet black when it was wet.

"Yes?" I asked after clearing my throat. Elijah looked me up and down with narrowed eyes.

"How are you feeling?" he asked.

I shrugged. "I've felt a lot better." My eyes dropped to the floor before I had the courage to look Elijah in the eye again. "Thanks for saving me. You didn't have to do that."

"You should have been more careful," Elijah growled. He turned on his heel and began walking down the hallway.

"Are those cuts on your knuckles from beating up your hostage or beating up Mike?" I breathed. Elijah kept on walking, and I knew I had to try another way.

"When are you going to set that man free?"

The silence that hung between us was deafening. I saw the muscles in Elijah's tattooed back tense up as he stopped, his hands in fists by his side. I knew that dropping the question would be the best course of action, the smartest route, but I couldn't be smart all the time.

"Are you *ever* going to let him go?" I hated how my voice trembled and cracked over the words.

I'd been wanting to ask Elijah about his captive for weeks, even though the answer seemed to become more and more clear every day. Elijah growled and turned around so he was fully facing me.

"Are you ever going to stop asking stupid questions?" he barked. I shook my head. Elijah's lips pulled over his teeth in a vicious snarl, and he raised his fists so that I could see.

"*These* are from dealing with that punk, Mike. He got what he deserved for what he was trying to do to you. And you know the rules. I told you not to ask me about that!" he roared.

So Violet had been right. Elijah had beaten the shit out of Mike when he'd found out that he'd been giving me drinks all night at the party. But what was it to Elijah? Why would he care, outside the possibility of me leaving vomit in the communal spaces?

Elijah turned to leave, and I grabbed the back of his shirt before I could stop myself.

"I think I deserve to know after everything!" I cried, my voice rising as I grew angrier. "Just be honest with me, Elijah. For once in your life, be honest."

Elijah cast me a look full of malice, then dropped his gaze to my hand, which still held tightly holding onto his shirt. Before I could pull away properly, Elijah grabbed me by the wrist and pulled me into my bedroom, his face a ball of fury. Without warning, he let go of me and sat on my bed while I stood in front of him, my arms crossed.

"What are you doing?"

"Get over my knee," Elijah snapped, his eyes dark with lust and sadism.

My heart burned in my chest, and I shook my head. I wasn't going to do that. My eyes fell to Elijah's crotch, noticing how his dick imprint was very obvious against his grey jeans.

"Why would I do that?" I shot back.

Elijah's frown grew deeper, and he bared his teeth at me. "You can either get over my knee or get on all fours. Pick one before I make you," Elijah snarled.

I felt my pussy clench at his words, at his deep and velvety voice. Elijah was serious. There was not one part of his face or his body that suggested otherwise.

Swallowing my pride, I walked towards Elijah, my heart thumping anxiously in my chest because his eyes were on me the entire time. I slowly lowered myself to the ground, so that I was facing his knees. I already felt degraded, less than human, and I knew that whatever Elijah had in store for me would only reinforce that feeling.

I draped myself over his knees and before I could get comfortable, Elijah grabbed me firmly with his big hands so that I couldn't move out of place.

"Now that's a good girl, following instructions," he purred.

The smoothness of his voice was at odds with his actions. Elijah grabbed the waistband of my sweatpants and roughly shoved them down my legs so that my bare ass was on show. He growled as he ran his hands over my ass, grabbing and kneading with all the possessiveness in the world.

"No underwear," he said darkly.

"It's healthy to go commando sometimes-" I breathed, but was cut off when Elijah's hand smacked my ass sharply.

"What did you do that for?" I whimpered. I tried to pull away from Elijah, but he held me fast.

"You're getting punished for getting too drunk last night-"

Another spanking. I flinched when Elijah's hands met my ass, but instead of cowering from the pain, my pussy twinged in response.

"But that wasn't my fault!"

It kind of was, but I wouldn't have gotten *as* drunk if I hadn't had to deal with Mike.

"You need to be spanked for asking too many questions too," Elijah growled as he brought his hands down on each of my cheeks.

His spanks were hard, quick and searing. I yelped each time his hand came down, but at the same time, heat rushed through my body and the space between my thighs grew warmer and wetter. Elijah's hands slipped between my thighs and caressed the folds of my pussy.

"I knew you'd love being spanked," he growled as he thrust his fingers into my wetness.

I moaned as Elijah grabbed my ass roughly and pumped his fingers in and out of me. I felt so slutty and submissive and loved the fact that he was in complete control.

It felt so fucking good.

My breathing sped up, as did my heart rate as I felt myself getting closer to orgasm. When I couldn't hold it back anymore, I gave into the pleasure and let the familiar ecstasy wash over me. Breathless, I tried to sit up and get off of Elijah's lap, but he held me firmly by the back of the neck so I couldn't move.

"Where do you think you're going?" he growled.

"We're done, now let me go," I said.

Elijah chuckled darkly. "I'm not finished with you, Grace."

Elijah brushed his fingers lightly along my sensitive folds before he thrust them back inside of me.

"Please, no, I'm not ready!" I cried.

My body shook uncontrollably from Elijah's touch. He really didn't believe in a cool off period.

"Oh, you're ready for me," Elijah growled. "Wet and moaning is exactly how I want you."

As Elijah's sexy voice caressed my ears and his heavenly fingers stroked at my insides, I felt myself convulse around him, my pussy pulsating around his fingers as Elijah forced me to orgasm again.

I loved how he had full control over my body, over my orgasm. When I tried to pull away for the third time, Elijah held me firmly and his growls became more aggressive as he made me cum twice more until I was crying out. I was relieved when Elijah pushed me aside onto the bed once he'd finally decided that he was finished with me.

My head felt cloudy and empty as the endorphins rushed around my body. Elijah's pupils were dilated as he scanned my body, his face flushed with longing. My pussy ached from the delicious torture it had been through, but it also ached for him. My eyes dropped to Elijah's crotch and my lips parted in silent request.

Elijah grabbed my chin and ran his thumb along my lips. The tenderness took me by surprise, especially considering how rough he had been only moments before.

"What do you say to me for punishing you?" Elijah purred. I dropped my eyes shyly to his tattooed hand before I looked back at his burning eyes.

"Thank you," I breathed. And I meant every word.

I hope he couldn't hear how loudly my heart was beating.

"Good girl," he growled. "Now, if you ever get that drunk or ask me those questions again, my next punishment won't be as kind."

Elijah squeezed my face forcefully in his hand to make sure that he got his message across before he released me and left my room without another word.

Why couldn't Elijah stay with me for even a moment after he'd degraded me like that? If he did, I knew I wouldn't feel as bad as I suddenly did at that moment.

Because he's not your boyfriend and you mean nothing to him.

Sure enough, he'd looked after me when I was drunk for reasons I couldn't even understand, but to expect anything more from Elijah was a joke and a dark path that would only lead me to get my feelings hurt. Elijah's last words had been a promise. And since I knew myself better than anyone else, I knew that the chances of me sticking to his requests were very small indeed.

23

GRACE

The next few days flew by and I barely felt present. I went about my usual routine, trying to keep to myself as I gravitated between the library and Violet's place before I eventually found my way back to my apartment. I was relieved that I'd been allowed to continue with my course and only had to make up the plagiarised essay with a new one. I tried to keep busy, to keep Elijah out of my head, but somehow he still forced his way to the forefront of my mind.

I didn't even tell Violet about how things had progressed between us, worried that if I verbalised my confusing feelings out loud, then it would make things too real, too scary. So I shot down her questions as best as I could and promptly moved the conversation onto her life, which she was more than happy to go on about.

After my afternoon seminar, I went back to the apartment, glad that Elijah was out so that I could have some thinking time. I had my leftover pesto pasta that was in the fridge before I went to my room.

When I was halfway through my movie, Mom called and I picked up because it had been a few days since we'd been able to chat properly. I got her up to speed with college and let her know that Violet was okay. I wanted to talk to her about Elijah, but things were way too volatile to mention him to a parent.

What exactly would I even say, anyway?

Hey Mom, you know that guy that ignored me in the hallway on move in day? Yeah, he's my roommate, yeah, the scary one with the tattoos. He enjoys giving me forced orgasms. Like a lot. Oh yeah, and he bought me this new laptop. But no, we're not boyfriend and girlfriend...

I bit my tongue and expertly skirted around questions regarding my roommate situation, choosing to answer them in the most vague way possible, even though all I wanted to do was spill my guts to someone.

Mom started updating me about her life, which inevitably came with updates about Dad, which still didn't get any easier no matter how much we spoke about it.

A few minutes into the conversation, I sighed and put my head in my hands. I already had enough on my plate and being in the middle of my parents' drama was the last thing I needed.

"Grace, are you still there?" Mom asked on the other side of the phone.

"I am," I said, trying my best to keep my annoyance out of my voice. "Why can't you just tell Dad yourself?"

"I'm just really busy today," said Mom. She had never been the best at lying. "Besides, this is just one thing you need to do for me. I'd really appreciate it, Grace."

I felt a pang in my chest at her words. She wanted to know if Dad was seeing anyone else and for me to bring it up in the most casual way possible. I had no clue how I was supposed to do that when we didn't exactly talk about relationship stuff.

"Please?" The slight desperation in Mom's voice made me feel guilty. I knew she wouldn't drop it until I agreed.

"Fine," I said after a moment. I just wanted the whole thing to be over and done with. When I'd picked up her call, I hadn't expected her request at all.

"Aw, thanks! Remember, try not to be too obvious about it. It's no big deal. I'm just curious."

Why was she so curious about what Dad was doing when she'd been the one to call everything off? My mom could be a confusing woman at the best of times, and I knew better than to question her.

"I have to go now, Mom, but I'll speak to you later."

"Bye, Grace."

I hung up the phone and tossed it on my bedside table. I lay back in bed and felt a massive weight sink into my chest. I'd tried not to think about the fact that my family was splitting apart, but I could only push away the thoughts for so long.

I felt helpless and confused and I wanted to shout at both of my parents, wanted to shake them until they saw sense- but I knew it was no use and that there was nothing I could do about it. The reality of my family situation did nothing to stop the tears from falling down my cheeks.

There was a knock on the door. I stared at the handle to see if he'd barge in or wait. To my surprise, Elijah actually waited for me to answer.

"Come in," I said. I quickly wiped my tears away and hoped that it wouldn't be obvious that I'd been crying.

I sat up quickly in bed and smoothed my hair down. Even though Elijah had had me in a very compromising position the day before when he was spanking me, I still felt inclined to look somewhat put together.

"Hey," Elijah said as he stepped into my room. The first thing I noticed was the way that his shirt clung to his muscles and the stubble dusting his chiselled jaw.

"What's up?" I asked before I could get carried away, admiring his looks.

Elijah flexed his jaw and joined me on the bed. I focussed on keeping my heartbeat and breathing normal.

"I was just checking on you after yesterday."

"Oh," I squeaked and I could feel my cheeks flushing red.

Elijah trailed his eyes up and down my body before they landed on my face. His eyes darkened, and I watched the muscle tick in his jaw.

"Why were you crying?" he asked.

"I'm not. It's just allergies."

"Don't lie to me, Grace," Elijah growled.

I cocked an eyebrow. "What? Are you going to spank me?" I snarked.

"If I have to," he shot back with no hesitation.

And he looked serious *as hell*.

It seemed stupid to lie about it or try to avoid the topic when my chest felt so heavy. And the way that Elijah was watching me with such intensity made me feel like he actually wanted to listen for once. I took a deep breath and let the words fall out.

"My parents are divorcing and it's just a really weird and shitty time. Don't get me wrong, I love them both, but I don't like the weirdness and feeling like I have to pick sides," I said.

Elijah slid his hand across the bed until his fingers met with mine. I flinched at his touch, but didn't pull away.

"That sounds... hard," Elijah said quietly.

"Yeah. They're living separately now and I'm not looking forward to going back home for the holidays. Like what the hell even is *home* anymore?" I sighed.

"Just remember that you can't do anything about it and you're lucky that you still have both of them around,"

Elijah said after a moment, a guarded expression on his face.

"I know, but that doesn't stop me from feeling bad about everything *right now*," I said.

"I know." Elijah squeezed my hand with his, sending warmth through my body.

"What's the deal with your family?" I asked once I'd finally built up the courage.

Even though we'd lived with each other for a while, I realised that there was still so I didn't know about him. Elijah pulled his hand away from mine and placed it back in his lap. It stung that he pulled away from me, but I tried my best not to let my feelings show on my face.

"There's no deal," Elijah said coldly. His eyes darted around the room as his eyebrows knit furiously together.

I'd touched a soft spot, but I didn't regret it. I wanted to know where he'd come from and who or what had made him into the dark prince that he was.

There was no way he's always been like this.

"I'm not going to judge you, Elijah. I just want to understand where you're coming from," I said gently.

Taking a deep breath, I slid my hand across the bed and let it rest on his thigh. Elijah stared at my hand as if it was a poisonous snake, but didn't move away.

It was small, but it was something.

I watched as Elijah's hands balled into fists and his whole body stiffened. I held my breath anxiously as I waited to see if he was going to open up or continue building up the wall between us. It felt like years before he finally spoke.

"I don't have parents anymore," Elijah ground out. "They were smack heads before they had me and even after I was born, they decided that they'd rather inject heroin than look after their kids."

"I'm so sorry," I gasped.

"Why are you apologising? It's not your fault," Elijah scoffed.

I opened my mouth to apologise again, but kept my mouth glued shut. He was right. It was his pain. His life.

"They both died of an overdose when I was six. I was hungry and went to ask them when it would be time to eat..." Elijah's eyes glazed over as he relived the memory.

It must have been so awful for him to find his own parents dead, but especially at that age. My heart hurt for Elijah and I stroked his thigh gently to show my sympathy, even though I knew it couldn't bring his parents back and couldn't reverse what must have been a horrific childhood.

"I remember feeling annoyed that they were asleep." Elijah chuckled darkly. "I tried to shake them awake as hard as I could, but they just lay there with needles scattered around them." Elijah gritted his teeth together.

"That's horrible," I said, my voice barely louder than a whisper.

"I remember hearing at school that you could call the police if you were in trouble and they were supposed to help. There was no food in the house and my parents weren't waking up, so it only made sense to me to call the police."

Elijah turned to me, a sad smile at the corner of his mouth. "You wouldn't believe my surprise when they showed up with no food and started asking all these questions that I didn't want to answer."

"What happened next?"

"Foster care," Elijah said bluntly. "I didn't know that shit could get worse, but it did."

I'd heard enough horror stories about the foster system to get an idea about how things must have been like for Elijah, and the thought made me wince. Another thought crossed my mind. I couldn't remember if Elijah had said he was an only child or not.

"Do you have any siblings, or is it just you?" I asked.

Elijah dropped his eyes to his lap, and I stared at the shadows that his thick, dark lashes cast on his angular face. The muscle in his jaw ticked furiously and no matter how hard I stared at him, he refused to look at me.

"I have a... sister," Elijah choked out after a moment. It seemed like he'd been deciding whether to trust me with the information, and I was glad that he had.

"How old is she?"

"She's nineteen."

"Are you guys close?"

The pained look that took over Elijah's face made me regret asking the question. But I'd waded too deep to pull back.

Elijah swallowed hard. "Maybe when we were younger, but not anymore."

"What happened?"

"You just don't know when to stop asking questions, do you?" Elijah snapped. His tone was no longer remorseful, and had resorted back to anger again.

"I'm sorry, I just-"

"You just what?"

I looked up at him with pleading eyes in the hopes that they'd soften his hardened ones.

"I just want to know you. The real you," I breathed.

Elijah's features were twisted with fury, but as the words came out of my mouth, they seemed to placate him, even if it was only just a little bit. Elijah shook his head slowly and grimaced.

"I let her down. I was meant to be there for her, but I wasn't. And now she hates me and I can't even blame her," he said quietly.

"What do you mean? What did you do?" I asked warily.

Elijah looked up at me in that moment, and the pieces started to click into place.

"Does that guy you're holding captive have something to do with your sister?" I gasped. "Is that her boyfriend?"

"Don't you fucking dare say something like that," Elijah roared, his eyes lighting up with fire. I recoiled into my pillow as I felt shame wash over me. Elijah sighed loudly.

"David is not her boyfriend. Stella would never willingly go after a piece of shit like that," Elijah spat. He ran his hands through his hair before he clicked his knuckles one by one.

The man's name was David.

I didn't want to say the wrong thing, or anything that would set Elijah off again, so I waited for him to speak even though I was bursting with questions.

"That foul, decrepit waste of space rotting in that storage unit," Elijah said, his voice dripping with venom. "That sack of human shit raped my sister and anything I do to him won't ever get him back for what he did."

My hands flew to my mouth, and it all made sense. Why Elijah had been so adamant about keeping everything secret, why he'd been so angry every time I sympathised with David or asked when he'd set him free. I'd thought that Elijah was the monster, but really, he'd been trying to get revenge on his sister's rapist. *The real monster*.

"I'm- I'm so-"

"Don't apologise," Elijah snapped. "It's my fault and I know it."

"How's it your fault?" I shot back.

I eyed Elijah up warily. Unless he'd made a deal with David or something... My stomach turned at the mere thought of something so disgusting. Surely Elijah couldn't be capable of something like that. Elijah pinched the bridge of his nose to steel himself before he looked at me.

"I was meant to meet Stella when she was coming up to visit me. We hadn't seen each other much since our shitty foster parents kicked me out the day I turned 18. They didn't let me visit, so Stella and I always had to meet somewhere else. When she left, she started working at this hostel and the gave her a room there. We were meant to have drinks to catch up, but I'd been drinking with my friends and I decided to blow her off. I told her to go home or to stay at a hotel, then we could meet the next day. Stella seemed annoyed, but that wasn't anything out of the ordinary and I was too drunk to care. The next morning, I got a text from her telling me that she didn't want to see me. I got annoyed because I thought she was just being difficult..." Elijah swallowed hard.

"I kept calling her, kept trying to get her to explain, to stop being avoiding me. She picked up after what must have been thirty calls and told me that she'd stayed at the bar that we'd agreed to meet at and then when she was walking back drunk to her hotel, a guy dragged her into an alleyway and raped her."

Even though I knew how the story ended, that knowledge didn't stop my heart from constricting in my chest.

"If I'd been with her that night, it wouldn't have happened. I could have protected her. I blamed myself for being so selfish, and so did Stella. And she has every right to."

"But it's not your fault!" I exclaimed. "It's that sick guy's fault for raping Stella in the first place. You couldn't have known that."

Elijah shook his head, clearly in disagreement with what I'd said.

"I should have been there for her," he said firmly.

"How did you find out that it was David who raped your sister?" I asked, deciding to move the conversation away from Elijah's self blame.

"Stella didn't want to tell me much, but all she told me was that he stank of gasoline and had these creepy blue eyes and ratty facial hair. So I hung around the bar and the alleyways near it for a few weeks." Elijah shrugged. "It didn't take long to find the son of a bitch. David works at the garage nearby and he has a penchant for following and harassing young women. Once I was sure that it was him, I knew that I couldn't just let him walk free. Not after what he'd done to my sister and probably to a bunch of other girls." Elijah's hands curled into tight fists.

"And that's why you've been sneaking off every night," I said, nodding.

"It was all going to plan until you showed up." Elijah's bitter tone made me shrink away.

I'd seen him knock David out and assumed that Elijah had been the one in the wrong. No wonder he'd acted so hateful towards me. It was one thing to get put into an apartment with a girl when he'd specifically asked for a male roommate, but it was a completely different ball game when that same roommate got involved in your business and didn't even understand the full picture. *Shit*.

"I didn't know-" I started to say, but Elijah held up a weary hand.

"There's no point apologising. What's done is done."

"When was the last time you spoke to Stella?" I asked.

"The day she told me she'd been raped," Elijah said through gritted teeth.

I could only imagine what Stella was going through and even though I didn't know her, my heart was full of sympathy. I also felt sorry for Elijah, for the burden and blame he'd been carrying all this time, as well as the guilt that clearly weighed him down each day.

"You've got to promise not to tell anyone about this, okay?"

"I guess if I don't, you'll make me," I said halfheartedly as I struggled to process everything he'd just told me.

The questions I'd had for so long were finally answered and they cast him in a completely different light. I didn't know how to feel now that I knew the whole truth. Especially when I was still surprised by the fact that Elijah had finally decided to open up. Elijah's eyes flashed, but his face remained as hard as granite.

"Promise me," he said, this time more forcefully.

"I promise," I breathe, unable to tear my eyes away from his fierce gaze.

I thought my answer would be enough to ease the tension in his body, but clearly it hadn't been by the way that he continued staring at me like there was something pressing on his mind.

"What's wrong?" I asked when Elijah wouldn't look away from me.

"What's wrong is that your pussy isn't wrapped around my cock," he said, his face unwavering.

"Oh," the small sound had barely escaped my mouth before Elijah pounced on me.

Elijah's rough hands were running up and down my body in an instant, grabbing possessively as he tore my clothes off of me. I moaned as his tongue licked against mine, the warm sweetness of him making my back arch. His mouth had taunted me for weeks on end, and finally, we shared our first scorching kiss. Holy fuck, it was better than I could have ever imagined.

"Fuck," he breathed when my bra fell to the floor, revealing my swelling breasts and hardened nipples. I suddenly felt subconscious and my hand flew to cover my stomach.

"Are you sure that you don't walk to talk some more about-" I started, but Elijah simply shook his head. His time to be vulnerable was over. His focus had switched to pleasuring me.

He pulled my hand away from my stomach and started stroking it gently with his hand, before he replaced it with gentle kisses.

"You're too beautiful to cover yourself up, so don't you dare," he growled.

Feeling a surge of confidence and warmth as a result of Elijah's words, I let him push me further up the bed. His mouth flew to my nipples, his tongue licking enthusiastically with the occasional bite that made me squeal, all while he palmed my breasts roughly.

"That's a good girl. I love hearing you squeal for me," Elijah moaned as he tore my panties off.

His eyes fell to my slit, which I could feel throbbing and growing wetter by the second. Unable to control himself, Elijah tore his own clothes off, discarding them on the floor as his eyes stayed on mine the entire time. The sight of his tanned skin covered in tattoos turned me on impossibly more. I bucked my hips impatiently, watching Elijah pump his thick erection with his hand.

"You're going to take all of this," he growled, a sadistic smile on his face.

"Are you going to hurt me?" I asked, my finger slipping between my folds to caress the ball of heat growing there.

"I'm not going to hurt you."

Elijah got onto the bed and lowered his body on top of me. He pinned my arms above my head with one of his hands and continued fisting himself, his eyes on me the entire time.

"You're lying," I breathed.

Elijah continued pleasuring himself as he watched me bucking my hips in frustration. The tension and heat between us continued to grow until it became unbearable.

Elijah smirked. "I might hurt you, but I'll make sure you like it."

I grew even more desperate to feel him inside of me, and he knew that. I moved my hips so that my slit was in line with his erection. I *needed* it. I needed the relief that I'd been denied for long enough already. Elijah's hand flew to my hip, and he pushed me away slightly so that there was an inch between our parts.

"Beg for it," he ordered, his eyes flaring with fire.

"Please," I said.

"Beg like you mean it or you're not getting fucked."

"Please, Elijah. I need you to fuck me!" I cried.

I felt so submissive, so slutty, lying naked beneath him, our warm bodies pressed up against each other, my arms pinned above my head. I didn't care what it took, I just needed Elijah's cock, *badly*.

"Be careful what you wish for," Elijah breathed. Elijah pushed himself inside of me without another moment's hesitation, making me gasp sharply at the size of him.

"Let me in, let me spread you," Elijah said as he pushed against my walls.

"I'm trying," I breathed.

"It's cute that you think you have a choice."

The pain and the pressure felt so good as Elijah forced his way inside. My walls stretched to accommodate him and once he'd firmly buried himself to the hilt, he begin rhythmically thrusting inside of me.

"Oh fuck," I moaned as Elijah pounded the life out of me. His lips met my neck, and he left rough kisses there that made me unravel even more.

"I belong here," he growled as he pushed himself inside me once again.

Elijah felt so fucking good inside of me and I started seeing stars as his dick forced me closer to an orgasm. All the fighting, all the games and cruel words melted away as our bodies rocked against each other. Our breathing grew heavy, our bodies warm and sticky with sweat as we got lost in the throes of our pleasure. Elijah removed his dick from inside me, making me moan in annoyance.

"Why did you stop?"

Elijah grabbed my legs one at a time and looped them over his shoulders before he thrust himself deep inside of me again.

"I needed to go deeper inside of you, Grace. I need you to feel my cock filling you up, deep and hard," he breathed.

I felt his balls slapping against my skin as he continued fucking me. Elijah's thrusts were so deep and hard that my brain was spinning. My body felt weak as I felt my orgasm approach.

Elijah wrapped his hand around my neck and started choking me, not stopping for even a second to give either of us a break.

"You're mine to fuck, mine to choke, mine to make cum," he growled. "You're mine, Grace."

Elijah's words were the push I needed to go over the edge. I unravelled in his arms, my hips bucking violently as my orgasm took over my body. When my pussy clamped down on him, I felt Elijah's legs stiffen and cock start pulsing as his orgasm took control of him.

We moaned in synchrony as he filled me up with his warm load, still shaking from the aftermath of the earth shattering orgasm we'd shared.

We separated and lay on the bed beside each other. I felt like I was in a dream, but no matter how many times I blinked, Elijah still lay beside me, tattoos, tanned muscle and all.

Fucking hell, I'd never had sex like that before.

Elijah's pupils were so dilated that his eyes looked even darker than usual. Now that we'd had sex, what did that mean for us? What did *he* think it meant?

"You okay?" I asked as I tried to catch my breath.

Elijah's eyes followed the movement of his hand up and down my thighs before he returned his gaze back to me.

"I hope you excuse my manners, but I need to fuck you again, Grace."

My breath hitched in my throat, my legs still quivering from the orgasm I had yet to recover from.

"Give me a minute to cool down, then we can go again," I said.

"I'm not asking, I'm telling you," Elijah growled, grabbing my arm roughly as I tried to roll away.

And before I knew it, he was on top of me again and my arms were pinned above my head as Elijah's hard erection teased at my entrance, his cum still leaking out of me.

"I need to fill you up with more cum."

Oh fuck. Good thing I'm on birth control.

24

GRACE

"Wait, start all over again, from the top. You and Elijah did *what*?"

I held my phone away from my ear while I waited for Violet to stop screaming.

"We had sex," I hissed sheepishly.

As soon as I'd picked up the phone, Violet had been on my case and had picked up that there was something "different" simply because of my voice.

"Tell me we're in a parallel universe right now because this is not happening." Violet's disbelief appeared to be going nowhere.

"I'm afraid to disappoint you, but we're *not* in a parallel universe and this is *absolutely* happening," I squealed, allowing myself to get excited for a moment.

"Well, I'll be damned," Violet breathed. "That explains why he swooped in and beat up that guy at the party. He probably had his eyes on you then."

"Maybe." I felt myself blushing, and I was glad that Violet couldn't see my face. "Would it be weird to ask him on a date?" I said after a moment.

There was a niggling thought in the back of my mind

that kept trying to convince me that Elijah was only interested in sex, and that he was *using* me for sex. Which wasn't a nice thought at all.

Plus, the way he'd looked at me while we'd had sex... he'd never looked at me like that before. I knew it was safer to guard my heart, but I didn't want to believe that Elijah was truly a monster anymore, and I wanted to give him an opportunity to prove that. Especially after everything he'd shared with me.

Violet burst out laughing.

"What?" I asked, a little more defensively than I intended.

"It's not weird at all. I just can't imagine Elijah being a date type of person," said Violet. She was probably right. Until recently, I hadn't even thought of Elijah as a people person. I sighed heavily.

"But there's no harm in asking," Violet said quickly, obviously picking up on my suddenly deflated tone. "I'm not trying to discourage you at all, just... be careful."

"I can look after myself, don't you worry," I said, chuckling. "And it's not like it's that big a deal. We just had sex. I'm not trying to trap him in a relationship," I added.

So what am I trying to do?

"Hey, whatever works for you. Look, I'm outside the office and I need to go to work, but I'll text you later, okay?"

"Sure thing."

Violet and I said our goodbyes before I hung up the phone. I caught my reflection in the mirror and realised that I looked way too cute to not go out on a date of some kind.

What kind of date would be the least offensive to Elijah? One where he couldn't get into a fight with anyone, and preferably one where there weren't too many people. He probably wouldn't like that.

It felt weird that I was getting so giddy thinking about

someone who'd previously frightened and repulsed me so much. As cheesy as it sounded in my head, something *had* changed between us.

Maybe I was mistaken, but it felt like the wall Elijah had tried so hard to keep up had slowly started crumbling down. Especially since he'd come clean to me about everything that had happened with his sister. It was like I'd seen a whole new version of him. It wasn't as simple as Elijah being a monster. If anything, he was a protector, just trying to seek justice. Even if the means he went to were fucked up.

I slipped into a crop top and nice flowy skirt, staring at myself in the mirror as I contemplated the outfit. My stomach poked out more than I wanted to and I almost changed into a top that covered up more when I remembered the sensation of Elijah caressing it with his hands as he stared into my eyes and called me beautiful. My cheeks were flushed again as I walked across the hallway and knocked on Elijah's door.

~

"Why would anyone choose to eat outside, on the floor no less, when inside is perfectly fine?" Elijah grumbled.

I lay out the picnic blanket for us to sit on before I placed the basket on top of it so that it stayed in place.

"Because the weather is nice, and it's good to get some air," I said cheerfully in an attempt to brighten the mood.

Elijah scoffed, but followed my lead as I sat down on the blanket. As he continued to complain about the outdoors, I started getting things out of the basket. Elijah helped me lay out the fruit, the biscuits, and the bottles of iced coffee that I knew we both loved.

"I made these, since I know they're your favourite of mine."

I pulled out the container of brownies that I'd made that morning. Elijah had been on campus while I'd hurried about, making sure that they'd be ready in time for our date, and I was relieved when I saw that they were still warm and gooey. Elijah narrowed his eyes at me and picked up a brownie between hesitant fingers.

"How do I know you haven't spiked them with something?"

I raised an eyebrow at him. "I think we can say we're even now as far as spiking goes," I teased.

Elijah took the tiniest bite ever, and I couldn't stop myself from laughing at how ridiculous he looked.

"Always got to watch your enemies," he said in a mock serious voice before he took a much bigger bite of the chocolate treat. "Mmm, okay, I don't know what you've put in this, but it tastes fucking magical."

I took an internal sigh of relief. I would have been horrified if that specific batch had come out poorly, but I was glad that I still had my exquisite baking skills.

"I'd hardly say we're enemies anymore," I said, picking up on the comment he'd made.

"No?" Elijah quirked a teasing eyebrow.

"I'd say we made a truce last night, wouldn't you?"

Elijah's hand slid onto my bare knee and slowly rubbed up and down, his eyes on mine the entire time.

"We could make another truce, right here, right now," Elijah growled, his eyes flashing with mischief.

I looked around at the other people sitting in the park. Even though Elijah's eyes and wandering hands promised a fucking good time, I wasn't going to end up viral online for public indecency. The scandal *would* be something that my parents could come together over, though...

"Behave yourself," I said. I placed my hand on Elijah's

and tried to push it away, but of course, he was stronger and held firm.

"Remember that *you're* the one who takes orders from *me*, Grace. So if anyone needs to behave..." Elijah ran his tongue over his bottom lip. "It's you. But I'd be more than happy to *make* you behave."

Elijah's voice was like silk in my ears and for a moment I regretted wearing a dress instead of trousers because I knew that the heat and wetness forming between my thighs would eventually betray me at some point.

Once Elijah had gotten his message across and decided to stop taunting me for a moment so that we could both eat, we turned the conversation back to our lives at Oakwood.

"It feels like you're asking me all the questions and I don't know as much about you," I said.

Elijah shrugged and took a sip of his iced coffee. "I don't like talking about myself as much as you do."

"Hey!" I didn't think I was *that* bad. But what was I supposed to do? Just shrug and sit in silence?

Elijah shook his head as he focussed his eyes on the two kids running around trying to catch each other. From the tight brunette curls and wide smiles that they shared, it was clear that they were siblings, possibly even twins.

"I didn't mean it in a bad way. I like hearing you speak," Elijah said, turning back to me.

"I like hearing *you* speak. I want you to tell me more about yourself," I said gently.

I knew that when it came to Elijah; I had to tread carefully. Most people jumped at the opportunity to talk solely about themselves, but the way that Elijah skirted around it was like an extreme sport. But I wanted him to trust me, and I was sure that a part of him wanted to be able to trust me, too. Elijah's eyebrows knitted together as he waged a war with himself inside his head.

"What do you want to know now?" he sighed. "You can ask three questions."

"Three questions? That's barely any!" I shot back.

"With that attitude, young lady, I might not even answer one."

I rolled my eyes but wracked my brain for the right questions to ask at that moment.

"What was foster care like?" I asked.

Elijah's eyes glazed over for a second before he shook himself out of what seemed to be a trance.

"It was horrible. I hated it. How was your childhood?" he said flatly.

I was annoyed at his clipped tone, and I was sure that he could tell from the expression on my face.

"If I ask you a follow up question-" I began.

"Yes, it counts as one of your three," Elijah said, cutting me off and confirming my thoughts.

"You're infuriating."

"But you love it because I give you mind blowing orgasms," he smirked.

Mind-blowing was an understatement.

Elijah nudged me gently and nodded towards me. "Tell me about your childhood."

I reached to grab another brownie from the box and then stopped myself, realising that I'd probably eaten too many.

"My childhood was probably as good as they come," I said sheepishly. I didn't want to sound like I was bragging or being insensitive, especially since I knew that Elijah hadn't had the easiest start in life.

My eyes darted towards the brownies and back to Elijah.

"I don't know what else to say. I grew up an only child. My parents were pretty nice and attentive. School wasn't the worst thing and now... I'm here." I shrugged.

"Sounds nice."

Elijah reached over, grabbed one of the brownies from the tin and pushed it towards me.

"Eat," he commanded.

"No, it's okay, I've had too many," I laughed nervously. My hand subconsciously flew to my stomach. Elijah shook his head, grabbed my hand, and placed the brownie inside it.

"There's no such thing. If you want it, just fucking eat it. I'm not going to judge you, Grace."

I flitted my gaze between the brownie and Elijah again.

"They're fucking delicious and you spent time making them and on top of that you look gorgeous both in and out of your clothes, so for the love of God..." Elijah's eyes trailed up my body before they rested on my face. "Just let yourself enjoy the brownie, Grace."

I don't know if it was Elijah's voice, and the tender way it danced over the words or the way that he looked at me as if I was the oxygen that he needed to breathe. Whatever it was, I felt overwhelmed by the few words that he had said and realised that he was right. *I should just let myself enjoy the brownie.*

"Yeah, what the hell? They taste fantastic, if I say so myself," I chuckled before I took a bite.

Elijah stroked my back and reached to grab one for himself. "Where were we with the questions again?"

"I still have two left," I said, covering my mouth as I finished chewing. "What do you want to do after you graduate?"

Elijah cocked his head to the side as he contemplated his answer.

"To be honest, I haven't really thought that far ahead. Especially recently." His eyes darkened, and he swallowed hard. "It depends on whether I'm in a jail cell or if I'm on the run in another country." Elijah chuckled bitterly, and there was nothing joyful about it.

"Of course it makes sense that your plans have been... put on pause," I said carefully. "That must be frustrating."

Elijah shrugged. "It needs to be done," he said, and I knew he believed every single word.

Who was I to tell him that there was another way to get revenge on his sister's rapist?

"I'm not going to tell if you're still worried about that," I said quietly.

"I'm not worried about that," Elijah said quickly. He looked at me sideways. "Next question."

"Don't you want to know what I want to do after I graduate?"

"I know what you're going to do." I raised my eyebrows at him.

"Oh, really?"

"You're going to be an amazing doctor, the best in the country and all your patients and their families are going to love you because you're so kind and caring and good at your job," Elijah said in one breath. He turned to me, his eyes daring me to challenge him. "That's what you're going to do."

"Maybe," I said, blushing. When he said it like that, it sounded so real. "That's if I even graduate."

"Don't give me that shit, Grace. You're the most intelligent person I've ever met, and you're way too hard on yourself."

"Thank you." I cast my gaze down to my hands. I couldn't believe that he'd said those words to me and meant it.

"It's true and you know it." Elijah tucked a strand of my hair behind my ear and looked into my eyes. "You have one more question."

I looked up at him through my lashes and thought carefully before I asked my final question.

"Have you ever been in a relationship before?" Even if the answer had the potential to hurt me, I wanted to know.

Elijah's features and voice didn't flinch. "No."

"No?" I asked. I was taken aback but also curious to know more. "Why?"

I watched the muscle in Elijah's jaw tick as he thought over my question.

"You've run out of questions," he said flatly.

"I think this is a pretty important one that I deserve to know," I shot back hotly.

Elijah sighed heavily. "You're relentless."

"And you love it. Now tell me why you haven't been in a relationship before."

"No. Now drop it," Elijah said forcefully.

His tone took me by surprise and the atmosphere between us instantly felt a lot heavier than it had a few moments before.

"Does this mean you were a virgin before yesterday?"

"Of course I wasn't a virgin," Elijah snapped. "Do you think a virgin could make you cum the way I do?" he growled. "Now drop it."

I knew I wouldn't get anywhere with him. The line had clearly been drawn.

"Do you want to go back home now?" I had goosebumps all over my skin and it wasn't because of the light breeze that had started up. "I mean back to the *apartment*," I added quickly, once I'd realised my mistake.

Of course, it wasn't home to either of us and that made it sound like we were a couple or something.

Isn't that what you really want, though?

Clearly, he had a thing against relationships and I'd be

an idiot if I didn't listen to all the explicit and implicit signs that Elijah had given me.

"No," said Elijah.

"No?" I couldn't hide the surprise and confusion in my voice.

Elijah wrapped his arms around my waist and pulled me close to his body. I melted into his warm embrace as he gently pressed his lips to my head. The cold moment before was not forgotten, but pushed aside for just a moment.

"Let's stay here a little longer," he breathed.

"Okay," I whispered, because I wasn't ready to leave either.

25

ELIJAH

I couldn't tell Grace why I'd never been in a relationship before. Hell, I couldn't even tell her why I'd never been on a date. I knew that my silence pained her, but that was one road I wasn't willing to go down.

Especially because I didn't know how she'd react if I ever revealed my true feelings to her and I wasn't going to risk her throwing my words back in my face.

I'd been wary when Grace had suggested a date. I'd never been one on before and had never had a desire to. But for some reason, I'd been willing to do it for her. Even though things at the start of our date had been awkward and rocky, as the afternoon had progressed, we slipped into things better and before I knew it we'd found ourselves bickering back and forth like normal, only this time it was with the added knowledge that we'd slept together.

There'd been a part of me that had thought that sleeping with Grace would get rid of my perverse fascination with her, but it had had the completely opposite effect. Instead of feeling repulsed and regretful at the sight of her like I usually did with other women that I'd slept with, I didn't want to let Grace out of my sight.

Every time she laughed, my chest felt a little lighter, and I wanted to hear her laugh again. The more I found out about her and the more time I spent with her, the more I wanted. From the moment we'd had sex and shared all those things with each other, my mind hadn't stopped racing and I felt like I was going insane. The only thing that came close to silencing the rabid thoughts was when Grace looked at me.

I knew things had started to get bad when she popped into my head as I dealt with David. For the first time since I'd kidnapped him, I'd started wondering what Grace would think about me if she actually saw what I did to him every night.

When I clipped David's nails right down to the bud, her bright, beaming face flashed into my subconscious. When I starved David for two days because he said some horrific shit about Stella when he thought I couldn't hear him, Grace's twinkling laugh entered my ears.

It was a new type of hell that made it hard to focus on what was in front of me. Grace was not only a distraction, she was my new addiction. And I realised I was so hooked on her that I'd started neglecting other aspects of my life.

∽

As I made my way home from the storage unit, my arms and legs felt heavy. It didn't make sense that I had been laughing with Grace only hours before while we'd been watching TV and then torturing David not long after. I knew it made Grace upset that I still held him captive, but at least she finally knew the whole truth. She said that she understood, but how could she really?

Even if everything I'd done was for Stella, how far was too far? I'd had David trapped for weeks, and I still hadn't made my mind up about whether I was going to kill him or set him free.

And I was supposed to believe that Grace still wanted to be around me?

I stopped in my tracks and looked down at my hands, noticing the remnants of dried blood there. The bright lights of a car driving past me shocked me out of my thoughts and I kept walking down the road, bracing myself against the cool night air.

Was I really about to slide back into bed with her and act like I was some normal guy?

I knew she expected me to, but I couldn't do that. *Fuck*, even though she had said that she understood why I did what I did, I couldn't believe her. The thought had niggled at my mind all week, and it only seemed to grow stronger by the day.

When I marched into our apartment at 3am, my mind was full of loud intrusive thoughts that mocked me for thinking that Grace could ever see past what I'd done.

Who was I kidding?

I wasn't a good guy, and I knew that. I'd prided myself in that from the beginning. Grace knew that I wasn't a good guy and yet she seemed to want to pretend that I was.

I knew what the feeling was, the heavy one that appeared in my chest every time I shut the door, or left at night or when Grace went to campus. It was the feeling of missing her, a sensation that only came when you cared about someone.

Caring about someone so deeply in that way, let alone someone I lived with, had not been something I'd ever planned to do, and for good reason. Because I knew it could never end well. I knew I couldn't put myself in a position again where Grace needed to rely on me and I let her down.

I'd been there before, and I was paying every single day for my mistake.

"Elijah, is that you?"

I closed the door softly behind me and turned around to see Grace standing in the hallway wearing one of my shirts, which completely dwarfed her.

"I thought you'd be asleep."

Grace shrugged. "I wanted to make sure you got back, okay," she breathed. The words made my chest feel tight, and I cleared my throat as I walked towards her.

"You can go back to bed. I'm fine."

She looked up at me with those big, beautiful eyes again, and it felt like she was looking into my soul. I tore my gaze away and focussed on opening my door.

"You want to sleep together tonight or...?" The rest of Grace's question hung in the air and from the slight wobble in her voice, I could tell that she could sense something was off.

"Let's sleep in our own rooms," I said gruffly. My chest twinged as I saw Grace tried to hide her disappointment. "I've got an early lecture tomorrow, so... goodnight."

I gave her one last look before I ducked into my room like a coward. Even though I wanted to feel her warm body pressed up against mine and inhale her sweet scent, I knew that would just be selfish and that I'd only be taking one step closer to madness and potential failure.

I peeled off my clothes and tossed them on the laundry pile. As I grabbed my things and went to the shower, I heard Grace sniff in her room. I couldn't tell if the sounds were because of allergies or because she was upset with me.

This is exactly why I don't do this shit.

I waited outside her door until the sounds subsided, contemplating on whether I should go in. A good guy would burst in and explain his fears, explain why he couldn't be with her and that he didn't want to hurt her. But I wasn't a good guy.

Turning away, I jumped into the shower and turned the water up to the highest heat. Even though I scrubbed myself repeatedly with soap, I still felt just as dirty as I had when I'd stepped in.

∼

"Why are you being off with me?"

I sat my coffee down on the table and turned around to see Grace standing at the kitchen door, her arms crossed over her chest.

"What do you mean?"

"You know exactly what I mean." Grace narrowed her eyes at me even though I could tell that she was trying to hide how disappointed she was.

Did she know that I'd been able to hear her crying through her door?

"Come here," I said, gesturing to my lap. Grace hesitated, and I felt a pang in my stomach.

Why had I even bothered offering? Of course, she wouldn't want to touch me after how I'd treated her the night before. In her mind, I probably didn't deserve to touch her if I wasn't willing to open up and tell her how I felt.

To my surprise, Grace walked across the kitchen and sat in my lap. I stifled a growl when her sweet smell hit my nostrils and tried not to focus on the feeling of her ass against my cock. I carefully wrapped my arms around her waist, a new sensation that I was slowly getting used to, and balanced my chin on her shoulder.

"Did I do something to upset you?" she asked quietly. I closed my eyes and sighed heavily. Of course she hadn't.

How was I supposed to tell her that she'd done everything *right*? That she'd been kind to me and patient despite the amount of times that I'd pushed her away. That she actually made me believe that she liked me.

I couldn't just come out and tell her how much that scared me. Not when I'd had knives held against my throat and had been in numerous life or death situations in my life. A *girl* couldn't be the thing that brought me more fear than all those other horrific incidents.

"You haven't done anything wrong," I breathed.

Except make me believe that you might actually like me.

Grace turned around and looked at me with her big, beautiful eyes.

"Are you sure?" she whispered.

Even though I nodded, because I couldn't trust myself to speak, I knew that if I let her get any closer to me, it would hurt even more when she realised what an awful person I was and inevitably decided to leave.

Grace ran a hand through my hair, making me grit my teeth tightly together. She knew I had a soft spot there, and I resented her for having that small amount of power over me.

"You have really nice hair," she said absentmindedly as she played with one of the strands. No one had ever told me that before.

"Thanks," I muttered.

I wanted to throw her off me to get her to stop because I knew it was the right thing, the safe thing.

"If I ask you a question, do you promise not to get mad at me?"

I stared at Grace. "What's the question?"

"Are you stressed out because of David?" Grace asked quietly.

I let the question hang between us and felt both our

bodies stiffen at the mention of that sick motherfucker's name.

"I know I'm not supposed to ask so-"

"You're right, I told you not to ask about it," I growled. "Get up."

Startled by the tone of my voice, Grace jumped out of my lap and I stood up to my full height, dwarfing her. I poured the rest of my drink in the sink before I slammed the cup down on the side.

"I just want to know if you're going to let him go or-"

"Or what?" I snapped, cutting Grace off.

I whirled around to look at her. I couldn't quite read her face, which caught me off guard because she usually wore her emotions on her sleeve.

"Or if you're going to kill him," Grace breathed.

My chest felt tight as dark clouds obstructed my vision. Of course, she wanted to know *just* how bad I was, how monstrous I could be. Then she'd decide if whatever was going on between us was worth it or not.

"Why do you even care?" I snapped.

"I-I-I-" Grace stuttered.

"If I kill him, does that suddenly mean your pussy is off limits?"

"What's gotten into you? Why would you say something like that?" Grace shot back.

I was ready to shoot back with something harsher, something that would hurt her feelings even more when I saw just how upset and angry she looked.

"I don't like it when you ask me about him," I sighed.

"Why? I just want to understand what's going on," Grace said quietly.

I shook my head. She didn't understand.

"I know you already think I'm a bad person for holding him in there-"

"I don't think you're a bad person!" Grace exclaimed. And from the look on her face, I could tell that she really believed it.

Shame held me in a chokehold, and I knew I had to get away from her as soon as possible, before I made another mistake.

"I need to go," I said.

"Wait, you can't just leave it at that!"

"I'm going to be late for class."

I couldn't tell if Grace believed me or not, but she didn't fight me as I walked out of the kitchen and left her standing alone.

The more she tried to convince me that I was a good person, the more proof I found that I was not. But if I stayed around Grace any longer and let her convince me otherwise, I wouldn't be able to exact my revenge on David without hearing her sweet voice in my ears.

No. I had to avenge Stella. And I had to do it properly. I had to focus. Focus on everything but my feelings. And to do that properly, I couldn't let Grace distract me or let me fall for her anymore than I already had.

26

GRACE

For three days and three nights, Elijah had avoided me and barely said a word. Every time I walked into the apartment, he found a reason to leave. Every time I tried to reach out and touch him, he flinched and found a reason to move away. He barely made eye contact with me when I was nearby.

It was like our date had never happened, like we hadn't shared those precious moments in bed together, like we hadn't started tearing down our walls, albeit slowly, for each other

My worst fears were being realised.

If your parents had split up after decades together, what makes you think that you'll have even the slightest chance with Elijah?

Maybe my conscience was onto something. Maybe Elijah *had* just wanted me for sex, which was ironic because it had been so long since he'd touched me. I felt like I'd been taken back to the start of the semester again, when Elijah had made every attempt to stand as far away from me as possible and made me feel like I had leprosy.

I struggled to sleep again, and I'd ran out of Xanax and

wasn't feeling like risking getting anymore. Since Elijah had called me out for it, I'd worried about growing dependent on the little pills. Once it had gotten to the third night with little to no sleep, I knew I couldn't keep living that way.

I'd broken through to Elijah and felt like we'd actually started moving forward. There was no way that I'd imagined his laughter when we'd been on our date or how kind he'd been to me in the week that had followed. I hadn't made up that soft look in his eye or the way that he'd gently caressed my thigh underneath the table. Yet somehow, it all felt like it had been a dream.

I heard his bedroom door shut and knew that if I didn't make a move and address the enormous elephant in the room, then I'd regret it and probably self combust. I rapped my knuckles sharply on Elijah's door and let myself in before he could answer.

He'd been about to sit on his bed, but turned around to look at me as I walked in. His eyebrows knitted furiously together on his forehead and the hardened look that I thought I'd never have to see again had returned once more.

"What's up with you, Elijah?" I said gently, even though what I really wanted to do was grab him by the shoulders and shake him until he turned back into the Elijah of the previous week. The one who'd started opening up, the one who hadn't been afraid to show that he cared about me. At least in private.

"Nothing," he said.

"Bullshit." I watched Elijah's muscle tick in his jaw and wished that I could just read his mind.

"What do you want from me, Grace?" The tinge of annoyance in his voice almost made my knees buckle.

Why was he making me feel like I was the one being weird and asking for too much?

"I want you to tell me why you're suddenly acting all

weird and withdrawn when everything was alright last week!" I threw my arms up in exasperation. I swallowed my tears and tried to keep my balance steady.

I expected Elijah to give me a reaction, but he simply stared back at me blankly. Unfeeling, uncaring. The familiar cold that I'd been subjected to from the day we'd first met had fully returned.

"Did I do something wrong?"

Elijah turned his back to me and started fiddling with something on his desk.

"You could at least tell me why you won't look at me, let alone touch me!" My voice was hoarse, but I couldn't hold back my emotions any longer.

Elijah's back tensed up, and he turned around to look at me, his nostrils flared and lips pulled back over his teeth.

"You want to be touched?" he growled.

It was like he'd been possessed by a demon or something, because the Elijah that stared back at me was not the Elijah that had kissed my collarbones and rubbed my back while I'd fallen asleep. He couldn't be the same guy that had said so many kind and affirming things to me.

"Not right now-" I'd barely gotten the words out when Elijah charged towards me, grabbed me by the waist and threw me onto the bed.

"If you want to be touched, that's all you have to say, Grace," he snapped.

I tried to get up, tried to get away from him, but Elijah pushed me back down and held me firmly on the bed as he tore my trousers off of me.

"Stop it! You're hurting me!" I cried, but Elijah wouldn't listen.

"Clearly, I haven't been giving you enough attention, so here it is."

Elijah's hands were on my breasts, kneading them

roughly, but it didn't feel good like it usually did. Not when I could see that his eyes were full of hatred instead of lust.

Tears ran down my cheeks as I fought him and he continued to violate my body with his rough hands. Elijah grabbed my thighs so roughly that I knew there were going to be lots of bruises on them later.

The sound of his zipper coming undone sent shivers down my spine, and I started sobbing uncontrollably as I awaited my fate. Elijah was going to make me pay for breaking the one rule he'd asked me to follow.

I'd asked about David when he'd told me not to, and he'd been pushing me away ever since that day in the kitchen. As I watched Elijah palm his hard cock in his hand, I realised that he was going to stick by his earlier promise- he was going to make me regret ever opening my mouth.

"If you do this, then you're just as bad as David!" I knew it was a low blow, but I couldn't stop myself as I was flooded with fear.

The guy that stared back at me through slitted eyes wasn't Elijah. At least not the one that I knew. I didn't know where the real one had gone, but I yearned to have him back.

"What the fuck did you say?" he gritted out, his expression changing slightly.

"If you have sex with me right now, I'll hate you and I'll think you're a monster just like him," I spat, and I meant every single word of it.

Elijah blinked rapidly, as if a cloud had been moved away. He released his firm grip on me and tucked his cock back into his pants.

"Get out," he said flatly. Elijah refused to make eye contact with me as he threw my clothes at my chest.

My heart raced faster than it ever had before, unsure

how to compute what had just happened. What had *almost* happened.

"Elijah-" I started. Even though I wanted to hate him, I wanted him to reassure me that he'd made a mistake and that he hadn't meant to hurt me.

"Go and talk to someone that actually cares and stop using me as a substitute for your parents," he snarled as he turned to me with bared teeth.

I felt my heart smash into a million pieces in my chest and felt like I was going to throw up. How dare he say something so cruel?

I grabbed my clothes and marched towards the door even though everything was blurry through my tears. I knew I had to leave before I embarrassed myself any further by begging him to explain why he'd started acting like an asshole again.

I walked out of his bedroom and was about to close the door when I turned over my shoulder and stared at him through the gap. Elijah's nostrils were flared, his hands in fists, his muscular chest heaving up and down as he breathed heavily.

"I wanted to believe that you were better than this, that you had a fucking heart," I spat. "But you're full of so much hatred and darkness that I can't even understand."

"Well, it's not my fault that you were stupid enough to believe your made up version of me," Elijah snarled.

"How's anyone supposed to love you if you don't let them?" The words came tumbling out of my mouth before I could stop them. "Just because you think you're unlovable, that doesn't mean I do." Elijah's face fell for a moment before it twisted into fury once again.

"Why the hell would I want someone like you to love me?" he snapped.

Splinters. My heart was in complete and utter splinters. I

wanted to turn back time. I needed to reverse everything, to give him another chance to change what he'd said. But Elijah stood firm, his lips pursed, refusing to take back the cruel words that had slipped between his lips.

Before he could break my heart again, I slammed the door in his face and ran into my room. Even though I put my earphones in and turned my music up to the highest volume, I couldn't drown out the words that had come out of Elijah's mouth.

Elijah didn't want to be in a relationship with me, and I'd been an idiot for thinking otherwise. Elijah didn't know anything but control and I'd fooled myself into thinking that his feelings towards me were anything more than that.

And if they were...

No. I couldn't think like that anymore.

Why the hell would I want someone like you to love me?

Elijah had confirmed my worst fears over and over again. He was never going to give me the love and safety that I was looking for. I was getting to the point where I wasn't even sure that it existed.

What made me even sadder was that Elijah would never open himself up and give me the chance to love him. My logical brain knew that his past had fucked him up and made him the way that he was and that I should blame that- blame his parents, the foster system- but they weren't around for me to blame, and the emotional part of my brain was only interested in directing all my anger at the one that had hurt me most. All my rage and tears were for Elijah.

27

ELIJAH

Grace had called me a monster. I'd known that it would only be a matter of time before she admitted her true feelings towards me, but that didn't stop me from repeating the words over and over again in my head.

Monster.

I couldn't shake the image out of my head of Grace lying on her back, her eyes full of tears, clearly so afraid of me. I hadn't seen that look in so long and I'd purposely made her scared.

I'll hate you and I'll think you're a monster just like him.

I'd lost it. I'd been overcome by so much anger and frustration that I had to make her back off. Grace expected too much, wanted too much from me, and it was about time that I showed her I wasn't the guy she was trying to convince herself that I was.

Monster.

I couldn't stay in the flat after she'd stormed out of my room crying her eyes out. I found myself doing something I'd never do. I went to Oakwood's student bar and drank until I couldn't feel anymore. That was the problem with

Grace. She felt too much and made me feel too much. I couldn't handle that.

I didn't care about the way that the bartender looked at me when ordered another round of shots. It was my money, and I'd spend it however the hell I wanted to.

Over and over again, I tipped the glasses back into my mouth because the stinging sensation in my throat was far more appealing than the thought of Grace. The thought of Grace's disappointment, of her kindness. The most fucked up part was the fact that even though I'd said those horrible things to her, I knew that she still thought that she didn't deserve someone like me.

Someone so... monstrous.

The alcohol in my stomach sloshed around as I shakily got to my feet. The world had started spinning a bit, and the guilt was slowly fading away. All I wanted was my bed.

When I got outside, the evening breeze tickled my skin as I made my way back to the apartment. I prayed Grace would be in her room so that I could avoid her sad eyes and disappointment.

It had been a mistake to let her in. Fucking hell, I'd made so many mistakes with her. Maybe if I'd been more careful when it came to David, none of the bullshit would have ever happened. Maybe I'd be much happier if she'd never been implicated in my mess, if she'd been nothing more than an annoying roommate.

But I knew that wasn't true. Being with Grace had made me feel warm, even if I hadn't been able to understand it. *Would I trade those memories, the feeling of her against my skin, for the awful emotions I felt?*

I'd messed up whatever we'd had between us, and I had to add that to the list of things I'd have to live with until the day that I died.

∽

As I reached the apartment block, I noticed a slim girl dressed in all black pulling at the door and peering into the window.

"Hey!" I shouted at her. When she turned around at the sound of my voice, I stopped in my tracks. It had to be a ghost.

I looked the girl up and down again, took in her dark hair and eyes that matched mine, the shining silver piercings that ran up the side of her ears that matched the one in her nose and the one in her eyebrow.

"Stella, what are you doing here?" I breathed.

I hadn't seen my sister in so long. I noticed the sleeve of her jacket riding up and spied the self harm marks there before she quickly covered them up again.

I blanched at the knowledge that Stella was hurting herself again. At least when we'd lived together, I'd been able to hide her razor blades every time I found them.

Stella swallowed hard and walked towards me. My eyes flitted over her again, still astounded by the fact that she stood in front of me, by the fact that she was even alive.

"This is where you live, right?" she asked, gesturing to the apartment.

My heart was struck with fear and dread. We Blackmoors didn't make small talk.

"Are you okay? Are you hurt? Why haven't you been answering my calls? I called your hostel, and they said you weren't there, so where have you been staying?" My mouth worked faster than my brain.

It was late. *Why was she here on her own? How had she gotten here? Where was she staying?*

Stella's face contorted into pain and then fury as she gritted her teeth together and stared me down. I got the sense that she didn't appreciate or want to answer any of my questions. My little sister could be just as stubborn, if not more so than me.

"I want you to stop calling and messaging me," she said flatly. The vice like grip around my throat tightened at her words.

"Stella, you don't fucking mean that," I snapped.

"I do," she sniffed. "I need you to leave me alone."

Hadn't the time we spent apart been enough? Maybe not enough for her to heal from what that sick psycho had done to her, but surely it had been enough time for her to forgive me?

"What can I do to change your mind?" I could feel my eyes welling up with angry and desperate tears. "I'm trying Stella, I know I can't change that night-"

"No, you can't," she snapped. "You can't change the fact that you were meant to be there for me and you weren't. But now I know that I'm the only person who's looking out for me." Stella swiped her finger along her cheek, displacing the tears that had begun to fall there. "Goodbye, Elijah."

"Wait, I have him. The man who hurt you, David Smyth. I tracked him down and have him locked up. I promise that he'll never hurt you again!"

Stella turned around sharply and faced me, her eyes blazing.

"What the fuck is wrong with you?" she hissed.

"I did it for you!" I snapped. Why couldn't she understand that everything I'd done had been for *her*?

"No, you didn't. You did it for yourself. I never wanted this. In fact, I wanted to forget that any of this ever happened!"

Stella marched towards me and shoved her fingers hard into my chest. "Don't you dare, for a second, pretend this was about me, Elijah. This was all about making yourself feel better because of your own guilt."

Her words cut straight through my chest, but I shook her off and took a step back. No matter what I said, she didn't want to hear it.

"That's not true-"

"Yes it is, and it's about time that you just admitted that to yourself," Stella snarled. "Did you really think I'd be jumping for joy hearing that my big brother is holding my rapist captive?" Stella barked out a laugh.

"I'll kill him for what he did to you," I growled.

"I sure as hell won't be visiting you in prison," Stella said sharply. "Kill him, let him go for all I care. It doesn't change what happened, what he did to me. You need to get a life and move on, Elijah."

My chest was getting so tight that I couldn't breathe. My brain couldn't process the words coming out of Stella's mouth quickly enough. It didn't *want* to process the words. If only I could make her see through her pain, see how sorry I was...

"I was doing the only thing I could think of. I'm sorry," I told her.

"Well, your sorry doesn't fucking change a thing," Stella snapped. "We're done here, Elijah."

My sister shot me one last look of disappointment mixed with disdain before she turned on her heel and left.

"Stella!"

I started running after her, but the alcohol slowed me down. There was a black car parked around the corner, clearly waiting for Stella's return. The windows were tinted and I couldn't see who was driving or if there was anyone else besides the driver inside it.

Stella slipped into the backseat, staring straight ahead as

she slammed the door shut and the car drove off, leaving me standing outside alone.

My knees threatened to buckle beneath me. The guilt that I'd tried to wash away with copious amounts of alcohol sprung up again as if it had been waiting for a chance to reappear. This time, the tidal wave of emotions was too strong and too much to bear.

I'd spent so long trying to suppress them, because I never wanted to give something else so much power over me. I'd convinced myself that I could fix everything, when in reality I'd been powerless since the start.

My darkest fears, the truth I'd known all along, had been confirmed. Grace had known it, Stella had known it, and I'd been stupid to think that I could push it aside.

I was a selfish, unlovable monster. The fact that my parents had chosen heroin over me, the fact that my sister wanted nothing to do with me and the fact that I'd driven Grace away, the one person who had consistently tried to show me kindness, was all proof of that. The only way that I could live with myself was by destroying everything around me. That was what I'd always been best at.

Even after what I'd done for Stella, she still hated me. I thought that when she finally decided to speak to me again, that she'd forgive me. But I'd been an idiot to think that I deserved that. I'd failed to protect her. I'd been a terrible brother. I deserved everything I got because of my stupid fucking mistakes.

I pulled out my phone and scrolled down until I saw Grace's number and picture. The sight of her pink hair and sunshine smile was enough to make my heart ache. Without thinking, I started typing out a message and sent it before I could stop myself.

I'm sorry for hurting you.

I waited 5 minutes, then 10 minutes for her to open the

message and respond to it. Grace always had her phone nearby, and I knew she responded quickly to messages because she didn't like people thinking that she was ignoring them. She was nice like that.

20 minutes passed, and I still hadn't gotten a response from her. For the second time that night, I'd been proven right again.

I threw my phone at the wall, picked it up from the floor and stomped on it until the screen was completely shattered.

I barely felt conscious as I walked and walked, allowing my feet to guide me wherever they wanted to go. When I found myself outside the storage unit, I realised just how sick I was in the head.

David. The one thing that had always been a good outlet for my anger and hatred. He couldn't do anything but sit there with all the cuts, bruises and various injuries I'd given him inside and out.

David's eyes were wide as I walked into the room. We both knew that I was a lot earlier than usual. Without making eye contact with him, I pulled out the sharp knife that I kept in my pocket and cut through his restraints until they fell onto the floor around us.

David stared at me, clearly anticipating my next move, anxious that there had to be a trick somewhere. He was too weak to fight back. Of course, I'd trained him to expect the worse, but I no longer had anything left to give.

I tore the duct tape off of David's mouth and my eyes finally met his. Eyes that also looked at me like I was a monster, when really we were a mirror image of each other. His body bore the proof of the torture I'd inflicted upon him, torture that still hadn't been enough to make things right with Stella. Marks that proved that I wasn't good enough for Grace and that I never would be.

"Go," I said.

"What?" David cried out weakly, confused.

"Get the fuck out of here and if I see you again, I'll kill you."

All I heard was the sound of David stumbling off as quickly as he could before I changed my mind and strapped him to the chair again.

In that moment, David was the last thing on my mind. All I could think about was how I was such a disappointment, such a failure. I'd let down Grace, and I'd let down Stella and they both hated me.

There was no point in anything.

28

GRACE

Two whole weeks passed, and I didn't say a single word to him. It was my turn to avoid Elijah this time. Which wasn't hard because every time I saw him, I was on the brink of bursting into tears. His words echoed in my head repeatedly.

Why would I want someone like you to love me?

It didn't matter how much chocolate I ate or how many tears I cried, the pain in my chest seemed to grow stronger every day. The knowledge that Elijah was only in the next room and could probably hear me as I sobbed as quietly as I could into my pillow, only made things worse, especially because he made no move to talk to me, even after the text he'd dared to send me.

I'm sorry for hurting you.

But if he was so sorry, why hadn't he said anything since? I couldn't believe that Elijah had thought that one text would fix everything, and I made a point of blocking his number in case he tried something stupid like that again. I felt like he was mocking me, playing with my head again.

Elijah said one thing and did a completely different thing with his body. I didn't deserve it. I fought every urge in my body to knock on his door and run into his arms, to beg him to explain, to reassure me, to tell me he was different. That things were different with me.

But shame and sadness kept me in a vice, and the days passed awkwardly in the apartment filled with stony, heartbreaking silence.

I got ready to go to campus, feeling completely detached from my body as I locked my bedroom door behind me on my way out. As I walked down the hallway, I noticed the TV was on. The TV was rarely ever on.

My blood froze in my veins as Elijah's dark hair and muscly back came into view. I snuck a sideways glance at him, but tore my eyes away when my heart threatened to shatter again at the sight of his cruel beauty.

Taking a deep breath, I ignored him and started walking past the sofa, hoping that he would let me pass in peace.

"Where are you going?"

Of course, Elijah didn't understand the concept of peace. For two weeks I hadn't heard his voice and in that moment, I realised just how much I'd missed it.

"Why do you care?" I said coldly, hoping that he could sense my disdain for him through every syllable. Elijah got up and stood in front of the door just before I reached it.

"Move, I need to get to class."

"Are you ready to talk?" Elijah growled.

Was *I* ready to talk? It's not like he'd tried to say anything over the last fortnight.

"I don't want to talk. I need to get to class or I'm going to be late for my test," I snapped.

"Don't lie to me, Grace. I know your class doesn't start for another 10 minutes and it only takes you two minutes to get there." Elijah's voice was more aggressive and it matched the fire in his eyes.

Of course, he knew my timetable off by heart.

I looked at him properly for the first time in what felt like forever. I saw how tired and depleted he looked despite the stony aggression that was ever-present on his face.

"Don't make this harder than it already is," I said as evenly as I could. I could feel the tears in my throat threatening to choke me. "It's bad enough that we still have to live together, so the only thing I ask is that you don't fuck up my future by not letting me past."

Elijah narrowed his eyes at me and stayed put. "You really hate living with me that much?"

I narrowed my eyes back at him. "I can't wait to leave."

I regretted the lie as soon as it slipped out, but for a second I wanted to hurt him just as badly as he'd hurt me. But when I saw the hurt flash across Elijah's face, I was about to take back what I'd said when he stepped aside and gave me full access to the door.

I slipped out of the door and moved my feet as quickly as I could, forcing myself to get as far away from Elijah as possible before I turned around and probably made a mistake that would cost me my sanity and my heart again.

∾

I thought I'd be able to breathe a sigh of relief after my exam, but the fact that I knew I'd have to see Elijah again only made my chest feel tighter.

This is exactly why you're not supposed to shit where you eat.

Instead of going back to the apartment like I usually would, I called Violet to see if she was around to hang out.

"Hey Grace, how did your test go?" Violet asked when she picked up the phone.

"I think it went okay, but I don't want to think about it. Are you free to hang out right now?"

"Aw, I'm really sorry, I can't today. I promised my mom that I'd have lunch with her and the twins. They're coming up today-"

"No worries, I completely forgot. I remember you told me the other day," I said quickly, cutting her off. "You don't need to apologise." It was my fault for focussing my attention on people that didn't deserve to be focussed on.

"I can definitely do tomorrow though, if you're not too busy?"

A small smile came onto my face. "Yeah, that would be nice."

"Are you sure everything is okay with you, Grace?" Violet asked, a concerned tone in her voice.

I swallowed hard, conflicted between telling her what was really going on in my head and my heart. I decided it wasn't fair to dump all my shit on her, especially when she was about to see her family. That was already going to be a stressful enough situation for Violet, especially considering everything that had gone down with her mom the previous year. I could wait one more day.

"Yeah, I'm just exhausted and I've got to go."

Even though Violet wasn't satisfied with my answer, she had to get ready, so we made a time to meet the following day before saying our goodbyes. I slipped my phone into my pocket and thought about what to do instead of going back to the apartment.

I didn't want to stay on campus in case I bumped into Elijah. Even if it was a big place, I didn't trust myself to react appropriately if I saw him again.

I walked down the path away from campus and towards town. It was a little colder than I'd expected, so I stopped on the side of the street and took my backpack off my shoulders.

I was relieved when I saw my scarf lying there waiting

for me at the bottom of my bag. I grabbed it and wrapped it around me tightly before I stood up straight again.

As I continued walking down the street, I could feel the hairs on the back of my neck standing up. I had an odd feeling of being followed. I glanced left and right, looked up and down the street, but it was just me and a woman in high heels and a pantsuit marching in the opposite direction. She spoke quickly and pressed her phone to her ear. It sounded like she was on a stressful work call.

I tightened my scarf around my neck and kept on walking. I'd walked down the same road to town plenty of times. I just felt paranoid and jumpy for no reason.

No doubt thanks to Elijah.

Feeling a sudden craving for caffeine, I popped into the nearest coffee shop and got a latte to go. My eyes flitted to the window every few seconds because I just couldn't shake the feeling that I was being watched.

"Is that everything for you?" the barista asked as she rang up my order.

"Yeah," I said distractedly, my eyes still on the window.

A man walked past with a knitted beanie pulled tightly down over his ears, his shoulders hunched over and his head bowed down. He looked into the coffee shop at the same time that I looked at him and I noticed the piercing blue of his eyes.

I would have sworn I'd seen eyes like those before.

"Are you paying by cash or card?" the barista pressed, clearly not for the first time. The tinge of annoyance in her voice made me tear my gaze away from the window and turn my attention back to her.

"Sorry," I said sheepishly. I dove into my bag and pulled out some money to give her.

As she counted it up and went to grab my change, I chanced another glance at the window, but the man was gone and in his place was a mother walking with her pram and a little toddler by her side.

I thanked the barista, grabbed my coffee, and headed outside. I still felt like I hadn't killed enough time outside of the apartment, so decided that I'd wander around town a bit more.

It was definitely the quietest that I'd ever seen it. Grateful for the warmth coming from my drink, I took a left, which I knew led to the car park behind a bunch of charity shops. I hadn't been to one recently, and I wanted to see if there was any cool jewellery that I could add to my collection.

I brought my coffee cup up to my lips as the car park came into sight. But before I could take a sip, a pair of hands had grabbed me roughly around the waist, knocking my cup onto the floor.

"Let me go!" I shouted as I struggled against the arms that held me in a tight vise.

I kicked and screamed and tried my hardest to get away from my assailant, but they were too strong and their grip was unrelenting. I tried to turn around to see their face, but they forced my head forward and shoved cool metal against my temple, which brought tears to my eyes.

A gun.

My heart stalled in my chest as all hope seeped out of my body.

"Quit the screaming or I shoot," a deep male voice growled into my ear.

"Please don't kill me!" I cried as tears streamed freely down my face. "I'll give you money if that's what you want. I don't have a lot, but you can have my purse."

My assailant pressed the barrel of the gun against my skin even harder, to the point that I was afraid it would split.

"I don't want your fucking money," he snapped. "But I could have some of this."

Suddenly, his rough, grabby hands travelled up my waist and squeezed my breasts hard. I cringed away from his touch, but he laughed darkly, a harsh noise that sounded like a knife cutting glass. I knew his laugh would haunt my dreams. *If I lived.*

My limbs shook uncontrollably as he preyed on my body like an uncontrollable animal given a raw slab of steak after being starved for weeks.

"Please, let me go," I sobbed.

"That's not going to happen," he said.

My heart plummeted in my chest and I saw my life flash before my eyes as he grabbed onto my body firmly again, this time ramming the barrel of the gun into my back.

"Get in the car," he snarled.

I felt dizzy, like I couldn't breathe and could barely see straight through my tears that I hadn't noticed the grey car.

I stood still, wracking my brain for anything that I could do to make this end, to go back to my apartment, even if it meant dealing with Elijah.

Elijah.

In that moment, with a gun pressed up against me, threatening my life, the first thing on my mind was him. Even though he'd hurt me in so many ways, not only did I wish that I'd just gone back to the apartment straight after class, I wished that I could take back the horrible words I'd said just to hurt him. But it looked like I'd never get the chance to.

Angry tears mixed with fearful ones and I started sobbing heavily as my kidnapper forced me into the back seat of his car. He climbed into the front and pointed the barrel of the gun at me, daring me to challenge him.

"Don't even fucking think about it," he snarled.

I held my hands up in surrender, shaking uncontrollably as I sat back in the seat and blinked up at him.

At those stark blue eyes. I gasped as realisation set in.

It was David. Stella's rapist.

Elijah had set him free.

Anger and confusion coursed through my body and I didn't even know what to think anymore. Had it all been part of some sick joke that I wasn't privy to?

Had Elijah been lying this whole time? When had he set David free?

There were too many questions and too little time, because David had started the car and still had a gun aimed at my head in case I tried to move.

David had been the one following me through town. When I'd seen him outside the coffee shop, I'd just thought he was a random man, but no. It had all been calculated. How long had he been watching and following me?

Up close, I could see the bruises and cuts all over his face, which I assume he'd tried to hide with the beanie which was pulled down tightly over his ears. His thin lips were busted, but pulled up into a sadistic smirk, which was surrounded by a hideous mass of facial hair, which looked just as bad as the strands of dead hair poking from beneath his hat. David was truly a thing of nightmares.

I assumed the marks on his face were from Elijah, but what if some of them had been from other victims?

David reached over onto the passenger seat, his eyes flitting towards me as he grabbed something from it. I watched, still as a stone, as he fastened a gas mask onto his face with one hand. It made him look even creepier than before, which I hadn't known was even possible. I cut my gaze to the windows and saw that they were firmly shut.

"No need to look so afraid," he chuckled darkly, his voice

warped because of the mask. "I'm going to take good care of you."

His voice made me sick, and I didn't want to find out what he meant. David lowered the gun and turned back to the wheel. As soon as I felt the car reversing, I lurched towards the doorhandles and tried to open the backdoor. But of course it was locked.

Hot tears burned my cheeks, but I struggled against the handle, willing it to open, needing to be set free. Even when I saw a weird coloured gas make its way through the car, I kept pulling on the door handle.

I need to survive.

My parents need me.

Violet needs me.

My hands grew weaker by the second and even though I tried to hold my breath for as long as I could, it was a matter of moments before the gas had filled up the entire backseat and everything had gone pitch black.

29

GRACE

I kept blinking in and out of sleep. My body felt so heavy and weak as if I'd run a marathon. My mouth felt dry, my tongue heavy and useless in my mouth. My throat was parched, but I had no clue if I was going to get any relief anytime soon.

"Hello sunshine," David crooned.

I curled away from him, as much as I could, realising as I fully came to, that my wrists and arms had been bound and I'd been tied to a chair. David crouched beside me and breathed his horrible breath into my face, which made me gag.

"Not in a chatty mood today? Don't worry, I'm happy to do all the talking."

Up close, I could see just how yellow and chipped all his teeth were, as if they'd never seen daylight, let alone a toothbrush.

"What do you want from me?" I croaked.

David stood up straight and barked out a laugh. He then turned to me, his eyes trailing up and down my body as he ran his tongue over his lips like a rabid dog. I shuddered as he sized me up, imagining all the horrible things that he was probably thinking of doing to me.

"Lots of things," he snarled. "The main one being, I want to make Elijah Blackmoor regret ever fucking with me and for being stupid enough to let me go."

"I don't know who that is," I lied through gritted teeth.

Smack. David's hand made contact with my face so quickly that I didn't even have time to register the fact that he'd slapped me.

"Don't even bother lying to me, sweetie," he growled. "I don't like being fucking lied to."

Hot tears ran down my burning face and I couldn't even wipe them away because my hands were tightly bound behind me.

"I've been keeping an eye on you over the last two weeks."

David twirled his gun in his hand and then stopped dramatically before he pointed it at me. He barked out another animalistic laugh at the fact that I'd flinched, and it only made me hate him even more.

"I bet you're wondering how I knew where to find you guys, huh?"

Of course I did. The fact that he'd known where to find me made me sick to my stomach and added to the violation I already felt.

"If you ask around this town and keep your eyes peeled, you can find out exactly what you want soon enough," he chuckled to himself, clearly satisfied by his 'achievement.'

I couldn't believe that he'd been watching us for so long. How many times had I been walking alone and given David the opportunity to hurt or take me? The thought alone made me shudder, and I was close to throwing up all over myself.

"I saw you going into his apartment three nights in a

row. I gathered that you either lived there or you guys were fuck buddies or something." David quirked a bushy eyebrow at me and stuck his disgusting tongue out between his thin, cracked lips

"We're not, we just live together," I ground out, forcing myself to keep my eyes on David's ugly face.

David barked out a laugh. He looked me up and down with his beady eyes, clearly undressing me mentally as he did so.

"You expect me to believe that he hasn't had you on your back fucking the shit out of you?" David snarled.

His words made my insides turn, but I forced myself to keep my face steady. He could make his assumptions and it didn't matter how close he came to the truth, I wouldn't give him anything that could make the situation worse than it already was.

"We just live together," I repeated.

"Fine, keep lying. See where that gets you. Anyway, isn't it funny that Oakwood doesn't have much security on campus?" David asked. "It was so easy to track you down and find out your name and the names of your parents and all your friends." He pulled his lips into a snake-like smile.

No, not Mom and Dad. Not Violet.

"There were so many times when I could have taken you, too. But they were too risky, so I knew it was best to wait. And boy, you made it so fucking easy for me," he chuckled.

"What do you want from me?" I breathed.

I didn't want to think about how long he'd been stalking me for or how much he knew about my life. I needed to know what he wanted and if there was a way to get away from him unharmed. David's face darkened again.

"Do you know what that son of a bitch did to me?" David spat. A glob of it flew out of his mouth and landed on my cheek. I shivered in horror and tried to wipe it away with my shoulder even though my restraints pinched at my wrists, which hadn't stopped screaming with pain.

I turned my attention to the floor, noticing how dirty and uneven it was. How many other girls had been in the same position before?

I shook my head in response to David's question and dropped my gaze to the floor. I'd thought about it every night that Elijah had snuck out. Horrible images had flashed into my mind, but I'd never wanted them to be confirmed. It felt easier to separate the Elijah who did *those* things to the one I lived with.

David hissed as he lifted his shirt and pressed his hairy chest into my face. "Look!" he roared.

I trembled with fear at the tone of his voice and disgust at the stench of sweat and gasoline that radiated off his body and threatened to choke me. I shut my eyes tight, praying and counting down the seconds until David moved away.

"I said look!" David grabbed a clump of my hair and pulled it so sharply that it snapped my head back and made me wince. My eyes involuntarily flew open, and I instantly wished that I could unsee what lay before me.

Tattooed deep into David's chest was the word *RAPIST* in jagged capital letters. The blood and pus leaking from the letters forced me to empty my stomach all over his shoes.

"Fucking bitch!" David slapped me across the cheek again before he jumped back. But he was too late. My vomit had already coated his shoes.

Had Elijah really done that to him?

"Do you know how hard I've tried to get rid of this?"

David stabbed his finger into his chest, drawing my attention back to the infected tattoo.

"I've tried everything, and it won't fucking go away.

Thanks to your boyfriend." He snarled. "And that's not even the worse thing he did to me."

I didn't want to hear it; I didn't want to know. My insides already felt constricted, like I couldn't breathe. I couldn't comprehend that the Elijah he was talking about was the same one I knew. The same one that held me and kissed me and looked after me when I'd been drunk.

The fire and hatred in David's beady blue eyes told me that the way I saw him was the same way that he saw Elijah. I curled into my chair and willed my breathing to go back to normal, but the smell of vomit was making it difficult.

"Just because I fucked his miserable slut of a sister, he kept me cooped up like an animal for weeks!" he roared.

"He's not my boyfriend. I knew nothing about-"

"Lying slut!" David lurched towards me, his hands on my body before I could try to shake him away.

"Please, get off me!" I cried weakly, even though I knew my words meant nothing to a monster like him.

"Don't pretend you don't want it," David growled. "Don't think I haven't noticed the way you've been looking at me with those big eyes and blowjob lips."

David ran his hands down the length of my t-shirt before he tore it apart with his bare hands, giving him full access to my breasts. Mortified and full of shame, I tried to shrink away from his touch, but there was nowhere for me to go as David palmed my breasts roughly with all the control of a wild beast.

"Stop!" I screamed, but that only made David more excited. His eyes lit up with sick delight as he reached down to his pants and unzipped himself.

Eyes wide with horror, I shook my head desperately as David let his small limp dick spring free from his pants. I'd never seen something so ugly in my life. My eyes scoured the room for anything that I could use to aid me in my escape, as I kept trying and failing to break free from my restraints.

"I'm going to give you the chance to open your mouth before I force you to," David snarled.

He forced himself between my legs, his sweaty and dirty body towering over me. I gagged, still tasting sick in my mouth, and shook my head. David grabbed my face with his rough and calloused hands and I tried to pull away as he forced me closer to his dick.

"If you want a chance at living, or if you want your family to live," David's eyes narrowed and his lips curled up sadistically. "Yeah, I know where to find them, Grace." I shivered. "Then you'll fucking suck my cock."

Tributaries of tears ran down my face uncontrollably and my shoulders shook, knowing that I couldn't risk my family getting hurt. I'd been the reckless one, and they didn't deserve to pay for my mistakes and poor judgement.

Weak and dejected, I opened my mouth just a crack, but David forced it wider as he slid himself inside of me. He tasted foul, like something that had been lurking at the bottom of a swamp. As David pumped his hips fiercely, grabbing the sides of my face as he did so, I tried to focus on not throwing up again.

"Yeah, that's fucking right," he groaned as he picked up the pace.

How could someone enjoy this level of degradation? Of violation?

I wanted to bite his cock right off, but that would only end badly for me and who knew what he'd do to my family then?

I focussed on counting and with each thrust I felt more and more sorry for myself. I thought about the warm bed I could be in. I thought about Elijah. Elijah's face sprung into my mind as David's thrusts became deeper.

He was getting closer to orgasm, and I didn't want to swallow him.

Even if I blamed him for the situation I was in, Elijah had been the only guy I'd let cum in my mouth, the only guy I'd let cum in *me* and I wanted it to stay that way. That was something that we'd shared, and I didn't want anyone to take that away from me. I pulled my head back, but David grabbed the back of my head and pushed his dick further down my throat.

"Move one more time and I'll kill you," he snarled.

I held deadly still as his legs went ramrod stiff and he emptied himself inside of my mouth. It tasted worse than I could have ever imagined. As soon as David removed his dick from my mouth, I spat his entire load out onto the floor before I could stop myself.

David zipped up his pants and gave me an unimpressed look. "Now that's not very polite, is it?" he tutted. I gritted my teeth together and stared up at him.

Had violating me not been enough? Did he really have to taunt me, too?

"Maybe I pity Elijah if those are the blowjobs he has to put up with," he scoffed as he pulled out his phone and walked towards the door.

"Where are you going?" I said, hoping that he was on his way to get water, or something for me to banish the taste of him from my mouth. David turned on his heel and gifted me that sadistic smirk of his.

"Is the little pink slut desperate for more?" he purred. "You're going to suck it better next time, none of that half ass shit," he snapped.

I gagged at the memory of his taste. We both knew that I'd rather gauge out my eyeballs than have another part of David touching me ever again.

"I was just warming you up, sweetheart. Get all the rest

you can right now, because I'm not going to go easy on you." His eyes narrowed, and he licked his lips grotesquely.

The haunting promise in David's voice forced more tears to roll down my face, but this only made him more amused. David shot me one last ugly smile before he closed the door behind him. I heard a key rattle around in the lock before his heavy footsteps melted away into the distance.

I stared at the thick door, wishing that I could burn a hole through it with my eyes. I screamed as loudly as I could, hoping that someone could hear me, anyone. But my throat soon grew tired and my voice weaker by the second when it became clear that nobody was around to answer my cries for help.

David had left me alone, strapped to a chair with my clothes practically falling off my body. I shivered from the cold, from the memory of what he'd done to me and the fear of what he'd do to me when he returned.

The horrors that awaited me only made my resolve to get free stronger, but the more I bucked against my chair and tried to break away from my restraints, the weaker I became.

My stomach growled angrily and my throat felt tight and scratchy. I hadn't eaten or had anything to drink in hours and I doubted my host cared. I was nothing but a pawn to him in the sick game he was playing with Elijah. Even though I blamed Elijah for setting such a dangerous man free, a small part of me couldn't help but blame myself for ever getting involved in Elijah's business.

A cacophony of shoulds echoed around my mind.

I should have moved out of the apartment when I had the chance.

I should have listened to Elijah's warnings.

I should have stayed away from Elijah.

I should have stayed in the coffee shop longer.

On and on, the voices taunted me and admonished me for my mistakes. But it didn't matter because for all I knew, I'd be dead before I could grow tired of the shame that held me just as tightly as the restraints binding me to the hard chair below me. I'd be dead after David had violated my body some more.

Even though I'd resigned myself to a fatal end and started picturing how devastated my parents and friends would be if they ever heard what happened to me, a small thought niggled at the back of my head and refused to be extinguished.

What if Elijah knows where I am?

Even if he did, there was no guarantee that he'd want to save me, anyway. Maybe he'd even had something to do with my kidnapping. My chest tightened at the possibility of Elijah's involvement. He'd told me time and time again that he wasn't a good guy and if his cruel words and actions hadn't been enough to show me that, then the fact that he'd set his sister's rapist free was evidence enough.

Elijah's darkness had been frightening yet so alluring, and I'd finally accepted that it was actually going to be the death of me.

30

ELIJAH

I'd gone out to a bar in town with Nate and Tristan. They'd both been surprised that I'd been the one to suggest going out. My mind hadn't been quiet since everything that had happened with Stella and Grace and the only thing that I knew would bring me relief, regardless of how temporary, was alcohol.

"Are you sure you're okay?" Nate asked.

He'd asked me twice already, and it was pissing me off. Nate didn't *really* care. We never spoke about that kind of stuff. Maybe he was the closest thing I had to what a friend was supposed to be, but that didn't mean I trusted him with information about my life.

"Why do you care?" I scoffed before I took another shot of tequila.

Nate's eyes flitted to my shot glass and then back to me, a judgemental eyebrow raised.

"I've never known you to drink so much," he said with a shrug.

Frowning at him, I downed the two remaining shots in front of me before setting them down loudly on the bar.

"So when I drink and everyone has a problem with it,

but Tristan is always high as shit and no-one cares?" I snapped.

"Calm down, man. It's just a question," Nate said.

"I don't want to answer your stupid fucking questions."

"What's wrong with you, Elijah? You're being more of a dick than usual and it's really fucking with my high right now," Tristan chimed in.

Tristan had been staring into space for most of the night, but of course the only time he had anything to contribute was when it was time to scrutinise *my* behaviour.

"As if I could give a shit about your fucking high," I snapped.

"Maybe you should take something to calm the fuck down," Tristan said as he sat back in his seat. "Maybe you'll be more fun to be around."

I snarled at him, but took another sip of my drink. No, I wasn't about to get into a fight. Even if he was asking for it. Tristan's eyes light up with mischief. He turned to Nate.

"I know what's going on with Elijah."

Nate raised an eyebrow. "Even if I tell you I don't care, you're going to tell me, aren't you?"

"He's mad that he's not getting pussy," Tristan smirked.

"You don't know what you're talking about," I spat.

I didn't want to think about Grace, not even for a second, but it seemed like it didn't matter where I went. I couldn't escape her.

"My guess is that she rejected you. The only question is whether you were lucky enough to fuck her before or-"

"Say one more fucking thing and I'll break your face," I lurched towards Tristan, who continued sitting in his chair like the smug bastard that he was.

Nate jumped between us and tried to push me away from Tristan.

"I didn't come out tonight to deal with you two pussies," he growled. "Stand down."

I stopped pushing against him, not because of Nate's command, but because I felt my phone buzz in my pockets. Even though Stella had made it very clear that she wanted nothing to do with me, I still instinctively reached for it to check if she'd changed her mind.

"He started it," Tristan said, but I didn't even care anymore.

The text that awaited me made everything else around me melt away into a blur. No matter how many times I blinked and refreshed the page, the words continued staring back at me in black and white.

Come and get your little pink haired girlfriend, unless you want me to give her the same treatment I gave your sister ;)

It was from an unknown number, but I knew exactly who had sent the text.

"What's wrong? Not such a tough guy anymore?" Tristan taunted.

"Shut up, Tristan," Nate snapped. He grabbed me by the arm, but I shook him off. "What's up, Elijah?"

"I need to go," I breathed, but I couldn't get out of the bar quick enough.

My knees felt weak and my chest was heavy, but I kept moving, kept forcing myself through the sludge of alcohol that clouded my brain.

David had Grace.

David had Grace.

And to make matters worse, it was all my fault. I'd put her in such a position because I'd been drunk, stupid and selfish and I'd lost my fucking mind. That was *if* David was telling the truth. I stopped for a second as I typed out a reply, staring at the screen impatiently as I waited for it to send.

Where is she?

The text bubble appeared to show that David was typing, but it was the picture that flashed up on my screen that made my jaw drop and my heart ache.

Sure enough, the pink hair and trainers that I'd seen her wear every day since we'd moved in together were a dead giveaway that it was, in fact, Grace. She had bruises all over, her hair was plastered to her face, her shirt was torn and she sat in a chair, her hands and feet bound tightly. Even in the picture, I could see how terrified and weary she looked. Like she didn't believe she was going to live.

Seeing her in such a state made me shake with rage, but what made it even worse was the gun that was pointed her way in the foreground of the shot. David's hand was holding it.

You have ten minutes to get here, or Pinky dies.

After that message, he sent me an address that I recognised lead to an abandoned warehouse on the edge of town. It took fifteen minutes to get there.

I had to save Grace. I wouldn't let her die for my stupidity. It was the least that I could do after breaking her heart. I'd failed already in protecting Stella, I couldn't fail again, so help me God.

I ran as hard and fast as my feet could carry me, through the haze of my drunkenness, towards the warehouse where the only girl that I'd ever let get close to me sat and awaited her death sentence.

∼

Sweat dripped off my body as I stopped outside the warehouse that David had directed me to. It didn't look like anyone was inside and I would kill the motherfucker on sight if I found out that he'd lied to me.

Before I could even catch my breath, I banged hard against the door, not caring who heard nearby. I banged again, followed by a few hard kicks with my feet. He was taking too long to answer. Using up time that I didn't have. Grace was relying on me. Well, maybe not *me*, but she was probably hoping that *someone* would help her. I'd let her down already, and I couldn't do it again.

I glanced at the time on my phone. I had a minute and a half to spare. My legs and shins burned from forcing myself to run as fast as I could through town. I hadn't cared how many people had stared at me. This was a life or death situation.

I hard the rattling of keys on the other side and as the door slowly crept open, David's ugly face and beady blue eyes awaited me. I raised my fist to punch him, but stopped short when I noticed the gun in his hand.

"Let's not be stupid," David tutted. "Empty your pockets." Gritting my teeth, I followed his instruction and handed him my phone, keycard and my penknife. He used the gun to point in front of him. "Walk."

"Where is she?" I snarled. "I got here in time, so you have to let her go." David shook his head and closed the door behind me. He jabbed the gun into my back and forced me to walk.

"*I* don't have to do anything," he growled. "If you want me to set your pretty slut free, then you're going to have to listen to me this time."

The sadistic glee in his voice was too much to bear. I wanted him dead. I needed him dead so that I could save Grace and get her the hell out of this place. But the cool steel pressed into my back meant that I had to play my cards wisely, or we'd both be fucked.

I let David walk me through the poorly lit warehouse. In

the dim light, I could see the remains of old furniture and random trash scattered about. Clearly, the place had fallen into complete disarray after the previous owners had moved out years ago.

I perked up at the sight of an open door where some light streamed out. As I got closer, my eyes landed on Grace, and I could feel my heart splintering in my chest.

She looked so weak and forlorn sitting with her head bent and her hair, which was usually so vibrant and alive, was matted with blood and hung limply by the sides of her face.

"I have a visitor for you, Grace," David sang out smugly.

Grace slowly lifted her head to reveal a cheek and eye that were slowly bruising. When her gaze met mine, I fell apart entirely. In those wide eyes, disappointment and dejection awaited me. It was like she barely registered who I was.

"Let her go," I snarled, turning back to David.

David shook the gun at me in the same way that one would shake their index finger when scolding a child. "You don't make the orders around here, remember?"

My blood boiled, threatening to spill out of me as I clenched my fists tightly together. If I had to listen to the sick fuck just to save Grace, then I'd have to keep my wits about me.

The last time we'd spoken, she'd said that she couldn't wait to stop living with me. Whether she still felt the same didn't matter. I still had to protect her. I wouldn't be able to live with myself otherwise.

"What do you want now?" I gritted out, my attention on David once again.

I didn't trust myself to look at Grace too long, in case her helplessness caused me to do something stupid that would cost both of our lives. David stroked his gun against his chin, his eyes glittering with mischief.

"I want you to feel as helpless as I did when you locked me up."

"Then it should be me sitting in that chair and not her," I snarled. "She has nothing to do with this."

David barked out a laugh. "Oh, but she does. She's made things a lot more interesting around here, haven't you Grace?" David said in a patronising voice.

I hated how her name sounded in his mouth. The familiarity with which his tongue ran over it made my muscles tense up even more.

Grace's eyes met mine. "You need to leave," she urged.

"I'm not going to leave you," I said.

And I meant it. Grace's eyes teared up, and I wasn't sure if it was because of my words or because she now knew what David was fully capable of.

"Grace has a great mouth," David chimed in. I tore my gaze away from Grace and turned to him, taking the bait that he had laid out for me.

David smiled his ugly, toothy smile. "Her blowjob game needs some work, though. You're obviously not a very good teacher," he snarked.

A growl escaped from deep within my throat and I knew that it was only a matter of time before I beat the shit out of him, gun or not.

"Stop fucking around and let her go, David."

"Alright, alright." David held up his hands in mock surrender.

With the gun still trained on me, he pulled my knife out of his pocket and walked towards Grace. I held my breath as I watched him cut off her restraints with one easy swoop. Grace slowly got to her knees, her hands flying to her exposed chest, her torn shirt hanging limply off of her.

I wanted to run towards her and wrap my arms around her, but I forced myself to stay put. It wasn't over yet. We weren't free until David decided we were. I watched David walk back around Grace until he was standing between the two of us. He flitted his gun back and forth, warning us not to move or try anything stupid.

"What now?" I growled.

"I want you to feel as helpless as I did when you locked me inside that room and tortured me for weeks."

A painful expression flitted across Grace's face. How much had David told her?

"Are you going to do it, or should I?" David's voice cut through my thoughts.

"What the hell are you talking about?" David licked his lips like a rabid dog, his eyes narrowed sadistically.

"Are you going to shoot her or do you want me to? Your pick, Elijah." His smile stretched out across his bruised, ugly face and I felt my heart pound incessantly inside my chest.

"You ruined my life!" he roared. "You took away my freedom, so I'm going to take away something that matters to you."

"Wait!" I cried out. David lowered the gun and shot me an impatient look.

"What?" he snapped.

"Take me," I said before I could stop myself. I put my hands out in front of me. "Set Grace free and put me in her place. This is between us, not her."

"Elijah, you don't know what you're talking about!" Grace cried out weakly.

I forced myself to stare straight at David, but that didn't stop my heart from buckling at the sound of her voice. The desperation in it. Something that almost sounded like... care.

No, I can't allow myself to think like that.

David smirked at me as he thought about my proposition. "So you'd really take this useless slut's place and let me torture you instead?"

I gritted my teeth together, forcing words that threatened to rise to Grace's defence to slide back down my throat. She had family and friends that loved and cared about her. It only made sense for her to be the one that got to walk free.

"Yes, set her free and I'm all yours."

I knew the fate that I damned myself to with those words, but once they were out in front of me, I knew that there was no way I could take them back.

"Haha! The only thing that would make this better would be if your sister was here to see it," David taunted.

My nails bit into my palms, but I focussed on David's face. He just had to say yes. One word and I could breathe. I would take whatever he wanted to give me as long as he let Grace go.

David's answer came after an agonising minute of silent staring.

"I decline your offer," he said with a shrug, the sadistic smirk on his face once again before he pointed the gun at Grace, his finger balancing on the trigger.

"No!"

My adrenaline spiked and in a split second I jumped onto him, but not before I heard and felt the gun go off with a loud *bang*. David and I fell to the ground together, smacking against the cool concrete below.

There weren't just stars in my vision, but planets, too. The entire Solar System swirled around as I struggled to see from the darkness that began clouding my vision.

Three gunshots rang out in the small enclosed space, followed by a blood-curdling scream. I could feel the bullet lodging itself deep inside of me, the pain sharp and all-consuming. The stench of blood filled the room and grew stronger by the second like a repulsive perfume.

Grace, where's Grace?

Everything went black.

31

GRACE

David's finger had danced on the trigger as he pointed the gun directly at me. I'd started counting down the last few moments of my life as I waited for the bullet to hit. The next few moments happened so quickly.

Elijah jumped in front of the bullet.

Elijah and David fell to the ground in a crooked embrace.

The gun flew out of David's hand and landed in front of my feet.

I didn't even know what was happening as I grabbed it and pointed it at him.

All I remembered was screaming Elijah's name so hard that my throat felt like it was being torn to shreds. My body shook so violently and I couldn't see clearly from all the blood.

So, so much blood.

Elijah's blood, slippery, wet and warm as it drenched my fingers, my clothes.

David's blood splattered on the walls after I'd shot him until I'd made sure he was dead. *I'd killed someone.*

With shaky, bloody fingers, I tossed the gun aside and

fumbled for Elijah's smashed phone to call for an ambulance. Once I put the phone down, I screamed and screamed until I couldn't scream anymore.

～

My knees wouldn't stop shaking as I fidgeted in the hard hospital waiting room chair. My gaze kept flitting towards the door, eyeing the nurses that came and went with announcements for everyone but us.

"It's okay, honey. He's going to be alright," Mom said gently as she squeezed my arm.

"What if he's not?" I croaked out. I'd cried so many tears over the past few days that even though I sobbed, barely anything came out.

"It's not healthy to think that way, Grace. We just have to wait," Dad said on the other side of me. "At the very least, we're so glad to know that you're okay."

Okay. That was the overstatement of the century. I didn't know if I'd ever be okay after the hell that had unfolded. I'd barely gotten any sleep because every time I closed my eyes, I saw David; I felt his arms grabbing me; I saw blood everywhere, and I saw Elijah lying helplessly on the floor. So my eyes stayed open, yet weary because I was too scared to shut them.

The last few days had been one hell of a confusing blur. One moment David had kidnapped, restrained and assaulted me and the next moment he was lying on the floor with Elijah. Both of them bled profusely, the only difference being that one was dead, and the other had a fatal bullet wound and was still fighting for his life.

When the police and ambulance had shown up, I'd been a quivering mess. They'd asked me a million questions about what had happened to me, but all I could think about was Elijah.

He'd found me, even after everything that had happened between us. He still cared enough to risk his life to save me. Clearly, he wasn't the monster that he'd wanted me to believe he was.

The police and paramedics had told me that because the gun had been shot within point blank range, the wound that Elijah had sustained was potentially fatal. There was a high chance that he wasn't going to make it.

After I'd had my minor wounds treated to, I'd sat in the hospital waiting room day after day, refusing to move until I heard news about Elijah and his operation. Even though my phone buzzed incessantly in my hand, the only people I responded to were my parents and Violet, who'd heard about what had happened on the news.

I'd rushed into my parents' arms as soon as they'd entered the hospital waiting room. I'd been grateful when they half forced me to eat something because I hadn't been able to trust myself to keep anything down except from the soggy toast from the hospital kitchen.

Mom and Dad tried to reassure me that everything would be okay even when the police came back and kept asking more questions. Even though my mouth moved and I appreciated all the support, all I could think about was if Elijah would live or not.

He'd saved my life and there was the possibility that he wouldn't be able to live the rest of his. I needed him to live. When I'd thought that I was surely going to die, seeing Elijah's face for what I thought was going to be the last time had made me realise just how much he meant to me.

And now I might lose him.

"Is Grace here?"

My head perked up at the sound of the nurse's voice. Dad stood up with me, but Mom motioned him to sit down.

"Come this way please," said the nurse.

I felt like I was drifting through a haze as I waved goodbye to my parents and followed the nurse down the hallway in silence. When we reached the door of Elijah's hospital room, she turned to me.

"He came out of surgery about an hour ago and he's taking pretty strong medication, but he's going to be alright," she said.

I felt myself exhale properly for what had to be the first time in weeks. I was just ready to see him.

"He's really lucky that it missed his heart. And you're lucky to have him." The nurse smiled.

I was at a loss for words, so I simply smiled back at her, grateful when she pushed the door open.

"I'll leave you two to have a moment."

The nurse ducked out of the room, and I walked towards Elijah's bed. My eyes trailed over the drip coming out of his arm. He looked so peaceful lying there, and his chest went up and down slowly, confirming that he was still alive. My gaze flitted to his heart rate monitor, relieved to see that it was stable.

Sitting in the chair beside Elijah, I brought my hand to his, and the tears began falling freely again.

"I'm so glad you're alive," I whispered.

"Speak up, I can't hear you over the machines," Elijah croaked.

I gasped when I realised he was awake and lifted my head to see that his eyes were open and focussed on me.

"I said, I'm glad you're alive."

"I know, I just wanted to hear you say it again," Elijah snarked. I chuckled lightly. I was glad to see that the gunshot wound hadn't eradicated his humour. Elijah stroked his thumb gently against the side of my hand.

"Thank you for saving my life back there. I really thought I was going to die," I said after a moment. "I can never thank you enough."

A pained expression crossed Elijah's face before it quickly melted away.

"I would do it all over again if I could. I'm so sorry that I put you in danger. It's all my fault. I shouldn't have let him go-"

"It's okay, you made a mistake. I forgive you," I said, meaning every single word.

"You do?" Elijah said warily.

"Of course I do! You saved my life. I think that's enough grounds to forgive someone," I laughed.

"Hmmm, I guess you're right." Elijah scanned my eyes. "I don't think I could thank *you* enough for saving my life."

I swallowed hard as the memories of the gun going off in my hand shot into my memory.

"You were so brave back there and you saved us both, even after everything. So thank you."

Elijah slowly brought my hand up to his lips, which he gently pressed against my skin. I allowed myself to melt against his touch. My eyes grazed over the thick bandages peeping out from his hospital gown. I still couldn't believe that he'd been shot in the chest and lived to tell the tale.

Even if there was still a small part of me that felt guilty for killing David, I knew it had been in self defense and had been to save us both. I needed to remind myself of that. And hearing Elijah's words had done exactly that.

"Grace," Elijah said gently.

"Yeah?"

"You know when you asked me why I've never been in a relationship before?" he croaked out.

"Yeah," I said slowly. "Why?"

Elijah's eyebrows knitted together for a moment as he decided whether he wanted to go on or forget about it again.

"The reason why I didn't want to tell you was because I was scared that you'd make fun of me or think I was a weirdo," he said after a minute.

"I already make fun of you already about a bunch of other stuff, but I wouldn't think you were any more of a weirdo because of *that*," I teased lightly even though my heart was beating at a million miles per minute.

"I'm being serious." Elijah laced his fingers through mine. "The reason I haven't been in a relationship before is because I've never allowed anyone to get close to me. I didn't believe that love existed, and I thought that if it did... that I wasn't deserving of it. Or that if I ever got a taste of it, it would be taken away. So I preferred being on my own. It was always safer that way."

Elijah sighed heavily, and I knew just how hard it had been for him to say those words. As I looked at him lying in the bed, I thought about his younger self. How much pain he'd endured at such a young age and how he'd carried that pain and darkness throughout his life and kept people at arm's length to prevent any more.

But I could also see how tired he was, and that he didn't want to push people away anymore. At least not *me*.

"I appreciate you telling me that," I breathed.

"I let you get close to me, even though I didn't want to," Elijah went on. "And it fucking scared me. The way you made me feel, the idea of you realising that I was an awful person-"

"You're not an awful person," I said, cutting him off.

"How dare you interrupt me?" Elijah chuckled.

"It's true!" I exclaimed. "You're not, and I don't want you to think that way anymore."

Elijah's eyes glazed over, but he blinked back the tears before they could fall.

"When I realised that I'd put you in danger and that I could lose you, I realised just how much you meant to me and how unfair I'd been to you because of my own fears. I never want to lose you, Grace." He chewed his bottom lip, and I held my breath.

"I love you, and I want to make sure that nothing like that ever happens again. I'm never going to let anyone hurt you." Elijah said in one breath. His words made my heart flutter and my tongue felt lazy in my mouth.

"I love you too," I breathed, realising that I felt the exact same way. The thought of losing him had been too much to bear. Even though we'd driven each other crazy over the past few months, our feelings were more potent and real than ever.

"Thank fuck for that, because if you'd told me to fuck off, I would have had to fake a seizure," said Elijah. I rolled my eyes and laughed, knowing that he probably would have.

"Don't expect me to watch *The Notebook* with you or anything," he said with narrowed eyes.

"Why would I get you to watch *The Notebook*?"

"I don't know. Isn't that the type of shit that girls get their boyfriends to watch?"

"I wouldn't know. I don't have one," I said coyly.

"Would you like one?"

I raised my eyebrows. If someone had told me that Elijah would be the one to bring up the relationship question of his own free will, I'd have slapped them before laughing in their face.

"You're not going to take no for an answer, are you?" I teased.

Elijah's lips spread into a heart-melting smile.

"Absolutely not."

I giggled and rolled my eyes, my heart feeling warm in my chest.

"I guess you can be my boyfriend," I said.

Elijah's smile grew impossibly bigger and mine couldn't help but do the same.

"Now be a good girlfriend and pass me some water," said Elijah.

"Only if you say please," I said in a patronising voice.

Elijah narrowed his eyes at me and pointed at the cup.

"Water, now."

I continued sitting where I was and gave Elijah a smug smirk. I was having way too much fun taunting him and had no intention of stopping.

"Come on, Grace," Elijah moaned when I still didn't move. "Are you going to make me regret jumping in front of that bullet?" Elijah snarked.

"Maybe." I smiled as I bent my head and pressed my lips against Elijah's.

It was only meant to be for a moment before I got him his long awaited water, but I found it impossible to pull away. It was the most gentle kiss that we'd shared, but it was as if all the words and feelings we'd been holding back flowed freely through that one kiss.

32

ELIJAH

"His medication makes him drift in and out of sleep, so I'm not sure if he's going to be awake," I heard the nurse's soft voice pierce through my dream.

"It's okay, I just want to see him," another voice replied, a familiar one that I hadn't heard in a while.

I peeled my eyes open just as the door shut to see Stella sitting on the edge of my bed, her eyes red and puffy.

"Hey," I croaked. My throat felt completely raw, and I looked around for more water.

I tried to reach for the glass beside me, forgetting about the bullet that had gone through my chest. The pain made me wince and fold back in on myself.

"Here, I'll get it for you." Stella grabbed the water and held it to my lips while I took a grateful sip.

"What are you doing here?" I asked once she'd set the water down.

Stella's eyes darted around the small hospital room, and her silence made my skin crawl. The last time I'd seen her, she'd told me to stop contacting her, to leave her alone for good. I'd been so sure that I'd never see her again that I became completely overwhelmed by the sight of her.

"You're my brother..." Stella said quietly. "And you almost died... I can't believe he almost killed you."

Stella's hand flew to her mouth as she started sobbing to herself. I wished that I could reach out and comfort her, but my body ached too much- it was like the painkillers weren't doing anything. And besides, we'd never been the type of family to hug.

"It's over now, and he can never hurt you again," I said. "That son of a bitch got exactly what he deserved, and he's going to rot in hell for what he did to you."

Stella looked up at me through her tears. "You shouldn't have put yourself in so much danger-"

Using all my strength, I held up a hand to silence her.

"It was my fault for not being there that night and I'm going to spend the rest of my life regretting that mistake. I know you're never going to forgive me," I said slowly, struggling to get the words out.

"I should never have blamed you, Elijah. It wasn't your fault. It was his fault for... for raping me. He could have done that at any time and to anybody. It just so happened to be me," Stella sniffed. She placed her slim hand on top of my tattooed one. "I forgive you Elijah, but just because you made a mistake, that doesn't mean you're a bad person, okay? You're still my big brother and you've been there for me more than anyone else."

I shook my head in disbelief at the words that came out of my sister's mouth. How could I believe what she was saying?

"Not recently. I've let you down."

It was Stella's turn to silence me with a hand.

"I needed time on my own. Time to heal, okay? And I'm still healing." Darkness passed over her face before she pushed it away again. "But I mean every word I said. You've been there for me when no one else was. Not Mom and

Dad, not our shitty foster parents. Maybe you slipped up one time, but you've always had my back, Elijah. And I can never thank you enough for that."

Stella threw her arms around my neck and collapsed into me, her body shaking as she let herself sob. I tore my focus away from the pain in my chest to my sister and brought my arm up so that I could rest my hand on her back.

"I couldn't bear the thought of losing you too," she sobbed, her warm salty tears splashing onto my neck. "You're the only person I have left."

"It's going to take a lot more than a bullet to get rid of me, Stella," I chuckled before the tears in my throat could overwhelm me.

Stella unravelled herself from me and sat back, her nose red to match her puffy eyes. We weren't perfect. But we still had each other, and that was the most important thing. Now that Stella had forgiven me, it was only right that I forgave myself. Even though the bullet had torn a hole through my chest and made my body feel like shit, Stella's words made it all bearable.

"She must be a really special girl if you were willing to take a bullet for her," Stella said with a teasing smirk.

I opened my mouth to speak, but was cut off by the sound of the door creaking open.

"Hey, I was just coming to check-"

She paused at the door and her eyes flitted awkwardly between me and Stella. Despite the bruises on her face that David had given her, which made me angry beyond belief, Grace still looked beautiful as ever. Seeing her standing there, shifting her weight between her feet, made my heart beat faster in my chest.

The girl who I'd taken a bullet for. The one who'd saved our lives. My *girlfriend*. Grace was truly mine, and I was hers.

"Sorry, I didn't mean to interrupt you guys. I'll go," Grace said sheepishly as she started backing out of the door.

"Don't be silly, come in," Stella said.

Grace bit her bottom lip, but stepped into the room and shut the door behind her.

"I was just coming in to see if I could get you anything to eat," she said to me. Grace turned to Stella. "I can get something for you too, if you like?"

Stella shrugged. "As long as it has a bunch of carbs in it in, I'm pretty easy. Same for him." She nodded her head at me.

"Carbs, got it." Grace smiled nervously. She cast a shy glance my way.

"Carbs sound good to me," I returned her smile.

"Good," Grace nodded and turned to leave again.

"Wait!" Stella exclaimed.

Grace turned slow motion and looked at Stella again. I almost laughed at the cute expression on her face. It was quite obvious that Grace was a bit intimidated by Stella, which was unsurprising since she was a Blackmoor. But it was funny watching Grace trying to conceal her nerves around my sister.

"I just want to say thank you for saving Elijah and for killing that psycho," Stella said gently, her eyes searching Grace's face.

Grace played with a strand of her pink hair and her gaze fell to the ground.

"Oh, I'm sure anyone in my position would have done the same thing," she breathed. "I'm glad he can't hurt anyone ever again."

Stella stood up and crossed the room until she was directly in front of Grace. Grace looked startled when Stella suddenly grabbed her by the shoulders.

"I'm being serious, Grace. What you did back there was fucking phenomenal, so don't you dare downplay it, okay?"

"Okay," Grace squeaked.

"He might not know it, but my brother is so damn lucky to have you."

Grace chuckled bashfully and her gaze slid towards me. "I'm lucky to have him."

I watched as the girl whose bravery had saved us both and the girl who I'd risked everything for shared an awkward hug. When they parted, Grace excused herself to get our food.

"I see why you like her," Stella said with a grin once Grace was firmly out of earshot. "So, is she your girlfriend yet?" she waggled her dark eyebrows at me.

"I'm not talking to you about this," I groaned. I didn't care if I'd been at death's door. I still didn't feel comfortable talking about my love life, even if she was my sister.

"Wow, I never thought I'd live to see you cracking an actual smile again," Stella teased. "But it seems like the ice prince's heart has been thawed."

"Maybe a little," I chuckled.

Even though I wasn't ready to bare my entire soul to Stella, and maybe I never would be, I was glad that I could actually admit out loud to somebody else how I felt about Grace.

I spied Grace's face in the window as she balanced the boxes of food in her hands. She laughed to herself as she stopped a box from falling on the floor. No matter how many times I heard or saw that sound, I knew it would never stop melting my insides.

I never wanted to go another day without seeing that beautiful smile.

33

GRACE

"Are you sure you don't want me to carry that?" I asked Elijah, gesturing to the bag slung over his shoulder.

"I'm perfectly capable, thank you very much," he scoffed.

"I mean, I don't know if a bullet wound in the chest is the same as being perfectly capable," I said pointedly.

Elijah stopped just outside the door of our apartment and turned to me, a lazy smile on his face. He brought his tattooed hand up to my face and gently caressed my cheek.

"I appreciate you looking after me, but you don't have to treat me like I'm going to break, okay?" he said.

I nodded. "I know, but you can't blame me for being worried for you, after... everything," I breathed.

Elijah pulled me into his warm chest and stroked the back of my neck. "It's all over, Grace. You're safe now."

I tipped my head up to look at Elijah and felt an overwhelming rush of emotions as I remembered how close I'd been to losing him. Elijah pressed a kiss to my lips before he turned and opened the front door.

"Surprise!" shouted Violet as soon as we stepped into the apartment.

I blinked a few times as I looked around and saw a bunch of people standing at the door with big, warm smiles on their faces. I recognised Nate and Violet and some other people from my classes. I assumed the unfamiliar faces belonged to people from Elijah's classes.

"What's all this?" I hissed to Violet, while I tried to keep a smile on my face.

I appreciated the lengths she'd gone to decorate the apartment with balloons and banners that said *Welcome Home*, but I would have preferred to hide out in my room for a bit after how draining the week I'd had.

"A party to welcome you guys home," Violet exclaimed. She threw her arms around my neck and I melted into her warmth and familiar smell, grateful that I was still alive and able to feel more of my friend's hugs.

"I heard about everything on the news." Her eyes were teary and her lips trembled as she pulled me into another tight hug. "Thank fuck you guys are okay!"

I squeezed her tightly and realised how much I'd missed my friend while I'd been in the hospital.

"Nate and I tried to make you a cake. It's probably not going to be as good as the ones you make but-"

"I'm sure I'll love it," I chuckled, cutting Violet off.

"You should have told me and Tristan where the hell you were going. We would have come and fucked that guy up!"

I turned at the sound of Nate's voice as he spoke to Elijah. Elijah rolled his eyes before he answered flatly.

"I'm sure your fists would have been a great defence against a gun."

"How much did getting shot hurt?" Nate pressed on, not even trying to conceal his intrigue. Elijah cut a glance towards me before he turned back to Nate.

"It could have been worse."

Nate sighed dramatically, annoyed that Elijah refused to

budge. Even a near death experience hadn't been enough to eradicate his friend's stubbornness.

"Come on, man, spill the details. You literally survived a *shoot out*. I know the news didn't tell the full story, so spill the beans!"

He punched Elijah in the arm and I watched Elijah hide his wince behind a stoic expression.

"Hey, sorry I'm late. But you guys look like you might need a pick me up."

Tristan appeared beside Nate and Elijah, looking worse for wear.

What was up with that guy?

I watched as he reached into his jacket pocket and was about to pull out something when Elijah held out a hand to him and shook his head.

"For fuck's sake, not here. Just give it a rest for a second," he growled.

Tristan narrowed his eyes at Elijah, and his lips became a thin line.

"He's right, let's just focus on the fact that Elijah and Grace are *alive*," Nate chimed in.

I noticed the muscle ticking in Tristan's jaw and the way that his hands curled into fists by his side.

"Are you guys trying to make me feel like shit or what?" he snarled. "I'm just suggesting we have a little fun, lighten up, and now you're acting like I'm the bad guy or something."

"We're taking this outside," Nate snapped, grabbing Tristan's arm as he spoke.

Tristan shook him off angrily and shot daggers at him. "Don't fucking touch me."

"Then go outside before we do a lot more than touch you," said Elijah forcefully.

Anyone watching carefully would see the tension

brewing in the guys' corner. I felt like I was prying by watching, but I wanted to know what was going on, too. After a few more hastily exchanged words and tactical shoving, Nate and Elijah shepherded Tristan out of the front door.

Maybe I'll ask Elijah about that later.

Shaking my head clear of what I'd just seen, I turned my attention back to the party and let Violet lead me through the throng of people milling about in the living room.

As I made my way through the party, marvelling at the decorations that were luckily not my underwear, the amount of people that wanted to speak to me overwhelmed me. Classmates, people I'd seen at parties, as well as people I didn't know. But all of them had something to say and were exceptionally curious about the kidnapping and shoot out that had gone down.

I tried to answer as best as I could, but quickly felt fatigued by the sheer amount of questions. I wanted to enjoy the party that Violet had thrown as best as I could, and I didn't want to relive that night all over again. Especially when I knew that the memory of it would await me when I went to sleep.

Excusing myself from a group of girls that were on the same course as me, I went in to my room to put away my things and to pull myself together. The music thrummed lightly through the walls and it still felt so surreal that I was back in my room, alive and well. Or as well as I could be after something so traumatic.

I pulled my hair back into a bun and checked my reflection in the mirror. I still had some bruises on my body and face from David, and I prayed that they'd go away soon.

It was bad enough that I had to deal with the memory of my kidnapping every time I shut my eyes or had a moment of silence to myself. I didn't need any more reminders.

"Grace."

I turned around at the sound of Elijah's voice, startled that he'd managed to sneak up on me while I'd been absorbed in my reflection and nightmares.

"Hey."

I let him wrap his arms around my waist as we pressed our foreheads together, our breaths and heartbeats in synchrony.

"I don't like parties, but surprise parties are the worst," Elijah said.

"You could have fooled me," I chuckled. "We should probably get back out there though, before Violet and Nate get worried and have a fit."

Elijah shook his head and pulled me closer, engulfing me in his all too familiar heat. I soaked up every inch of his smell, making sure not to press my head against his bandages too much.

"I'd rather stay in here with you," he growled.

"*Elijah*," I teased.

"*Grace*," Elijah purred as he began lowering his hands slowly down my body until they were resting on my ass. "I know you'd rather stay in here, too."

Elijah pressed his soft lips to my neck and my head involuntarily tilted back as he started kissing up and down it gently, leaving little fires everywhere his mouth touched. I moaned into his embrace, feeling my resolve to go back to the party diminish with every second.

"You're a menace," I whispered as I let Elijah pull down my trousers.

"And you love it," he chuckled, his voice like honey in my ears.

It wasn't just lust that took over me, but the overwhelming sensation of love and excitement that I could finally express my true feelings without being scared that Elijah would pull away.

I pushed Elijah onto my desk chair, giggling when his eyes widened as I slowly peeled off my clothes.

"I can't believe I was so close to never seeing this again," he breathed.

"Consider yourself lucky," I teased.

I pounced on Elijah, sweeping my tongue across his as he wrapped my legs around his waist. Running his fingers across my slit and over my clit, I felt the wetness and heat build up between my legs at his touch.

"That's my good fucking girl," Elijah growled as he pulled his cock out of his pants.

He was already hard and throbbing for me as I lowered myself onto him. Moaning into his mouth, I gasped as Elijah pressed himself deep inside of me, filling me up just the way I liked.

"Fuck," I breathed.

"You want to thank me for saving your life, then grind that pussy on me real good," Elijah growled, my hair wound tightly around his hand.

His velvety voice turned me on to no end and I started grinding on his cock with everything in me, loving how he felt inside me.

Three knocks at the door. "Grace, are you in there?"

I stopped grinding my hips into Elijah and was about to jump off so that I could get dressed and pretend to have a modicum of dignity before Violet barged in and caught us in a very compromising position.

But Elijah had other ideas. He started bucking his hips, driving himself deeper inside of me, filling me up to the brim so that I could barely speak or think clearly.

"One minute, I'm getting changed," I breathed as Elijah kept on fucking me.

"Why are you getting changed? You look fine," Violet called back.

I stifled a moan as Elijah pinched my nipples between his fingers and started pulling on them hard. He gave me a challenging look, daring me to make a sound, but I bit down on my tongue and continued riding him even though it was getting too much.

I heard awkward laughter from Violet on the other side of the door when I didn't reply.

"Oh, I see. I'll leave you two in peace," she chuckled before she left.

"Are you ready to take my load?" Elijah breathed into my ear, his breath warm and sensual on my lobe.

"I'm ready," I cried.

Clutching onto each other tightly as if we'd never see each other again, Elijah and I bucked our hips against each other quickly, fucking like wild dogs that had been set loose.

I clamped down around Elijah's cock as my orgasm tore through me, and I felt his warm cum shoot into me, his dick throbbing as he filled me up with his seed. Pressing our lips together, we moaned into each other's mouths as we rode out our orgasm together.

"Fuck, I'm never going to get over how amazing your pussy feels," Elijah moaned.

"I could say the same thing about that cock of yours," I breathed. I climbed off Elijah and reached for my clothes. "I'm going to jump in the shower-"

"No, you're not. You're going to put on your panties and put on the rest of your clothes and go back out to the party."

"No, I can't do that!"

"Yes, you can, and you will, because you're mine, Grace." Elijah pressed his forehead to mine. "Isn't that right?"

"You're ruthless."

"Say it," Elijah ordered.

"I'm yours," I breathed.

Elijah pressed his lips to my forehead, then each of my cheeks, before he brushed them against my lips.

"Good girl," he smirked. "Now get dressed and go back to the party."

Hearing those words and knowing that his load was still inside me made me feel like Elijah's little slut and I loved it.

After many more lingering and desperate kisses, I got dressed and went to find Violet while Elijah disappeared to find his friends, or maybe a corner to lament his hatred of people and surprise parties.

"I was starting to worry about you!" Violet exclaimed when I walked into the kitchen. She looked me up and down and quirked an eyebrow at me.

"From the glow on your face, I'm pretty sure that Elijah had something to do with it."

"Maybe," I teased.

My phone buzzed with a message and I pulled it out quickly while Violet updated me on what had happened while me and Elijah had been in the hospital. It was from Elijah.

I love knowing that you're walking around with my cum leaking out of you.

My cheeks burned, and I tried to keep my face as neutral as I could. Thank God I was wearing trousers and not a skirt, because I would have felt even more humiliated than I already did. Instead, the feeling of Elijah's warm load trickling out of me and down my thigh was a secret reserved just for the two of us.

I loved how Elijah could turn me on with just a few words, hell even just the memory of him, the memory of his touch, of him filling me up from the inside...

It was the type of insanity that I craved and what made it

even better this time around was that I knew he was entirely mine and that I was his and that nothing could get in the way of that. I tucked my phone into my back pocket and willed my cheeks not to go red.

"Thank you for doing all this," I said to Violet. "You really didn't have to."

"Don't be stupid, you almost died, Grace." Violet's eyes welled up with tears.

"But I didn't because Elijah saved me," I said, my heart and voice full of extreme gratitude.

I could never express just how much Elijah meant to me or how grateful I was that he'd saved my life. I knew I'd spend the rest of my life trying, no matter what it took.

"I might not be his biggest fan and he's definitely not mine, but that definitely earns Elijah some brownie points from me!" Violet teased.

"He might grow on you, eventually," I chuckled, even though I knew from personal experience that it took a *lot* for Elijah to warm up to anyone.

"Regardless of my relationship with your new lover-" I went to punch Violet in the arm playfully, but she blocked it before I could do any damage. "I'm just happy that you're happy and well, and that's all that matters."

A flash of tattoos and dark hair caught my eye as Elijah walked past the kitchen. He gave me a lazy smirk before he continued walking down the hallway. Even though the moment was brief, it was enough to fill my heart up to the brim with sheer love and adoration.

"You're completely right," I said to Violet, turning my attention back to her.

I wasn't just happy that I was alive; I was happy that I was in love with Elijah and that he was in love with me, too. After surviving the worst possible thing imaginable and having finally opened our hearts to each other, I knew we could get through anything and that the rest of the year spent living together would be a hell of a lot more fun than before.

For the first time in a long time, I felt truly hopeful.

34

EPILOGUE

A *couple months later*

"I really appreciate you driving me."

Elijah looked sideways at me and placed a big, firm hand on my thigh. "I'd rather drive you than have you struggling with your bags on the train," he said with a smile.

My heart started beating a little quicker as I saw the signs that lead to home. We were only a few minutes away, and I was overthinking things again, as per usual. I hadn't been back since I'd left at the start of the semester and even though I usually looked forward to Christmas, this year I felt anxious about what Christmas would look like with Mom and Dad being legally separated.

"I didn't realise you lived in such a fancy area," Elijah teased as we pulled up onto my road.

"It's not fancy!" I said, feeling defensive. "It's just well kept." Okay, I had to admit that some houses on my street *were* pretty damn fancy.

"That one's mine."

I pointed out the house with the green door and directed Elijah to park on the drive in the empty spot where Dad's car used to be. I felt a twinge in my chest when I saw it empty, but pushed it away as I focussed on the task at hand.

"Is your mom in?" Elijah asked warily as we got out of the car and he started unloading my suitcases from the boot.

I looked up at the window and saw a faint outline of Mom's silhouette through the lacey drapes that hung in the kitchen window.

"She is, but she's nice, remember? You don't need to be scared," I teased, nudging him in the arm. Mom and Dad had seen Elijah really briefly at the hospital before they had to leave to get back to work. Unfortunately, Elijah had just taken another dose of his medication and had passed out before they'd finished the introductions.

"I'm not scared," Elijah scoffed. But his body was significantly tenser than usual. "I just don't know how to do... parents. I've never done this before."

A nervous laugh came out of his mouth, and I felt an overwhelming urge to wrap my arms around him. The same Elijah that had held his sister's rapist captive and taken a bullet for me to save my life was the same guy that was nervous to meet my mom properly. It was kind of sweet that something so small in comparison could cause him so much anxiety. But it made complete sense considering his past.

I linked my fingers through Elijah's and led him to the door.

"It's going to be okay, just be yourself," I said. "Maybe a little less grumpy," I laughed.

"Right." Elijah took a deep breath and waited with me outside the door for Mom to open it.

"Welcome, welcome!" Mom exclaimed as she flung the

door open, a big, friendly smile on her face. I was instantly filled with love and realisation of how much I'd missed her.

"How was your journey?" she turned to Elijah. "Thank you so much for driving Grace down. I know you were really heavily sedated last time we met, but it's nice to see you looking a lot better, Elijah. Remember, you can call me Linda."

Mom held out a hand to Elijah and I could tell that she was bursting with questions. She gave me a not-so-subtle wink that told me she'd be bombarding me with many questions later on.

"Nice to see you again, even though I don't really remember our first meeting, I'm afraid," Elijah said with a nervous smile. He pointed a thumb towards the car. "I'm just going to get the rest of Grace's bags."

"Thank you," I said. Elijah squeezed my hand before turning back to his car, leaving Mom and me on the doorstep.

"You two make quite a pair," Mom said with a nudge. "He seems like a nice guy, easy on the eyes, too. I can tell why you like him so much."

"Mom, let's not have that conversation right now, especially when he's right here," I said as I followed her into the house.

As Mom lead me to the kitchen, I realised how much tidier the whole place looked. It was practically a clutter free zone. The clutter must have mostly belonged to Dad.

"Would you like me to get you and Elijah some tea?" Mom asked. She filled the kettle with water before she turned it on and the water started boiling.

"Tea would be nice," I said.

"Actually, I will probably pass on the tea since I need to get going," Elijah said. He'd finished bringing in my stuff and was standing in the kitchen doorway, looking quite uncomfortable.

"Oh, come on Elijah. There's no rush! Stay for as long as you like," Mom said, flapping her arms at my boyfriend.

Elijah's eyes darted all over the place as he scratched his neck and tried to figure out how to decline Mom's offer.

"No, I should leave you to have family time for the holidays." Elijah's lips stretched into a wan smile.

"Elijah, we want you to stay for Christmas, if that's something you'd like," Mom said more gently. She looked down at me, a hopelessly romantic look in her eye. "I think Grace would like you to stay too."

A smile broke across my face because I really wanted Elijah to stay, but had tried not to guilt him since he had been so insistent on spending it on his own. On top of that, I hadn't been sure how Mom would react to meeting him properly.

Knowing that she liked him enough already gave me the confidence to turn to Elijah with pouted lips and puppy dog eyes.

"Please, will you stay for Christmas?"

Elijah's eyebrows knitted together, but slowly loosened as he struggled with the smile that threatened to consume his face.

"I guess I can stay," he said after a moment.

I cheered, stood up, and wrapped my arms around Elijah. When I pulled back from our hug, I got up on my tiptoes and kissed him on the lips.

The holidays were about to get *a lot* better.

～

"What's Stella doing for Christmas?" I asked once we'd settled in.

I blew on my second cup of tea and took a sip, setting it down when I realised it was still too hot.

"I'm not sure. We didn't really talk about it," Elijah said quietly.

"Why don't you invite her over?" I asked, surprising myself.

Admittedly, I found Stella a bit intimidating because she radiated super-cool-but-could-also-beat-the-shit-out-of-you-if-you-crossed-her energy. Regardless of my feelings towards her, I still thought it would be nice for her and Elijah to spend more time together after the crazy year that they'd had.

Elijah narrowed his eyes at me and set his mug down. "What are you plotting, Grace?"

"I'm not plotting anything!" I said defensively.

Elijah raised an eyebrow at me and gave me a teasing, yet suspicious, look.

"I don't trust you."

"Look, I just thought it would be nice," I said with a shrug.

"So you want me to invite my sister over?"

"That's what I said."

"The same one that you're scared of?" Elijah chuckled.

"I'm not scared of her!" I said, slightly too quickly. I looked down at my tea and then back up at Elijah. "I'm just not sure if she likes me."

Elijah reached his hand out and placed it over mine. "Of course she likes you." He tipped my chin up with his finger and stared deeply into my eyes. "It's kind of impossible not to."

"You're biased," I said, before I let him press his soft lips against mine.

After we shared a kiss, Elijah stepped outside to call Stella while I unloaded the dishwasher.

"She said she'll get here in like an hour," he said once he came back inside.

"Great."

Mom called us into the living room because *Home Alone* was on and it was her favourite Christmas movie. Elijah and I sat on one sofa while she sat on the armchair opposite, mouthing along to the lines of the film that we'd watched at least a hundred times already. To my surprise, Elijah had never seen it and his eyes were glued to the screen right from the start.

I jumped up when I heard a knock at the front door. It wasn't like I was racing anyone, because Mom was too focussed on the movie and Elijah didn't live at my house. I pulled open the door to see Stella standing there with a backpack slung over her shoulder and a box of chocolates in her hand.

"Hey," I said as calmly as I could.

Somehow, she looked even more gorgeous than the last time I'd seen her and I'm pretty sure she'd gotten a new nose piercing, too. *Damn, those Blackmoor genes are intense.*

"Is it still cool that I came over?" Stella asked warily.

"Of course, come in!" I blurted. "Mom and Elijah are in the living room."

I gestured to the open door where Elijah had appeared, a big smile on his face when he caught sight of Stella. Stella's smile matched his as she walked towards him. I was about to close the door and join them when someone cleared their throat on the other side, making me open it back up again.

"Dad!" I exclaimed.

Dad stood outside the door with two bags full of wrapped presents and a crooked smile on his face. I felt my heart soar in my chest at the sight of him. I hadn't expected him to visit, especially since he'd mentioned doing a Christmas lunch on a separate day, for just the two of us.

"Hey sweetie," he said. "I thought I should drop these off before the big day." He gestured to the bags.

Even though I appreciated them, I didn't care about the presents. I was just so happy to see my dad. I flung my arms around his neck and gave him a kiss on both cheeks. I hadn't realised just how much I missed him.

"What are you doing on Christmas day?" I asked him once I'd pulled away.

Dad grimaced slightly and shrugged. He opened his mouth and was about to speak when Mom's voice cut him off.

"Violet, who's at the..." Mom's voice trailed off when she appeared behind me and saw for herself.

"Michael," Mom breathed. "I wasn't expecting you."

Dad sheepishly looked down at his feet and scratched the back of his neck. "I was just dropping off the presents and saying hi to Grace. I'll be off in a minute," he said quickly.

I gave Mom a pointed, pleading look while she chewed on her bottom lip.

"We can set an extra place at the table for you if you want to stay for dinner," she said after a moment.

"Are you sure?" Dad's face lit up.

"Why not? It's Christmas," Mom said with a smile. "Plus, you can meet Grace's new handsome boyfriend properly and his gorgeous sister." Mom nudged my arm and waggled her eyebrows at me.

"Boyfriend!" Dad exclaimed, a dramatic expression on his face as he looked at me. "I came at the perfect time then."

I stepped aside to let him in and watched as my parents awkwardly moved around each other and engaged in small talk. Even though they were separated and no longer wanted to be married, that hadn't been enough to eradicate the care and love that they clearly still had for each other. The fact that they were able to put aside their problems for one day to be with me meant so much.

Of course, there were the awkward introductions between Dad, Stella and Elijah, which I think went as well as they could. It seemed like Dad was a bit taken aback by the piercings and tattoos, by the way that his gaze kept lingering on them, but I was grateful that he didn't make any comments.

We put on another movie while Mom made dinner, but we mostly spoke over it as Dad updated me on what I'd missed since I'd been away at Oakwood and he also got to know Stella and Elijah a bit better.

∽

When dinner was ready, we all sat around the table eating, Mom and Dad at the heads like old times and Elijah beside me while Stella sat opposite.

Once the wine had gotten into our system and everyone had settled down a little more, things almost started to feel normal again. Elijah's hand was constantly on my thigh, stroking and squeezing it to let me know that everything was going to be okay.

Mom got exceptionally chatty when she was drunk and bombarded Stella and Elijah with lots of questions. I had to stifle a laugh when I saw the knowing looks that they exchanged with each other. I knew the Blackmoors well enough by now. They didn't like questions.

"I just want to raise a toast," Mom said, her words slightly slurring.

"It's been one hell of a year, but we're all alive and well

and that's better than I could have asked for. Even though we all live in different places, I'm thrilled to see you all sitting around my table," she said, holding her wine glass out in front of her.

"Even me?" Dad asked, a teasing lilt in his voice.

Mom rolled her eyes and did a dramatic sigh. "Yes, even you," she said with a light-hearted laugh.

Dad pretended to wipe sweat off his brow before he raised his glass, too. Elijah, Stella and I also lifted our glasses and clinked them together.

"You three in particular have all been through so much recently, so please let yourselves relax, okay?" said Mom. The three of us nodded. "Whatever's going on, you're always welcome here, no matter what," she added.

I knew she was directing the last bit of her message to Elijah and Stella, but it was nice to hear it all the same. Especially since I'd been so worried about coming back to a home without Dad.

"Thank you for having us," Elijah said.

"Yeah, we really appreciate it," Stella added.

Mom's smile went from ear to ear, and I could see the tears glistening in her eyes. If she started, I knew I wouldn't be able to stop.

"Is anyone up for playing a game of Monopoly after dinner?" Dad chimed in to ease the tension.

"Dad," I groaned.

"Come on, won't you let your old man play *one* game before he has to go?" Dad said in a sympathetic voice. I rolled my eyes and shook my head.

"How about you, Elijah?" said Dad.

"Sure," Elijah chuckled.

Glad that he had one person on side, Dad turned to recruit Mom and Stella to the cause. Meanwhile, Elijah squeezed my hand and leaned in to whisper in my ear.

"I hope your dad won't cry when I beat him," he purred.

"Try to go easy on him," I chuckled, but I was only half joking.

"I think you know better than anyone, Grace, that I don't do easy."

Elijah smirked at me and squeezed my hand.

I felt a notification come in on my phone and I pulled it out to look. A smile broke out on my face as I saw that I'd gotten the results back for my most recent exam.

"Someone's looking happy," Elijah teased.

I turned my phone around and showed him. "I got the highest mark in my class!" I exclaimed, unable to hold back my excitement.

"That's my little doctor!" Elijah said before he pressed a kiss to my forehead.

"You tried to sabotage me, remember?" I snarked.

"Yeah, but you're my little fighter and I always believed in you," Elijah smirked.

The news from my exam only made a good day impossibly better. I passed my phone to my parents, who wanted to see for themselves, and blushed as they congratulated me profusely. I was grateful when the conversation moved away from me and back to Monopoly.

The table had been cleared, so Dad pulled out the board and started setting it up with all the pieces on the table. We all ended up joining in, with Mom choosing to be the Banker. Watching the people I cared about together in one space, laughing and chatting and teasing each other despite all their differences, made me feel warm and cosy inside.

I glanced sideways at Elijah, watching as he exchanged game talk with my dad. The curve of his cheekbones, his thick dark eyelashes and angular jaw, not to mention the tattoos that ran down his neck and all over his body, still made me swoon no matter how many times I stared at them. He was truly the guy of my dreams.

The Christmas holidays had always been my favourite season and getting to spend it with my favourite person was the best wish that I could have possibly asked for.

∼

THE END

THANK YOU FOR READING!

Thank you so much for reading *Ruthless Sinner*! Please consider leaving a rating/review as I'd love to hear your thoughts on this book. Reading your reviews also helps me improve as an author and I'm so grateful to those of you who have reviewed and will review for the help your feedback gives me!

WHERE TO FIND ME!

CLICK HERE to get a FREE copy of one of my books instantly & to stay in the loop about upcoming releases.
Follow me on Instagram @ivyblakeauthor
Want to connect with me & other readers and talk about our favourite unhinged alphaholes? Join my Facebook Reader Group which is a safe space for readers like you! Join Ivy Blake's Reader Group
Click here to join my ARC Team!
My Amazon Author Page

PREVIEW- SAVAGE GOD

Violet

"I guess you're in here because you want to suck me off, right?"

I peeled my hands away from my face and shot daggers at the asshole who had entered the bedroom with me. Even through my drunken haze and with the speakers thumping from the next room where most of the partygoers were, my ears had still registered the crude words that had flown out of this stranger's mouth. A hot stranger, mind you.

As if this night hadn't been long enough already.

Even though there was only a small, dim lamp to light up the room, I could still make out his tall and muscular silhouette and the curve of his plump lips, which were curled up into a cruel smile. A smile that posed a challenge I was *not* in the mood for.

"Don't fucking flatter yourself," I spat as I got up from the bed and made my way to the door where he was standing.

Big mistake.

"Where do you think you're going?" he asked as he stood

in front of me, closing the door behind him with an intimidating *click*.

My heart froze in my chest and I stepped to the side, but of course, he followed my every move, which meant that I was trapped. *Fuck*.

He was practically twice my size and probably had triple the strength that I did. That meant I'd have to play dirty. *If* the time came, of course. As I drew closer to him, I couldn't help but notice his sweet masculine scent and intimidating stance, which had me both intrigued and unsettled.

"Move," I growled as I cast him my most scathing look.

There's no time to be thinking about which cologne he uses. Just get out before something bad happens, my subconscious warned me.

He let out a fierce chuckle, a dangerous sound that was absent of any sort of joy. It was a warning sound. Whether or not he was joking, I didn't have time for any of this shit and I wasn't just going to heed to his crude desires.

"What the fuck is your problem?"

"You're trying to leave," he shot back instantly.

His sapphire blue eyes flashed with danger and as I lurched towards the door handle, he grabbed me roughly by the arms.

"Get off of me, or I'll scream!" I exclaimed as I squirmed in his tight grip.

My tormentor stood calmly as I struggled as if I wasn't causing him any discomfort at all. If anything, he looked amused. At first I was pissed off, but as I continued to struggle and he continued to tighten his grip, my anger quickly turned into fear.

"I'd love to hear you scream," he purred as he squeezed my arms in his big hands. I shivered at the sound of his voice, and from the threat that it held there.

The party was too loud for my screams to be heard at this point, and the guy who held me in his arms knew that. Unless he changed his mind or gained a shred of empathy in the next ten seconds, I was in big trouble. My heart beat frantically in my chest as I saw the hunger growing in his eyes. I imagined how things must have looked from his perspective. I was a vulnerable, drunken mess in clothes that probably made guys like him think that they were entitled to me.

All I'd done was break away from the party to get some air, nothing more. And now I'd found myself in a potentially dangerous situation and I felt like the only person I had to blame was myself.

Why had I agreed to this stupid party, anyway? I don't even know whose apartment this is!

"Good girl, you've stopped fighting." His deep, velvety voice took me off guard and I realised that he was right.

I was standing still, my eyes level with his chest and realised that my body was frozen stiff. The only problem was, I couldn't tell if it was from shock or if I had simply accepted my fate.

I shivered as I felt his hand travel up my throat before his finger tipped my chin up so that my eyes met his. What lay behind them was nothing but pure, unadulterated hunger. An insatiable hunger that acted without morals, without empathy or regard. I tried to break away from his grasp one more time, but there was no point.

The hunter had caught his prey, and now he was ready to feast. He pulled me closer to him and smashed his warm lips against mine, fighting his way into my mouth with his warm, wet tongue. Palming my breasts roughly with one hand and grabbing my waist with the other, I was stunned into compliance as he took control over my body. My lips complied and even though I was shaking, it wasn't just fear that was keeping me in place. The space between my thighs was betraying my mind and true feelings and was growing hotter and wetter by the second.

I was terrified of the heat that was building up in my body, the heat that he'd put there without my permission. I was scared of what that meant for me and what *he* thought it meant. I didn't want to enjoy this; I wanted to get out- so why was I melting into his arms instead of kicking him in the balls to give myself time to escape?

As if he could hear my thoughts, he slid his hand beneath my skirt and traced the seams of my thong, disarming me even more. My breath hitched in my throat and I was paralysed with fear and desire. I needed it to stop before things got out of hand. I needed to get control back, to get my mind back. His kisses grew more furious, and I gasped as he applied pressure to my clit. *Bastard*. I tried to swirl out of his grasp once again, but he simply spun me around and pinned me against the door as if I was nothing but a ragdoll.

The combination of alcohol, his intoxicating scent and overpowering strength meant that it was so much easier to surrender and melt into his arms than fight a losing battle.

"The wetness between your legs tells me that you want to be filled up," he growled in my ear as he slipped a finger into my panties.

I froze again as he invaded my private parts, fighting to bite back a moan as my body grew hotter against his touch.

"I can feel how badly you want it," he purred against my lips.

He grabbed my hand and pressed it to himself, and I could feel just how hard and how big he was.

He was expecting me to put all of *that* in my mouth?

The bratty part of me never turned down a challenge

and was curious to see how hard I could make him cum until my conscience snapped back to action.

I didn't want it and I'd said as much when he'd first come in here.

What the fuck was I doing? I wasn't that desperate for attention and it didn't matter how good his lips or fingers felt- there was no way in hell that this was going to happen. A knock on the door nearly made me cry out in joy. It was as if my internal cries had been heard.

"Nate, someone's thrown up on the couch!" said the person behind the door.

Nate. So the devil had a name.

Nate growled and took his hands out of my panties, much to my relief. He pushed me aside and opened the door, but I was unable to see who was behind it.

"It's really bad," said the messenger in a shaky voice.

"Well, go and fucking clean it up then," Nate retorted.

Ah yes, that was exactly what I needed. Further confirmation that the guy in front of me was the biggest asshole I'd ever encountered. And probably the owner of this apartment. No wonder he'd felt so entitled to me.

"And you, get on the bed," he ordered me, his voice impossibly darker than it had been before as he turned over his shoulder.

"You want me to get on the bed for you?" I said in a sickly sweet voice.

"That's what I fucking said, isn't it?" Nate snapped.

"Well, I want you to burn in hell," I shot back before slapping him as hard as I could across the face.

I felt a rush of adrenaline and satisfaction until Nate let out a dark laugh. Not the reaction I was expecting, but I was honestly getting very unsettled at the psycho vibes he was giving off.

"It's not *my* fault you enjoyed it," said Nate.

I choked on my own breath as I struggled to come up with an appropriate response. Instead, my body kicked straight into flight mode. I felt like a passenger in my own body as I ran out of the room as fast as I could before the feelings of humiliation could fully settle over me whilst still in Nate's presence.

That sick bastard would probably thrive off my humiliation.

Maybe he was right, maybe a small sick and twisted part of me had enjoyed what he'd done, what he'd stolen from me. I pushed past people to get to the front door, ignoring the couples that were trying to make out because I needed to leave and I didn't care who else's night I was ruining in the process.

I'd explain to my flatmate Grace, who'd brought me to this dumb party, that I had to leave early because I felt sick and I'm sure she'd understand. It was basically the truth, anyway.

My shaking had become uncontrollable, and I knew it wasn't just from the cool air. Once I got outside the apartment block, I took lots of deep breaths as I tried to fill my lungs up with oxygen again.

With shaky hands, I shot Grace a quick text as I walked the perimeter of campus to get to my apartment. I tucked my phone away and couldn't help but notice the way that my lips still tingled with the memory of Nate's lips on them.

I hated how I couldn't and probably wouldn't ever be able to shake my mind free of the way that he'd taken something I had not willingly given to him. At least not at first. I'd hated the way that his eyes and hands had shown that they would take and take no matter how many times I denied them. I was lucky and relieved to be out of there, even if Nate had left me feeling incredibly pent up.

What would have happened if we hadn't been interrupted? I felt sick to my stomach, but I couldn't shake myself of the morbid curiosity. I just knew that I never wanted to see that jerk again.

Nate.

∽

Read the rest of the book on Amazon

ALSO BY IVY BLAKE

SAVAGE GOD

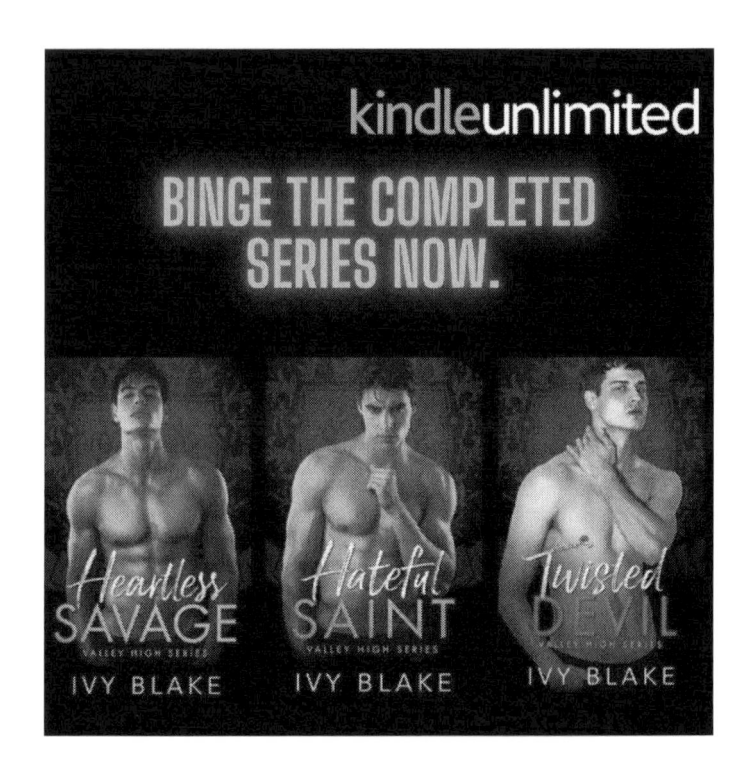

HEARTLESS SAVAGE

HATEFUL SAINT

TWISTED DEVIL

Printed in Great Britain
by Amazon